STEM & STONE

by Jessica Ferrara

Tea With Coffee
— Media —

Contents

Chapter 1

"The dog's still missing," Petra commented, peering out into the elements. "It's been a week."

"Do you think the witch got him?" Emil asked, a slight waver in his voice.

The wind howled outside, threatening to rip long splintered shingles from a cracked and leaking roof. What had begun as a tame pitter-patter of lonely drops coalesced into a mighty downward push, filling buckets in the hall. A flash illuminated the somber faces of two children, a slender boy, and a plump girl. Although she was the elder by three years, they were within an inch of the same height, with older eyes than years between them. The storm surged without and the two wondered within. It was suppertime. Yet neither child had the stomach to eat. Not while haunted by scenes of their friend, soaked and shivering, or worse, tied to a stake in the old bat's basement.

"Is that what your friends are saying?"

Emil nodded. "If ever were we to save him, now's the time. She won't hear us over the thunder."

Petra shook her head, turning from the pane as it quaked. "Absolutely not. If the witch doesn't kill us, Atla will."

"Please. Like she's gonna get home before midnight. It's early yet. Let's go now, while she's out."

Petra opened her mouth to say no, she was his elder and he'd better listen, but Emil had already turned away. The more she put her foot down, the softer the ground. Better she followed after, kept him safe. Besides, she missed Foss too. Every day, he met her across his fence, rolled the ball beneath for her to throw. Every day, he charged for, then caught it, racing as though to bring it to her, before turning away at the last instant, proclaiming, "Mine!" Until he didn't. She'd done her part, putting up signs, walking Emil from door to door, so he could knock, inquire as to whether Foss had been seen. It hadn't escaped her notice that the witch alone hadn't answered, had drawn her curtains closed, like Petra wouldn't see.

While he pulled his boots and jacket on, Petra did likewise, eyeing the gaps at his ankles, where the pants ended. Her jacket too, zipped no longer. She belted the middle, tying it closed like a robe. Her outfit was restrictive, her front more exposed to the frigid air than her back, but there was nothing for it.

Petra made doubly sure the front door was locked before they slipped out the back. Then they darted across their mud swamp yard. Her foot caught in one of Emil's holes, and she cursed him as they squeezed through the gap in the mildew fence. He hadn't heard or didn't care. She knew he often feigned the first on account of the second. Either way, their yard was a minefield of tripping hazards. Reaching the gate, Petra again considered the consequences were Atla to return early. Located in their own backyard, if damp, they'd barely get a lecture. Caught off-property in the middle of the night, however? Breaking into their neighbor's house? It would be months before Petra's meager allowance was reinstated.

"Do it for Foss," she murmured, swinging the gate wide for Emil, before locking it.

Next door lived an older boy. He was a recent addition to the block, his family having just emigrated from *abroad.* His bedroom light was off, elsewise Petra might've had Emil knock on the glass, lure him out with the promise of heroics, adventure. Afterall, there was safety in numbers. Instead, the children didn't dally, creeping from tree to tree, ducking behind the shed when they mistook a car horn for an alarm. They weren't going far.

The backlight flashed a fluorescent warning as they crept around the next yard. Motion sensors, Petra assumed. Her eyes peeled for adults, she puzzled over a plausible explanation for their presence. She'd heard a cry for help? Emil was sleepwalking and she'd set out to bring him home? Was either convincing?

There was a pool, but it wasn't warm enough for swimming, not that they cradled delusions regarding their abilities to swim. Giving the seasonal cover a wide berth, the children slunk on. Nobody burst out to investigate the light.

Hopping a short rustic fence, as opposed to opening what Petra suspected was a creaky gate, they arrived on enemy land. Creeping, they passed squares of squat rhubarb and strawberries. Swallowing the urge to whistle, call for their friend, Petra whipped her gaze from each dark shape to the next. Was he tied to a tree? Chained to a small shack? Hurt? Rushing ahead, darting behind foliage, wishing for better night vision, Petra gestured for Emil to hide behind what appeared to be a raspberry bush. Crouched low in the mud, windswept brambles slashed at her face and fingers. Squinting, wiping her vision clear, Petra saw no sign of Foss, nor much else, and they hadn't brought a flashlight. As for the backdoor, neither bordering window was dark. However, the faint light wasn't so bright as to be electric, unless it came filtered from a farther room. No witch shaped shadows darkened the panes.

For their plan to work, they had to enter when thunder hit. Could they predict thunder? Maybe. Petra watched for lightning, then counted up to the inevitable bang. Ten seconds, at five seconds per mile, meant the bolt struck two miles away. But where was the storm headed? Signing for Emil to wait, she counted out from the following flash.

Petra's ears were fast numbing, rain seeping down her collar, when a scream pierced the thunder. Emil looked to Petra, who scanned for the source. There erupted a second cry, shriller than the first. Then another.

The children strained to see in the dark, hands posed in tremulous salutes. The bushes, the trees, even the distant fence posts, were trying to escape their earthly bonds, sashaying as invisible hands pulled upward. The wild choreography was illuminated by the arc of Thor's great hammer, and for the briefest instant, the children saw they were not alone. At the edge of the plot, concealed from the street, were livestock. The witch raised pigs. Massive beasts, boars really, they thrashed against their brittle wire restraints.

In stories, pigs were cute, friendly, innocent, but most of all—weak. Wolf chow. The great fairytale writers of yesteryear must've grown up in cities. Petra'd seen wolves before and was confident those pigs wouldn't have made easy prey. If they escaped, she and Emil were in danger of being trampled. Or eaten. Anything could happen with beasts so crazed, angry, and *free*.

Petra turned to Emil. She had to shout over the storm to be heard.

"Let's head back!"

"What?!"

"I said we have to go!" she bellowed, gesturing across the property. Whether in misunderstanding or rebellion, she couldn't tell, but Emil appeared to brace himself. Then, without warning, he leapt to and ran opposite the direction she'd indicated, to the house. Choking back a curse, Petra followed.

She wasn't above tackling her baby brother. Rather, she recognized the futility. If she tried, she'd end up with mud to cushion the blow, but certainly not any limb of his. He was kneeling beside the stoop when Petra caught up. Nervous of the writhing mass of snouts, hooves, and teeth lurching not far enough away for Petra's liking, she hissed at him to come home *now*. If it weren't the pigs, it would be the witch herself. Emil opened his mouth to protest as the backlight flickered on.

He stood so fast he knocked Petra's chin on the way up, but the door swung open, revealing two spindly hands that grasped them by their shoulders before they could flee.

"Now, what have we here?!" the witch rasped, yanking them backwards, inside.

She slammed the door, shutting out the wind and screams.

"No," Petra cried. Whether out loud or within, she couldn't have later said, wondering what the witch would do to them.

"Trespassers!" the witch snarled. "Trespassers!" she accused, flicking the light switch on.

From beneath the angular sagging of paper flesh, the witch glared with her one eye. She'd neglected to don the embroidered patch she daily wore over the other, and both children stared transfixed by the crimson void. Her hair was more cobweb than silver, both in color and style. Wisps erupted from the unruly mane, nets for gathering debris. When she shook her head, seething, tangles fell loose, cloaking her face in shadow. The witch's nightgown was of dark velvet, the elbows faded. When she spoke, flecks of spittle flew from her mouth, and her nostrils flared.

For their part, the children said nothing, blinking at the brightness. That they hadn't taken anything wouldn't be hard to prove, but neither expected the chance to defend themselves.

"How dare you defile my property with your grimy little hands!"

Emil's eyes fell with defeat, not shame, but an old witch couldn't be expected to discern the difference.

"Oh, so I bet you're sorry now, are you? Traipsing in here, covered in mud?!"

"We were just leaving," Petra grumbled in her head. "You yanked us in. We would be home now, if not for you," but ranted in silence. When an adult decides they're right, there's no reasoning with them. Even little Emil knew to keep his mouth shut.

"Well, you should be! Brats! Trampling my lettuce patch, scaring my poor piggies! You know, I could do anything to you, and nobody would be the wiser—in a storm like this. I bet your parents don't even know you're out. They sent you to bed *and you just disappeared.*"

The old bat grinned, but her threat didn't incite the desired fear, not in Petra. Everybody knew everybody, and anyone familiar with their folks knew they were dead. Maybe Petra and Emil could get home without alerting Atla of their neighborly mishap. The witch couldn't tattle if she didn't know who they were.

Unaware of the magnitude of her ignorance, she prattled on. "My, how mysterious! You could be anywhere. Or nowhere!"

She concluded with a cackle which turned into a cough that trailed off into choking. At last, there was a lull. Emil opened his mouth but shut it, at the shake of Petra's head.

The shock of their capture wearing thin, her gaze wandered beyond the irate banshee. No dog in sight, and given that the only dirty footprints were their own, she doubted Foss was concealed nearby. The room was frilly, smelling of lavender and mildew, but certainly not of wet dog. Two matching love seats and a couch circled an oval coffee table, where atop a doily, sat a bowl containing apples, peaches, and pears, their dingy diadems suggesting waxy centers. The wallpaper featured yellow filigree, tendrils spiraling beyond round-framed paintings of citrus fruits and cotton-candy colored sweets. Above the fireplace lay a hefty mantle, where a rifle was held aloft by porcelain laborers.

The gun was the only object Petra saw that didn't quash her expectations. Even the pokers beside the fireplace had dendritic handles, yet Petra found no comfort in the cushy ambiance. Would the witch have shot them, had they run?

As if reading her mind, though likely just following her eyes, the witch snarled, "I could shoot you right here, right now."

In emphasis, she lifted the rifle. Her adjustments clicked metallic, and she aimed the muzzle at Emil, whose pupils dilated as his face drained of color.

"That's right. I could kill you. One shot each would do it."

The witch boomed with her mouth as she mimed firing on each child.

"I could hang you upside down, let your blood drain, and your meat soften. That's the way. Boiling's faster, but why rush the process? Cooking is an art. And you should never rush art." Her voice became more rasp and less yell with every word.

"What's one week for—" She looked them up and down, estimating their weights, her finger never leaving the trigger. "Call it, oh, 60 kilos of sweetmeat? Just think of the steaks and pies! You kids could make me fat. And your parents would never know. Children's bones look just like pig bones. Isn't that funny?"

Again, she cackled. Should they laugh? Would it help? Petra didn't know, and she was pretty sure Emil stopped listening the second the muzzle swung his way.

"We're very sorry," Petra said, enunciating every syllable.

Adults don't like mumbly kids, and it was of the highest importance that she be likable to the crazy lady brandishing a deadly weapon in her baby brother's face. Emil said nothing, his mouth slightly agape, eyes unblinking. There was a boy who was coming to terms with his mortality. Petra again tried to draw the witch's attention to herself.

"We didn't mean to make trouble. How about I clean this floor right now? Do you have a mop?"

The witch turned to her, finally bringing the rifle around. Emil breathed. Had he not been breathing?

"A mop? No. You may have a rag, each. And you will get on your hands and knees to clean this floor. Do not move."

That said, she left the room, firearm still in hand. Emil gestured to the backdoor, but Petra shook her head. A bullet to the back sounded like the opposite of fun.

"Unfun, if you will," Petra muttered to nobody in particular.

Looking longingly at the exit, she noticed an oddity she'd missed during her initial inspection. On the window sill sat a potted plant. While the pot was of the unremarkable baked clay variety, the plant was anything but. She inched closer to behold the alien beauty. A golden stalk rose and diverged into the narrower stems of seven violet leaves. Golden veins illuminated their edges, trailing to the points of each leaf. How many points did the leaves come to? She counted. Seven again. From above, the leaves formed a mandala, the tiniest bud peeking from where the stems split off. What would the flower look like when it bloomed? Petra wondered. Emil too, observed the unusual sprout. Careful not to touch it, he leaned in for a whiff.

"Doesn't smell like a flower to me. More like pastries. Sweet, anyway."

Facing away, they didn't notice the witch's return until she cleared her throat, reminding them of the threat at hand. Turning, they watched the witch's face crack into a lopsided smile.

"Ah! I see you've taken a liking to the St'Avgull. Funny that. Sat it out front all summer, and may as well have kept it in a box, for all the attention it got."

Petra wasn't surprised to hear that, as with the exception of the current hunt, she and her peers maintained a healthy aversion to the witch.

"Humpf. You children could do with a lesson in responsibility, to understand why you must respect other gardens! Save me the trouble of accounting for your bones. Yes." The old bat nodded to herself, pleased. "When you get home, put her in a window that faces east. She needs what light she can get. Water her once daily, just enough to darken the soil. If the soil looks dry before you go to bed, water her again."

Petra wasn't old enough for the annual school trip to the Grasagardur Botanical Garden, so her knowledge of botany was especially limited, but she suspected the "St'Avgull," was rare and precious. Why would the witch part with something valuable of her own free will? And to give something so fragile to two imprudent children? It didn't make any sense, but she wasn't about to argue. Whatever adults said, went, especially when those adults were as loony as they were armed.

True to her word, the witch handed them each a damp rag and set them to scrubbing. While they worked, she sat at the coffee table sipping her tea, one eye following their efforts, the rifle tucked under her arm. The children forced the grime from between the cracks in the floorboards, earning Petra a splinter in the process. At least she didn't need to use the bathroom. The acid sting of cleaning chemicals announced scratches lining her palms, some deep. She must've sliced herself on the raspberry thorns when the pigs squealed. In the cold, she hadn't noticed.

Once the floor was clean and dry, the children stepped back so the witch could review their work. Petra half expected her to keep them there all night, making them scrub and scrub at nothing until the sun came up, but instead, the witch nodded. She accepted the browned rags, handed Petra the St'Avgull, and bade them a blunt "Go home," before ushering them out into the storm, slamming the door at their backs.

Emil wanted to keep looking for Foss but Atla would be getting home soon.

"And anyway, we would've heard him if he was being kept in her house."

"But what if she fed him to the pigs?"

"Then there's nothing we can do."

The children entered through the back on the off chance Atla was home and unaware of their absence. The instant the door snapped shut, a wraith rose from the gloom. Under the sputtering bulb, the elder Kristjandottir appeared decades past her youth. Lines shifted over indiscernible brows, emphasizing the droop of her jowls. How long had her complexion been so jaundiced? Her cheeks and lips were rouged, but their rosiness only emphasized the dusky half-moons under her eyes—wet eyes, yet not brimming. Atla wore an oversized T-shirt, the sleeves shielding her upper arms. Below was red with bites. She must have had a hard shift.

"Where have you two been? You should be in bed."

Unable to meet her eyes, the children stared at their feet.

"Sorry, Atla," Petra said. "We were looking for Foss."

"At this hour? Are you insane? Playing dog catchers after dark during a thunderstorm?!"

Petra had the sense not to answer that, but Emil lacked her restraint.

"We figured the thunder would keep the witch from hearing us come in."

Atlas palmed her brow, before looking to the ceiling. She took a long breath, then spoke. "Tell me you did not break into our neighbor's house."

"We didn't! Honest! She pulled us inside!" Emil insisted.

Petra, her eyes glued to the floor, could feel the burning of Atla's attention.

"I can't believe what I'm hearing. Petra, you're eleven. Too old to fear imaginary witches and certainly old enough to know better than to jeopardize both of your safety on behalf of some dog."

"I'm sorry," Petra replied, "but you weren't there when she wouldn't come to the door, when she was watching us from behind her curtains."

"What would she even want with some old mutt?"

"I don't know. Maybe she wanted to eat him or use him in her potions."

Atla sighed. "Again, she's not a witch. Not every old lady who lives alone is up to nefarious deeds. Her name is Gunndis, for the last time." Rubbing her forehead, she continued, "So, what's this, then?" She lifted the pot from Petra and held it to the light. That bulb would need changing soon. In the meantime, Petra's head began to throb. "Huh. The stem looks metallic." She pushed it ever so slightly, to see if it might budge. When it did, she gasped. "I've never seen a plant like this. Where did you get it?"

The children explained their bizarre punishment-gift and the ranting that preceded its bestowal, while pulling off and putting away their outerwear.

"A rifle? You're saying Gunndis pointed a loaded weapon at you?"

"Yes!" Emil exclaimed. "She kept saying how she could eat us because our bones look just like pig bones."

Atla's brows could rise no higher, but her lips thinned, and her jowls grew sharp. For a moment, nobody spoke.

"Okay. So. Don't go near her again. I mean it. Not anywhere near her or her property." She uncurled her fists, like talons, before continuing. "Stop trespassing in other people's yards. The neighbors don't like us as it is. You're kids now, so nobody has pressed charges, but eventually, someone will, and then the CPA might take you away. This is serious. You guys don't under—" Her earnest spiel was interrupted by frantic knocking at the front door. Somebody wanted in, urgently, but who at this hour? "Do not leave this room." She commanded, placing the St'Avgull on the dresser and closing the children in behind her.

The children exchanged alarmed glances and rushed to listen at the gap in the doorway. Emil got there first, so Petra leaned against the crack above him, and both strove to achieve silence. Was it the witch? Had she followed them home? Had she brought the gun?!

No, it was a male voice, booming to compete with the storm.

"WHERE WERE YOU?! YOU WERE SUP-POSED TO—"

"I. Told. You. Never. To. Come. Here. Leave now. Before I call the police."

Atla's tone was barbed, likely pronounced through gritted teeth. They'd thought she was mad at them, but *that* was nothing compared to the hate she spewed now. If a tone could kill, the reaper would've raised his scythe.

"You wouldn't dare you dirty—"

"The hell I wouldn't. You and I had nothing planned tonight! That was last night and you never showed. My kids are home. I will see you tomorrow!" Her say concluded, she slammed the door shut, and judging by the metallic clicking that followed, set the deadbolt.

The man yelled something else, but the children couldn't make it out between two doors and the wind. Footsteps approached, and they both lunged for their beds before Atla slipped in. Her face shone red and her hands were clenched. The children did not ask about the unwelcome visitor. She spread her fingers and took a deep breath.

"Where was I? Ah. You are not going to bother Gunndis ever again, and this is the last time you sneak out. Period. Am I clear?"

The children nodded.

"Good. Now about tomorrow—Petra, I'm going to show you something. Emil, stay in bed. You should already be asleep."

Petra kicked off her blanket and followed her big sister. Atla's bedroom had seen tidier days. Band T-shirts, jeans, and undergarments carpeted every surface. The pervasive musk may have come from the walls. They'd been dealing with a mildew problem for some time. Atla got on her knees, brushed aside frayed socks, and tapped the floorboard she'd revealed.

"See this? It comes up. I carved a tiny 'X' into the corner so we can always find it."

From under her mattress, Atla pulled a pocket knife, which she wedged beneath the wooden corner and lifted. Therein was a stack of cash atop several manilla envelopes. Atla reached in, counted, and handed Petra a tidy sum.

"I need to catch up on sleep tomorrow. This should cover groceries. Next time we run low on milk, eggs, you know—the staples, money is here. Don't buy more than we need. This is for our bills."

Petra nodded, solemnly accepting this new responsibility. Atla's face was fading back to its usual pallor.

"You can go to bed now."

"Okay—but ah, Atla. Which side of our house is the east side?"

Atla considered, her hands pointing every which way while she made mental calculations.

"The window by your dresser should face east."

Before she tucked herself in, Petra lifted the blinds and moved the St'Avgull to the sill. Her headache from the flickering, buzzing light, had abated. In the dark, with no one to judge her fidgeting, she squeezed the little doll she always carried on her person. It wasn't much to look at, worn with a simple genderless face, no hair, and a cartoonish body, but the rubber flesh had give, and the limbs were posable. It had been a gift once, but so long ago she couldn't recall why, nor who from. Finally, toy in hand, she fell asleep.

Chapter 2

Petra was careful to observe the needs of their plant. Never having had a pet, this was an opportunity to showcase just how grown up she and Emil were. Every morning, Petra watered it before they walked to the bus stop. Foss reappeared on her route the day after the storm. When Emil asked where he'd been, the boys said only that he'd returned in the night.

Petra took to setting alarms even on their off days to maintain a regular schedule. Emil didn't appreciate being woken early when he had nowhere to be, but they both desperately wanted a dog of their own and he believed Petra when she said this was how to earn one. Afterall, she was the one Atla confided in, the reliable one, who always did her homework and read ahead, in her textbooks, for fun.

After forgetting to re-open the blinds one evening, the children took to changing in the bathroom, so they wouldn't have to close them at all. At night, before they turned in, Petra made sure to check the soil, providing extra water when necessary. If Atla was impressed, she gave no sign. They persevered regardless, optimistic she would notice and concede that they were ready for a puppy.

Beneath their watch, the St'Avgull's leaves grew wide, its stem tall. In a matter of weeks, the insignificant bulb bloomed. Petra expected the petals to open steadily over a day, perhaps two. What she did not anticipate was for the flower to open suddenly one restless night, its petals elongating, reaching beyond the confines of the narrow sill. Upwards, outwards and downwards, softly rustling, it spread to encompass much of the surrounding wall, floor, and ceiling. Its veins emitted a golden light. In the span of minutes, not hours or days, half of the children's room was engulfed by the alien flora, which bore a crevice, where seeds should have been.

"Emil?!"

He groaned, rolling over. The blossom's growth slowed, and ceased, leaving his bed untouched. He was in no danger of being overwhelmed physically, but she wanted him awake to bear witness. They say misery loves company, she thought. Well, maybe that was true for incredulity as well.

"Emil," she said more sternly. "Wake up. You need to see this."

His dreams proved more enticing than her command. Undaunted, it was with small steps and eyes on the eerie canopy, that she grabbed and shook him.

"Ugh. Not okay, Petra. I'm trying to sleep."

She shook him again, reiterating that he would regret missing *this*. He sat up, shoved her aside, rubbed his eyes, opened them, and let out a low whistle.

"Wow." He closed them again, rubbed and looked. "Still there."

Petra sensed that he spoke more to himself than to her. "Yup. We're not dreaming. This is happening. This is real."

She moved aside so he could view the entirety of what lay before them.

"How did that happen?"

"I don't know. I couldn't sleep. Then I heard it brushing the wall as it started to grow."

"And you didn't wake me up?!"

"What do you think I've been trying to do?!."

"Let's check it out!" he cried, kicking aside the bedding, hopping down, and charging for the tunnel.

"Wait!" Petra insisted, rushing to block him.

Fortunately for her, the room wasn't big, so he hadn't his typical gains.

"Let me take a peek first to see how deep it is before we go in."

At her urging, Emil backed off, his eyes glued to the abyss. Skirting around him, she eased first her fingertips, and then gingerly, her arm into the hole. Bracing, she poked the inner flesh. Unbit, she applied pressure. The rim felt closer to rubber than stone. She eased her entire palm against the side, pressing firmly. The surface was smooth, not soft, and in no way pliable. Pulling back her unscathed hand, she tried both hands, arms, and eventually, her entire head. She couldn't see much but was sure if they climbed in and clambered down, they'd find themselves far below the floor.

Withdrawing, she peered around the honeyed gloom, mulling over what supplies they'd need. In the light of the St'Avgull, they compiled a list. Petra jotted down food, water bottles, Emil's watch, their cereal box compass, flashlights, and their mother's remaining spools of yarn. Emil wasn't thrilled about using those, but Petra explained they would be no trouble to reroll during the return journey, and he dropped his objections. If the wool got dirty though, it was on her head.

First checking that Atla wasn't home, the kids packed and changed into daywear. Petra stole some laundry from Atla's room to make sibling-shaped lumps under their blankets, and on second thought, grabbed a box of Band-Aids. That ought to do it. They'd only be gone until it was time to wake for school. As long as they kept track of the time, Atla would never suspect they'd left.

Emil wanted to dive in, but Petra cautioned against it. She tied one of the spools around a leg of her bed. The rest she kept in Emil's bags for easy access. Adjusting the straps of her backpack, she crawled in first, more to ensure Emil didn't jump down, than because she wanted to lead. Easing herself in, she just fit, shimmying to advance. Gradually, the tunnel widened until Petra observed the roof was tall enough for them to sit without bending their necks, but standing wasn't an option. Emil too, pulled himself beyond the tight entryway before shifting to a crawl.

Anticipation spurred them on. They progressed quickly, keen to see and learn what could be gleaned from this space between places.

On their hands and knees, they moved farther from the vivid light that had beckoned them in. Narrow veins illuminated areas of wall, the entry point reduced to a bright pinprick at their backs, until it wasn't. Used to darkness, they opted not to turn on the flashlights just yet. This they agreed upon until the glowing tendrils disappeared and they couldn't see at all. Only then did Emil flip his on, keeping it low. What batteries the duo possessed lay in those metal tubes, and if they died, they'd be adventuring blind. In time the lit veins dimly returned, but suspecting Emil was loath to turn off their preferred light source, Petra pretended not to notice. The stem's glow was inconsistent, regardless, slipping into and out of the rubbery earth.

The path leaned perceptibly as they crawled. What had been an eraser-like consistency gradually gave way to the cracked texture of pumice, and the children had to move with care not to scrape their knees. After what must have been at least an hour, Petra became aware of a curved aperture, rim gleaming, a ways ahead and to her left.

"There's something there," she said, assuming he couldn't see past her.

"What is it?"

"Dunno yet."

The faint hoop appeared nearer than it was. She scrambled forward with the renewed vigor of curiosity. The monotony of their trek had worn her excitement thin.

Eager to reach any destination at all—Petra bumped her knees and elbows in her frenzy. Those would bruise. She arrived at a circle of what appeared to be fogged glass within a faintly lit amber setting. As she had with the St'Avgull's seedless center, Petra poked it. Soft, pliable, the window could be maneuvered. This wasn't glass. It was some kind of organic membrane. What would happen if it tore?

"Well, what is it?!" Emil repeated. Moving her yarn aside, he leaned his face over her shoulder.

"A window?"

"I think it's skin," she replied. "—maybe of the plant. We shouldn't play with it. It doesn't look like a way out."

She shuffled on, content to leave that mystery where it lay. Emil however, opposed abandoning their discovery. Approaching the filmy screen, he pointer finger across the smooth surface. Testing its resistance, he pressed more firmly with his palm, sure he felt a tear forming. Then, with all the forethought one might expect from am eight year old boy, Emil punched it.

He cried out as his arm tore through, freezing from fist to elbow. What he considered his death cry was eclipsed by the deafening peal of bells sounding from the fresh puncture. The instant passed, and retracting his arm from the arctic, Emil checked he was intact before wondering if the chimes had died down. Had they damaged his hearing? Was he deaf?! Fortunately, the shrill scolding of one Petra Kristjandottir cleared up that concern. Inspecting the window, they found it resealed, a fist-length scar marking the momentary rupture. The tunnel main continued, and so too did they, leaving other flesh windows be.

By the fifth screen, Petra called for a halt, to rest, eat, and check the time. Such were their goals. In practice, Emil found that either his watch or time was malfunctioning.

"Should we turn back now?" Petra asked. "It has to be getting late, and Atla will be upset if the school calls while she's sleeping." She squeezed the doll in her pocket, attempting to relieve anxiety.

Emil shrugged. "We've come this far. "

"Was the watch working earlier today?"

Emil stared at the cartoon face, willing its two-dimensional gloved hands to move.

"I think so."

"You're not sure?"

She passed him a banana and he handed her a water bottle.

"I'm pretty sure," he answered. "Anyway, we can handle Atla. She's not going anywhere. This path, though—it might not stay for long. What if by tomorrow night, it's shrunk back to normal?"

He bit into his banana. Was it rude to litter in a place that shouldn't exist, with garbage that would naturally decompose?

"Isn't that all the more reason to turn back now? What if it shrinks while we're in here?"

He watched Petra fold her peel and tuck it into her bag. Sighing, he followed suit.

"I don't know. Aim for one of the windows and hope it's warmer than the last one? We've come this far. Don't you want to know where it goes?"

"Of course I do. But what if it doesn't go any-where? What if it just loops around forever or stops at a dead end? Maybe those windows are it—the only way out."

"I don't think so," Emil answered, considering. "We didn't have to tear anything to get in."

"No. We didn't." Petra peered forward, squinting, looking for the light of an exit, listening for signs of life. "What time does your watch say?"

He told her, and she thought back to when the rustling caught her attention.

"That's about when we first climbed in. Can I have the compass?"

"Here you go," he said, passing it along.

The flashlight reflected off the glass surface, but despite its opaque sheen, they could see the point-er spinning wildly, flicking first this way, then that.

"Maybe time doesn't happen here. Or maybe in this tunnel, certain devices just don't work," Petra considered.

"The flashlights are fine," he argued.

"Yeah. But we're also inside of a giant glowing plant. None of this makes sense."

Maybe Atla was right, she thought. If the stem *was* metallic, however flexible, then it could be magnetic. Petra was fairly certain compasses worked by interacting with the magnetic pull of the North Pole. That's what the cereal box said, anyway. If the entire stem was attracting the needle, that would explain the spastic swiveling under the glass plate. Could a magnet break a watch? She didn't know.

"Okay. So we keep going?" Emil asked.

"I guess so, but let's sleep first," she suggested. "We have enough food to hold us over for a few days if we're frugal. Water, though—That's the issue. Once we're half out, we're heading home no matter what."

"Alright. Did you bring a blanket?"

He wasn't cold but blankets were as much for security as warmth. Unfortunately, the plan hadn't been to spend the night.

"Nope," Petra said.

They attempted to shape their bags into pillow-esque lumps, but it was useless. Water bottles and flashlights weren't soft. All they accomplished was squishing their meager supply of bread. Petra kicked off her shoes and laid them atop the yarn marking their return route. Then she rolled onto her side, turned off the light, gave her rubber doll a few calming squeezes and fell asleep. Emil scooted until his back was against hers, and then he too, drifted off.

He woke first, shooting upright and bumping his head before he remembered why he was splayed out over the hard ground in the dark. In his surprise, he'd knocked Petra aside, so she was instantly alert. Patting the ground while grumbling at his clumsiness, she reclaimed the flashlight and flicked it on. They shared a light meal before setting off, backs stiff and knees sore.

Breaks were seldom and they kept their water intake to a minimum. Neither child wanted to have to turn back early. Plus, as Petra pointed out after she woke up, there weren't any bathrooms in a flower. To which Emil'd responded, "This is nature. Everything is a bathroom." Brave though his words were, he had no desire to relieve himself in front of his sister, and there wasn't so much as a curtain of coverage in the tunnel. It was fortunate they hadn't had to deal with the bathroom issue thus far, but neither child was so naive as to believe it wouldn't come up before their next sleep.

As they crawled, they unspooled more yarn, carefully tying each new thread to that preceding. Petra was counting the windows and was at twelve when the path forked.

"Well, this is it," she said. "We have to choose. Left or right?"

Instead of answering, Emil turned off the flashlight and closed his eyes, allowing himself to become fully accustomed to the dark. Opening them, the choice was clear.

"Left. It's lighter farther in."

He flicked his light back on, and Petra nodded, scurrying into the chosen corridor.

"Wait right there a second," Emil said, his bladder calling. Handing his business a wall away, he returned.

"Smart," she said. "I'll be right back."

Who knew when their next chance would be?

Then the children pushed on. Before long, Petra observed an upward slant to the ceiling. Yards ahead, she cautiously and successfully attempted to stand. Emil followed suit, pleased at the opportunity to stretch. With increased height, so too those veins grew broader and more plentiful. Emil turned off the flashlight, putting it away. There was a grating noise ahead. Sounds like metal on metal,

Petra though, blinking back tears at the sudden pain that erupted along her crown. She quieted her steps to better determine the source. Emil heard it too and it sounded like freedom.

They sped up, thinking not of water nor food nor bathroom breaks nor school nor even of Atla. After what, to them, must have been at least a day underground, they thought of the sun, of being outside, of wide-open spaces. A field perhaps. Or a beach. Just a nice flat expanse where they couldn't reach from one boundary to the next.

The ground grew smoother. Petra broke into a jog and then a run, holding the yarn high above her head. Emil swallowed his frustration at having to move at her pace, but she was in the lead. He couldn't pass her without a word or a shove, and she wouldn't let him exit first. Being the elder, she assumed responsibility for his safety. How he felt was inconsequential. So she ran, and he jogged until suddenly her foot found air, and she tumbled out. Slowing, Emil reached the drop and jumped, landing with a thud at her side.

They took in their surroundings, Petra's right hand in Emil's, her left clinging to the way home. Visions of endless plains could not have been further removed from reality. The duo stood within a monumental dome, the center of which was a massive skylight, framing the barely-perceptibly waning moon above, which shone emerald, tinted by the aurora borealis' tidal dance. Opposite them, and at level, were fiery arches. At their feet, the ground sloped steeply downward, providing the children with a nearly unimpeded view of the sprawling crypt beyond. A labyrinth of stalagmite walls spiraled outward from a reflecting pool, mirroring the skylight both literally and in scale. The labyrinth's ridges were illuminated by the moonlight, amber veins, and distant lanterns. Stalactite ceilings swung low over narrow enclosures, eliminating opportunities for spying on the inhabitants. Here and there, condensation dripped, landing with audible splashes in the wake of distant banging. There was movement between the stalagmite rows. Figures were approaching. The children's arrival had not gone unnoticed.

Petra released Emil's hand and stepped in front of him as the welcoming party neared.

"Hello?" she said, her voice cracking.

What or who, perhaps, stood before her was of diminutive height, with pointy ears, a long snout, small dark nose, and wide obsidian eyes. Its gaze reflected the children in unsettlingly stark relief.

The creature, reminding Petra of a fox standing on its hind legs, had grey fur. There were bald patches, likely of illness or age, if the shining coats of its gathering peers set a basis for judgment. Their fur ranged from black to beige. Instead of paws, their limbs ended in hands and feet, their fingers and toes elongated by talons. The nearest was hunched, its knees curving inward. Above its nose and over its brow line, sat a cracked red gem, like a pineal eye. The others wore many such stones, theirs in better repair. Stacked necklaces and bracelets jangled in step, over chainmail of varying complexity and ornamentation, which hung almost to their knees. They wore no pants, nor shoes, and were armed with staves.

The nearest growled as the children were surrounded. Their snarl turned syllablic, and Petra was sure this was speech, though she knew not the tongue. More sounds followed and there came a word she recognized. "Bonjour." She was sure that was it. Then, "Ni Hao." Another greeting? Oh!

"Hello. How do you do?" she inquired, hopefully helpfully, in Icelandic.

There was a pause.

Then "Hello," said the beast. "I bid thee welcome to Josalfar."

Emil crept from her shadow to better face those whose home they'd intruded upon.

"Thank you," said Petra, unsure how to respond.

Commonly when meeting a new person, she would introduce herself and encourage Emil to do the same. She'd heard tell of demons though. Their names held power. In those stories, scarier tales than gram was supposed to tell—knowing the demon's name granted the speaker control of said demon. Did that imply the opposite was true? Petra wasn't sure if these were demons or fairies or if the *name-power-thing* applied to both. She also doubted asking would garner an honest response. So she lied.

With no way to explain to her brother without being overheard, she said, "I'm Marta, and this is Kristjan." Emil nodded, confused. "We've come a long way. What is this place?"

Emil caught the lie and, without Petra's reasoning, opted to trust her judgment. Doubtless, she would explain why they wore their parents' names later.

"Josalfar is the capital city of Stornalund, home of her Majesty, Queen Siv. May she reign infinite." the creature growled. "I call myself Roth. Humans rarely walk among the star people unbid. Have you a guide?"

Petra shook her head, and then considering that Icelandic was not Roth's first language, so likely western body language wasn't either, she emphasized the *no* verbally.

"Then it is for me to lead you. Food does not grow on the golden path. Drink does not flow. I have food and drink. Come."

A figure to his left barked and Roth yipped in response. A dog's bark could mean many things. A demon was altogether more foreign, and the children couldn't gauge the mood of their host. Without further ado, Roth turned from crowd and children alike, skipping a route, his stride, more hop than step. His companions parted so the children could follow, and without a better alternative, they did. Petra held the yarn aloft as she examined the maze from within. Looking back, Emil saw a swathe of shiny black eyes tracing their progress.

What did Petra know of fairytales and legends? The might of names, sure. That was a rule, but there were others. Before Emil was old enough to listen and care, their gram told stories about everything fantastic. "Think," Petra, she told herself. "What did gram say?" Star people—that's what Roth called them. Had gram mentioned star people? Not that Petra could remember. Would demons call themselves star people? Perhaps. Wasn't Lucifer named for the morning star? Demons lived in hell, which was to say, underground. Josalfar was that. But what of fairies? Where did fairies live? In other realms? Were demons and fairies the same? Or were the star people something else entirely? Damn her for not having paid better attention to gram's fairy lore.

As Roth ushered the children into a valley between geyserite dividers, Petra saw the dais covered in fruit and remembered the most important rule of all—do not eat fairy food. Maybe it was because the food was enchanted? Or poisoned. She couldn't remember the *why*, so the *what* had to suffice.

Petra wanted to communicate this crucial concept to Emil without informing Roth that she was on to him. Luckily the creature turned to the dais when he next spoke, and she shook her head emphatically, her finger pointing to the feast before making a slicing motion across her neck.

"Eat, children," Roth said, his tone guttural. "Your journey has been long. I shall send for drinks. Don't be shy. You need your strength."

With this, he yipped at a passerby, who raised a clawed hand in acknowledgment. The other stepped away, tail fanning behind him. Was that a sign of disgruntlement? Or an expression of puppy-like joy? His ears were up. With the non-anthropomorphic fox variety, that did not indicate a desire to play.

Emil caught her warning, would have been blind not to, but boy did he wish he hadn't. A kid could only live off stale sandwich scraps and bananas for so long. A platter of free goodies would have been tantalizing on any old Tuesday, but given what they'd gone through to get here, it was agonizing not to dive in.

"No, thank you," Petra said, and Emil gritted his teeth, frowning.

Yes, Atla taught not to take food from strangers, but surely she'd support an exception in this instance! They'd come so far and now—what?! Petra would have them leave not just empty-handed, but with bellies as barren as they'd come? Why were they here, if not to experience the world below?

"We're quite full from the food we packed for our trip. We appreciate the offer, though."

Emil could have kicked her. If she were two steps closer, he would have.

The other returned with a companion. While he carried small earthenware bowls of what may have been wine, but could also have been blood—neither of which were likely to sate their thirst—his peer brought only his staff. With glossier fur and embellished armor, including a split chain mail skirt that reached to his ankles, the children took the newcomer to be of greater renown than the star people they had yet encountered. An abundance of rubies radiated a halo around his head, casting bloody pinpricks of light across his wide slanted eyes. While the bowls were handed to the children, this third beast snarled, then roared at the cupbearer and Roth both. Perhaps admonished, the cupbearer parted ways, head and tail hung low, unspeaking. Their guide was not so easily dismayed. As the children pushed their undrunk bowls onto the dais, maybe-blood far less appealing than the meal that called to Emil, Roth yipped back. Growling ensued on both sides, as they smacked the stone floor with their staves, emitting cascades of sparks. With Petra distracted by the conflict at hand, Emil reached for a gooseberry.

In that instant, a decision was made. The staves again met the ground with a resounding *crack* that made Petra jump. A bolt of electricity burst from beneath Roth, knocking him back, sending static arcing across his armor, as he cried out in pain. Singed, he righted himself, snorted at onlookers and foe alike, and left without another word. The victor watched him go before acknowledging the children.

Turning, he looked first from the undisturbed dais to their bare hands. Then he wobbled his head from side to side, in what Petra took to be a nod.

"Hello, children. I am called Temil. Josalfar is home to Alfarians and adult humans. You are too young. Have you eaten of these plates?"

Both children shook their heads.

"Have you drunk of these cups?

They reiterated their nonverbal no.

"As it should be. You must leave now." His tone left no room for discussion. "I will show you the way."

So saying, he swept from the dais back in the direction from whence they came, until they stood at the edge of the dome before a pockmarked and varicosed wall. Petra first, then Emil, spotted the end of their yarn jutting from the solid rock.

Questioning, they looked to Temil. In answer, he turned, reaching for the charm at his neck. Lifting the spiral, he spun the central ring, and then the outer in the opposite direction. Temil whistled, rumbled, and sang, his breath glowing, not unlike his forehead gems. Then he leaned forward and placed the device in a divot beside the yarn sprout. Unseen bells tinkled as the wall split. This was not the crack and thunder of stone shattering against stone, but rather a symphony of chimes as the surface flexed and morphed. In moments their yarn hung from the base of a child-sized crevice.

"Step inside and move forward. Do not pass this way again while you have your youth."

Petra thanked him out of politeness, hefting herself up and in. Emil gave one last lingering look to the city underground, and then, with the optimism of a child clinging to a fresh secret, he too climbed inside. No sooner had Emil entered the cavern than the entrance sealed shut, the chimes echoing far ahead. Petra peered back, alarmed, but her fear was hers alone, for Emil's spirits couldn't be dampened. Sticking out her chin, Petra inhaled, allowed herself a moment of introspection, squeezed the doll in her pocket, and began the long trek home. True to her word, she re-raveled the yarn as she went. When the veins thinned, Emil pulled out his flashlight, absentmindedly shaping shadow puppets while he walked, stopping only when he was forced to crawl.

Petra paused, taking her time unknotting each chord from the next, passing them to Emil for safekeeping. He hummed tunelessly, accepting and storing this piece of their mother, taking little notice of their pace. Life was good. Adventures were good. Soon they'd be home, and you know what? He thought—home was good too.

Petra realized they were crossing greater distances more quickly than before, as she collected the yarn bundles, but she half expected them to have multiplied in their absence. Both children kept their eyes peeled for the bizarre windows of the prior journey but found none.

The light of their walls grew bright, and not ten minutes later, Petra tumbled into their bedroom, followed quickly by Emil, in a lopsided summersault. They turned to watch the rapid shrinking of the St'Avgull until it was no more substantial than the average house plant. Acknowledging the end of their odd journey, Petra untied the yarn from her bed frame.

Chapter 3

"Where have you been?!"

Petra turned first, Emil's cheer adding lag to his spin. His optimism left nowhere for Atla's voice, shrill with hysteria, to claw and clasp. Her negativity slid away like drizzle on an oil slick.

Rising from Petra's covers, Atla appeared to have aged rapidly during their brief absence. Her face was lined, any softness leached away. When had she last eaten? She looked hungrier than Petra felt.

Were those the same pajamas Atla wore last night? She smelled like spoiled produce, and the neon pink of her attire cast her that much paler, in contrast.

"I've been worried sick! I told you both not to go outside after bedtime. So what do you do?! What is wrong with you?!"

If Petra was hoping Atla's anger would be evenly distributed, she hoped wrong. Those bloodshot eyes glared at her and it was she who had to respond.

"I'm sorry, Atla. Really! It was—it was an accident! Did you see?! You must have seen the—the flower! How big it grew?! We didn't know the tunnel went so far, or we'd never have set out! Honest!"

"What are you babbling about?! I almost called the blasted police! Blaming a plant! *What tunnel?!* Are you insane?! Do you think I am?! Where were you?! Now. I want names. I'll be at their house faster than you can blink. Names. Now!"

Petra sought an answer that might quell Atla's wrath, but her attention was caught by nearly inaudible humming. She looked at the St'Avgull, to use the melody as evidence for her otherworldly claims, but found herself staring dumbfounded at her idiot brother, a toothy grin plastered across his stupid face. He wouldn't have been smiling if Atla blamed him! It wasn't fair. Petra wasn't *that much older* than Emil. Why was she expected to be responsible for everything he did? Was he not his own person?! Had Atla left the room, Petra would've given him a swift kick in the shin.

Disregarding hum and bum alike, Petra turned back to her big sister. She was careful not to squeeze her rubber doll, the perceived distraction sure to exacerbate the elder's fury.

"Really, Atla. The flower opened up and we crawled inside. It brought us to the star people—elves, I think. It's like the stories gram used to tell. I'm sorry we left. We shouldn't have. It won't happen again."

"Fairytales. You disappear for three days and I'm supposed to believe you've been with fairies this entire time."

Three whole days?! No wonder she was mad!

"Not fairies exactly. They look more like fox people and I don't think they can fly—"

"Enough! No more nonsense! No stories! You took off and I didn't know where you were—if you were alive or dead! Where did you go?! Who has been keeping you?! Tell me!"

"I'm telling the truth! Ask Emil!"

Emil started at the sound of his name. "What?"

Had he been tuning them out this whole time? What was with him?!

Atla's anger momentarily redirected, she asked, "Emil. Where have you two been?"

"Oh," said Emil slowly. Thoughtfully. He beamed at her. "We've been on an adventure! There were elves, Atla! Except they weren't like elves we've heard—"

"Stop! Stop it, both of you! This is madness. Go to bed. I'm going to bed. If either of you thinks of stepping foot outside of this room, so help me!"

Unconcerned, Emil shrugged. "Can we go to the bathroom?"

"Fine. Yes. You can use the toilet. Don't go outside. Don't touch the windows. If anyone knocks, don't answer. I need to sleep. We will talk about this tomorrow, and tomorrow I expect some serious answers. Good night!"

With that, she slammed the door and stomped away.

Petra and Emil exchanged glances. She wanted to change into pajamas, but found none in her dresser. She didn't want to exacerbate Atla's fury by pulling from what clothes hung drying outside. Instead, she changed into a loose dress, once Atla's, and climbed into bed. That Emil mightn't have been aware of Atla's misplaced anger eroded the sting from his amusement. As long as he wasn't smirking at her, Petra thought. Although—had Atla's anger been misplaced? They did sneak out in the middle of the night. Emil likely wouldn't have ventured into the tunnel if she'd forbidden it.

"Emil, can you turn off the light?"

He hadn't moved more than a step or two from where he'd initially landed.

"Okay," he said and did so.

She listened, waiting for her eyes to adjust, and heard neither the protest of their aging floor nor the crinkle of plastic sheets wrapping his bed. Sure enough, an Emil shaped shadow stood stock still beside the light switch.

"Emil we've walked a lot—a few days' worth, I guess. You should get some rest."

The shadow's shoulders rose and fell.

"Yeah. You're right."

The floor flexed and buckled, its cry replaced by the whisper of his comforter and sheets as he tucked himself in.

"Petra—do you think we'll ever get back there? The tunnel is gone."

"Maybe when we're grownups? I think we should forget about Josalfar though. Temil said not to come back while we're kids. I think we were in danger. Roth was bad news."

"Why?"

"The way we were warned—how Temil made us leave? Kids aren't supposed to be there."

"But what could they do to us?"

"Anything they want. I didn't see any police. Did you?"

"No."

"Maybe they eat kids like the witches in stories."

He was quiet. "I don't think I know those stories."

He wouldn't have, would he? She thought. Gram died when he was little and Atla wasn't one for books.

"Most of them revolved around people having to outwit the fae. Look, let's go to sleep, alright? You've got to be tired."

"Okay."

They were quiet except for the shuffling of covers.

"G'night Petra."

"G'night Emil."

The children woke late and Atla woke later. Guilt battered Petra, thinking of how awful Atla must've felt all alone. When Petra heard Atla's standard waking cough, she set about making breakfast. The rye had grown stale while they were awol but there was spam and crackers. In the fridge, which reeked of fart, there was cheese, skyr, butter, orange juice, salad dressing, three carrots, and a ball of lettuce. Lettuce was almost food. In the freezer was an ice tray of three jello cubes. Petra shrugged.

First off, she opened the skyr, took a whiff, gagged, and dropped it in the garbage. Wincing, she drew the drawstrings tight and lugged the bag out back. Had Atla not been in the kitchen in days? How'd she not notice the rotting fridge?

Returning to the kitchen, Petra turned on two burners. She let the gas hiss before setting each flame. Into one pan went the spam, and then cheddar over top, once the meat was crispy. Cheese quickly melted, she scooped the slices onto crackers. In the cast iron, she cooked carrot bits in butter. When they were soft, she placed pleasantly unwilted lettuce and carrot around the sandwiches, drizzling a spoonful of dressing across the lackluster salad. It would do. She'd have brought it to Atla, but suspected her presence would cause more stress than that of little Emil, so she ran to get him.

"Hey. I made Atla breakfast. I can make you some too if you like, but can you walk this up to her now? Be careful, please. She's had a rough time."

"Okay," he said, his voice hoarse.

Really? No argument? She'd asked him to do something, hadn't she? Putting the plate down, Petra reached for his forehead. It was hot.

"Emil—you're burning up. Never mind Atla. Go back up to bed. I'll be in with breakfast and orange juice in a few minutes."

"But!"

"At least lie down for a little while? You'll just get sicker if you don't."

He sighed, defeated. "Fine."

She watched Emil slump away before she carried the food to Atla's room. The door was partially open, but it was polite to knock.

"Come in," Atla called.

Petra did so, clambering over the corpses of a laundry massacre, wincing at the smell.

"Good morning. I made you breakfast."

"Thank you. We're still going to have a long talk about what happened though. You kids can't just keep running off and disappearing."

"I know. I'm sorry."

"Where's Emil?"

Petra flushed, convinced his condition would be her fault, and maybe it was.

"He has a fever so I sent him back to bed."

"Did he catch something from the people you were with?"

"You don't believe me, but no, I don't think any of them—they called themselves Alfarians—were sick, but we weren't there long."

"Petra, you're too old for fairy tales. I need you to be serious. The people you were with. Do I know them?"

"I am serious. We weren't with any people. I'm not sure what they were, but they weren't human."

Atla's face scrunched dramatically, reminding Petra of the painting her art teacher, Mrs. Halonen, had posted of her bulldog. Then Atla's features smoothed as she took a long breath.

"Thank you for breakfast. When you're ready to tell me what happened, I'm here. But I need to know the truth. If you were with other grownups—whatever happened—I'm mad at them. You can tell me about them. You can tell me anything. Do you understand?"

"Yes, Atla."

"Is there anything you want to tell me?"

Nothing you'll believe, Petra thought. "No. Sorry."

"Alright then. Has Emil eaten yet?"

"No. I was just about to make him breakfast."

"I won't keep you then."

Nodding, Petra left and returned to the kitchen. Later she thought she heard the gasp and quake of sobbing coming from Atla's room, but lacked the courage to confirm for or against. That sound could be anything, Petra told herself, scrubbing without looking at the dishes.

When she checked on Emil, she found him asleep, his food untouched. Weird. He was always hungry, even while quite ill. Heck, she remembered when he had eaten half a rhubarb pie their parents hadn't hidden well enough, right before a football match. Halfway through the game, he'd abandoned the field to let loose his forbidden dessert. And how did he celebrate when his team won? By eating the other half, naturally. Concerned, she reached for his forehead again. He shot upright the instant her palm made contact, his eyes wide as he gasped for air.

"The shine!" he erupted. "We have to dig deeper!"

Petra placed her hand on his shoulder and with her other, guided his chin until he was facing her.

"Emil? It's okay. I'm right here. You were dreaming."

Wildly, he peered through and past her, casting his gaze from side to side. In moments the fluttering settled and his breathing normalized.

"Oh. Hey. Sorry I shouted"

"It's okay," she said, relieved he hadn't cried out for either parent. There was no relief from those nightmares.

He nodded, peering down at his patterned and faded blanket.

"Want some juice?" Petra asked, changing the subject.

"No." He shook his head. "Can you stay for a little while?"

And so she did. Neither child left the room except to eat, drink, or go to the bathroom. Even Atla didn't work that night, instead destroying them in rounds of cards. It was a game of her making, dubbed *Lindu Buff*. The rules made no sense but it made them laugh.

"Why does Jack beat the king, again?" asked Emil, rightfully confused.

"Because J comes before K, remember?" Atla responded, clarifying nearly nothing.

And on they played. The evening stretched cozily on until sleep won.

At dawn, Petra awoke. Not naturally an early riser in a house of those equally aversed, she moved to the living room to not bother Emil. She wasn't hungry, so she pulled a puzzle from under the mantle. Large chunks remained assembled from the last time they'd attempted to complete it but she pulled those apart and began anew. Her attention would have been better spent on makeup assignments for the school, but Atla hadn't mentioned any and likely they hadn't been sent home.

Atla joined Petra in the living room around noon. They built much of the border, then busied themselves putting together a light breakfast. With breakfast on the table, Atla set her coffee down and observed the late hour.

"It's already half-past one. Is he still in bed?"

Petra got up to check and sure enough, Emil was out cold. Sick or not, it wouldn't do him good to sleep the day away. Quietly, she said his name, and then again, but louder. She reached forward, shaking him awake. His eyes opened and he groaned, muttering about *having to get home,* but there was no screaming.

"Hey, bud. Time for breakfast. Then you can go back to bed."

"What time is it?"

"One thirty."

"In the afternoon?"

She laughed.

"Okay. I'm up."

He kicked his blankets off and stood dizzily, almost falling back into his bed.

"How are you feeling?"

"My head hurts and I'm thirsty."

Petra felt his head. Still hot. Missing more school wasn't ideal but it wouldn't be right to send him tomorrow if there wasn't any improvement.

They ate in the kitchen. Mid-afternoon, Atla left for work. She was going in early to make up for the previous night off. Emil went to bed, Aspirin proving ineffective thus far.

He had no history of asthma nor allergies, so this was likely a cold brought on from the conditions of their trip. In a few days, he'd be right and dandy. He just needed rest to recover was all. Keeping quiet to not disturb him, Petra read ahead in her textbooks, making assumptions about what she'd missed. The last thing she needed was her classmates thinking she was stupid. They already liked each other better than any one of them liked her. It was math, the dullest of subjects, that tugged at her eyelids with sleep.

Monday came. Petra went to school and Emil did not. She came home with stacks of work for them both. After toiling through her own smaller pile, Petra helped Emil tackle his. Come Tuesday, she took his temperature but he looked worse, not better, which the reading reflected. Wednesday, Atla was concerned enough to drive Emil to the family doctor, or to the doctor who had been the family doctor, back when they'd been a family who scheduled annual physicals.

The results were largely negative. Emil was small for his age, far smaller than their parents' heights should dictate. Dr. Johnsson in no way hid his fretting when Emil informed him that Petra and he shared a height.

"Are you not feeding them?"

Before Atla could respond, Emil spoke up, frowning. "We eat plenty. Atla works hard every night to put food on the table. Don't be mean to her! It's not her fault the bills never stop. Take it up with Mr. Gunnarsson."

Atla shushed him halfheartedly but Dr. Johnsson bade him continue.

"Who is Mr. Gunnarsson?"

"He leased me a car," answered Atla. "The payments aren't too high. Don't worry. And Mr. Gunnarsson isn't a bad man. He's always been fair with us. They do eat plenty, but I'm going to make sure they get more protein and iron in their diets. We're going to start eating more meat," she stammered.

Whether this statement mollified the situation in his opinion, Dr. Johnsson did not say. Instead, he regarded her coolly before returning to the focus of their visit.

"Humph. Well, as far as symptoms go—a headache, lethargy, and fever all point to a cold. No cough though? Hmm. If he was older I would consider mono but—that's unlikely. We can treat the symptoms, but antibiotics won't help. If he isn't better in a week, stop back in and see me. Do you have cold medicine?"

"I'll pick some up on the way home."

"That's fine." Then he turned to Emil. "Do you mind sitting in the waiting room for a moment while I speak alone with your sister?"

Little Emil puffed his chest out proudly, ready to refuse, but Atla looked sternly at him and nodded.

"Fine," he grumbled, climbing down from the paper covered chair-bed and letting himself out the way he'd come.

"Atla—I imagine things have been hard since the accident. If you need help, there are organizations who can assist you."

"Thank you but really, we're doing fine. We just haven't been eating enough meat, I guess. All those health gurus are always talking about the pros of fruits and vegetables, but growing boys and girls need their protein."

Dr. Johnsson's brows stretched for his hairline, and a decade prior, would have snagged it at the obvious lie, but alas. He wasn't in his twenties anymore. Or his thirties, to his constant dread.

"Well, then I'm glad to hear you and the children will be eating more balanced diets. And when will I be seeing Petra? She is long overdue for a check-up. As are you, for that matter."

"I'll have her in soon. And I'll make an appointment for myself too, on my next day off."

At the mention of her dubious work schedule, the doctor's gaze lingered over her long sleeves in his heated office. Rather than ask what she did for work, he merely nodded and reiterated the importance of proper nutrition and regular physicals before bidding her adieu. He was a busy man and Emil wasn't his only appointment.

The week passed without any obvious improvements to the boy's condition. Perhaps this was more than a cold, after all, contended Dr. Johnsson on his second visit. Emil's lymph nodes didn't appear enlarged and there were no sores despite the pain in his throat. While his voice was hoarse, he had only a minor cough.

"Could be the flu," Dr. Johnsson finally announced. "Antibiotics won't help. This should run its course on its own, but cold medicine will help with the symptoms. It's too late for antiviral medications to have an effect, I'm afraid. He should be drinking lots of fluids and getting plenty of rest."

Again, he said to return in a week if Emil wasn't any better.

Petra continued bringing Emil's makeup assignments home and helping to finish them during his waking hours, but those hours became gradually fewer. During his third visit, Emil was exhausted and Dr. Johnsson was alarmed. Atla had waited almost two weeks to set this appointment rather than the one recommended. Through no fault of her own, she defended herself inwardly, her shifts had been running later and she had to sleep when she could. That her sleep schedule, and Dr. Johnsson's office hours, overlapped was unfortunate, but what was she supposed to do? Maybe her prioritizing didn't look great on the surface but as far as she'd seen, Dr. No-Meds had zero intention of writing Emil a prescription for anything that would make him feel better. What was even the point of these visits?! She had half a mind to skip out on ol' Johnsson, and bring Emil straight to the emergency room, but she knew he'd be waiting hours before being seen.

Surprisingly, Dr. No-Meds didn't bother chastising her.

"Look. I'm going to be frank. I'm not sure what the problem is. He has all of these symptoms, but given how long they've persisted, I would expect to see them worsening differently. He is more tired than he was, but his lymph nodes are fine. His nose isn't running. I see no sores. His ears are clear. Even his breathing sounds normal. There are several things this could be and I'm going to need to run some tests. Can you come back tomorrow?"

Satisfied they were finally getting somewhere, Atla agreed. Tomorrow they would finally have an answer. Soon her brother would be back to normal, *forgetting* to do his homework and digging inconveniently placed holes once more.

Emil hadn't been paying attention during the appointment and barely noticed his feet moving him from the office, to the waiting room, and into the car. He was likewise dumb to the severity of his situation, and Atla's ramblings, which ranged from concern to relief during the drive home. As he settled into bed, Atla relayed Dr. Johnsson's uncertainties to Petra, who kept her face blank while internalizing the news, careful not to reach for the doll in her pocket. She would feel her feelings later. Atla had struggles enough without having to comfort her.

While Emil was up, Petra served him canned soup and a glass of juice concentrate. Atla had become religious about always having a full stock of fruit juices and hearty meat stews. In time, she hoped they'd gain the inches they'd somehow missed those past few years. She was a good parent, or she wanted to be, which was almost the same thing, Atla thought.

Once Emil was done, Petra carried his dishes to the sink, and cleaned them. Later, she finished her homework in bed, the pages shifting from white to primrose, as twilight crept along the window panes, painting her room. She swept eraser shavings to the floor, ignoring the ink on her sheets.

Atla entered as Petra was finishing up a grammar assignment and tucking it away. She took a seat on the edge of her little sister's bed and leaned her back against the wall, looking at least as tired as Emil.

"Do you want to go to the doctor tomorrow? You haven't had a check-up in ages. He's going to need a bunch of tests so we should be there a while. I'm sure they could find time for you, too."

"That's okay. I feel healthy. Whatever he's got, I haven't caught it."

Atla sighed but she didn't argue. They changed the subject, debating how to celebrate once he was better, listing what snacks to buy, what park to visit, whether he'd prefer a trip to the aquarium over the zoo.

Later, Petra awoke with a start to the room brimming with golden light and Atla missing from her bed. Leaping from the tangled covers, Petra rushed to the receding St'Avgull bloom as its opening sealed shut. In under a minute, it had returned to its usual size.

"No! Nonononono—" she cried, lifting the pot from the sill, as if access to the tunnel lay out of sight, just underneath.

Then she ran to Atla's room, throwing open the door and flipping on the lights. There was a mayhem of things, familiar and homey as they were dingy, but no Atla. Could she have gone to work? Maybe, Petra hoped.

Then she prayed. She didn't know who to pray to but did so anyway, throwing herself to her knees and clasping her hands.

"Please don't take my sister. Let Atla be at work. Let her come home. Please let her come back to us."

Petra's eyes were wet, but the pooling refused to overflow. She repeated her prayer, half begging, and half mantra until her words came rougher than Emil's of late. She clenched the doll until the surface lost its rubber smoothness on one side, roughened by the stabbing of her nails. Then she abandoned her floor post for a glass of water in the kitchen.

The water assuaged her thirst but failed to cool the burning drum between her ribs, or the other of her skull. She paced from the living room to the kitchen and back. The creeping dawn spread from the windows to the floor and still she paced, squeezing her doll until she feared the wire skeleton might pierce its rubber flesh. Please, she whispered. Not my sister too, she prayed. If anyone was listening, they did so in secret. The alarm sounded upstairs so she altered her route to turn it off. There had been many mornings when exterminating kept Atla until noon. It wasn't unheard of for her to be out this late, but Petra knew that wasn't the case this time. Atla wasn't at work. Atla wasn't coming home. She'd gone to stay with the fairies—Alfarians—whatever—and being an adult, they weren't going to let her go. Petra's skin wept, a rancid moisture contaminating the fabric under her arms, where neck met shoulders and along her lower back, when her eyes could not.

Her stomach rumbled and her feet grew sore, but she was possessed by the wordless sense that if she stopped pacing, let the doll drop, if she stopped praying, her sister would be lost forever. Then the phone rang and Petra ran to answer it. Was it Atla? It had to be! Nobody ever called!

"Hello?"

"Good day! This is Harpa Einardottir. I'm the receptionist at Dr. Johnsson's office. Am I speaking to Atla Kristjandottir?"

"Oh." Petra was numb with disbelief. "No. This is Petra."

"I see. Petra is it? Well Petra, is Atla home? She had an appointment scheduled a half hour ago for a Mr. Emil Kristjanson and neither have arrived."

"No. She's not home. Sorry."

"Alright then dear. Can you have Atla call us back when she gets home?"

"Yes ma'am. I'll be sure to do that."

"Thank you. Take care, Petra."

"You too Mrs. Einardottir."

Petra hung up the phone and sat on the floor, defeated. Of course, the prayer hadn't worked. Just because star people and flower tunnels existed didn't mean magic was real for humans. She sagged against the wall for support. Petra stared unseeing, felt unthinking, and blinked back tears that never fell. She couldn't tell where the injuries of her soul ended and her suffering body began.

Emil stepped into the kitchen, yawning, a question. "What's the matter?"

Atla was gone. Probably forever. And here was Emil who should've been at the doctor's office getting blood tests. That he was concerned for her in his state was laughable. Or would have been, were the cause anything less.

"Atla's gone."

"Gone? Where—what do you mean? Gone?"

"The St'Avgull opened up last night. She must have crawled in."

"Oh."

He paused to digest this information. Petra waited to see if he would reach the same conclusions she had.

"But—but she's a grown-up."

Petra nodded.

"We have to go in after her!" he shouted, his cry a sorry rasp.

Petra sighed. "I don't know how to get it open. And the star people—blast them—they aren't like us. They have magic. How are we supposed to get her back if they don't want her to go?"

"I don't know. But we have to try."

She nodded. "Well, *we* don't have to do anything. You're sick. After you eat, go relax. I'll see if I can find her."

"How?"

That was a good question. Petra had only just arrived at the idea and hoped it had merit.

"Gunndis."

"The witch?"

"She gave us the flower. She has to know what it does. And maybe she'll know how to open it!"

"I'll come with you!"

But she put her foot down. She couldn't worry about him and reason with a grown-up witch. It was too much. Instead, she made him oxtail soup, gave him a glass of water and another of orange juice. Then she sent him back to their room, leaving in such a hurry, she forgot her too-small jacket.

The witch answered on the second knock, the door swinging open so abruptly Petra's hand was in the air, prepped for a third.

"That plant kidnapped my sister. Tell me how to get her back."

The witch glared at her with her one eye, the other veiled by the customary patch. Today, she was in a ruffled floral dress. She tilted her head, then nodded after a brief pause, leading Petra in.

"Would you care for some tea?" Gunndis asked, guiding her to a sofa.

"No thank you. I'm in a hurry."

While her statement was true, she also feared the poisons at the witch's disposal.

Gunndis tsked. "Well, my dear child, rushing will do you no good. And it will do your sister even less. I do suppose you mean your older sister, yes? The child you trespassed with two moons past was a boy. Were they not?"

"Yes. That was Emil, my brother. Atla, our older sister, is the one missing. She's our legal guardian."

"There's nothing you can do. They've recruited her and she won't be returned. You and your brother will need a new guardian."

Petra stood up, bumping her legs on the hardwood table.

"There must be something. They let *us* go!"

"Of course they did. You're too young for mining. It's not illegal, per se, but her Majesty frowns upon enlisting children. And what the Queen says, goes."

"How do you know this stuff?" Petra asked. The witch held up a finger, warning Petra quiet while she pieced her thoughts together.

"I'm like you and your siblings. I can see slivers of a world that others cannot, and have been to places that coexist with our own. I spent many years in your sister's shoes. There's nothing to be done. They won't release her until she's long past use."

"We've been to Josalfar. We went in and came back out. She can do the same. How do we open the flower up? How do we get back?!"

"You don't understand what you're asking me. Your sister isn't coming home. They have her now and she won't want to leave. If you and your brother return underground, they might change their minds about recruiting children. Is that what you want?"

"No. I want to bring her home. They can't just take people!"

"Nobody took your sister. She went of her own accord. As I did."

"You—you worked for the star people. How? What was it like? How did you escape?!"

"Escape? There is no escape from Josalfar, not from Alfarians. You were given leave so you left. As was I, in time. Nobody will let your sister go for many years, not that she would want to. I didn't."

"Why didn't you want to leave?"

"Do you want my story? My life before I became your neighbor?"

Petra needed information and this was a lead. "Yes."

"The St'Avgull caught your gaze, did it not? Its gold-tipped leaves and stem? Remarkable! That's what drew me in. I was young then, likely younger than your missing Atla. I came upon the sprout while seeking mushrooms for my family. The economy wasn't what it is now and we were hungry."

She paused, gesturing for Petra to return to her seat. Sighing, Petra complied.

"Anyway—I found the plant and resolved to share it with a scholar in my village. His name—oh, it doesn't matter. I haven't seen him in decades. He may well have died. But I was smitten and thought my discovery merited his special attention. Retracing my steps to the plant, I potted it the next day. The scholar was unimpressed, rejecting my gift and me. He couldn't see the sheen I described and perhaps thought me disturbed."

"Shamed, confused, I brought it home. Bedridden for drama's sake, I abandoned my studies. When I arose, lifted up by parents who had no patience for such nonsense, life pulled me in the usual directions, and I mostly forgot about the oddity on my sill, except for its daily watering."

Pausing, she turned to the sil, where until recently, a baked clay pot sat. A stain marred the paint where water must've long leaked from the base.

"Then, one night I awoke to a wordless whisper and a bright light filling my small room. The St'Avgull had grown wide and there laid a gaping hole at its heart. A wiser person would have risen to wake their parents. Maybe paid a nighttime visit to the town priest. Instead, fool that I was, I climbed inside."

She offered a small smile in return for Petra's red-rimmed glare.

"I won't bore you with the details of the journey. You've done it. You know. Suffice to say I was hungry, thirsty, and tired, when I dropped out at the end. Old enough for mining, I was led to a stone table where I could eat and drink as much as I wanted. From there, I was taken to the laborers' barracks. My clothes were filthy, so I changed into the plain dress they provided. The Alfarians bade me sleep and I did."

She blew on her tea and sipped. Petra kept her hands flat on the table. Hitting would not bring her sister back.

"When I next awoke it was to the shake of another laborer. They explained my new life to me while we gathered for our morning meal. They kept me out of trouble in the mines. You may wonder, why was I so agreeable? Why didn't I fight? Or try to run?"

Gunndis waited for Petra to nod, and she did.

"It's the food. The food makes things better. As long as they're fed, laborers are happy complying with the Alfarians' demands. Skipping meals leads to illness, and eventually, death. Atla won't live long if she leaves."

"Why did you give us the St'Avgull? And why are you helping me now?"

"When my host assessed that I was too frail to continue in my position, he set me to task in my birth realm."

She paused to tap her eye patch in case Petra had forgotten it.

"They take and transform an eye from every laborer into a ruby. You must have seen them lodged in their heads. Through those, they see what we see, and direct us from afar. My duty is to find, and send, more laborers to Josalfar, so I raise and plant St'Avgulls. You expressed interest in my sprout so I gifted you the trap, knowing it would soon be sprung—just as I was instructed."

Petra had a new mantra circling her skull. Must not hit. Do not hit. Must not, do not.

"My actions sent you to Josalfar and tradition sent you back. No harm can come from explaining these facts to you now, but a lot of damage could be done to your sister if you succeed in pulling her from home."

"Do you still need their food to live?"

"My work being less strenuous, I don't require as much food as I once did. Periodically, I find a package in the kitchen or on the back stoop, bearing provisions."

"Do you have a St'Avgull right now?"

"If I did, I wouldn't give it to you, but I don't. The climate has shifted since I was a girl and they don't grow well out of doors here anymore. You took my last sprout."

"When will mine next open?"

"Yours? St'Avgulls bloom during the full moon, but yours never will again. The magic is spent. They last just long enough to catch a single laborer, in the best of circumstances. Now that they have your sister, the Alfarians will let yours wilt and die."

"Will they be bringing you more?"

"Who can say? I sent them a laborer and found them a familial line to provide more help in the coming decades. I've done my duty. I don't know other retirees I could ask, and my host isn't one for responding to the petty inquiries of a human."

Petra had a thought. It wasn't good. It was altogether bad, in fact. Before she could follow it through, she had to finish her interrogation.

"How'd you get this house? And all of this stuff?"

"The Alfarians are a well-connected people, and retirees aren't so useless as to let us starve in the streets. Once returned to my birth realm, I was given money and directed here. You see, this house was my parents' until their deaths. With no children left to inherit, it should have become the property of the government, yet was officially claimed by me ages before I was relieved of duty. Someone was keeping an eye on the bureaucratic happenings of this small town while I was laboring underground. Someone kept this house in good repair while I was away. Someone kept it for me."

Gunndis paused, stroking her chin. "If you'd like, you and your brother are welcome to stay here. Otherwise, the Child Protection Agency will split you up and send you away."

"Thank you, but I can't trust that your boss wouldn't make you send us below, eventually."

Gunndis nodded. "Eventually, yes."

Petra stood. "Thank you, for explaining all of this to me. I need to be getting back. Emil's alone."

"But of course. Would you like to bring him some cookies?"

"No thank you. They might be fairy food."

Gunndis shrugged, stood, and led Petra to the door. "Good luck," she said.

"Goodbye," Petra replied, that no-good thought wriggling at the back of her head.

Free of the bizarre juxtaposition of kind comfort, and dangerous magic, the immensity of their issue settled on her shoulders. Emil had eaten something. It couldn't have been big, but he was going to die. Death or enslavement. Those were his options.

Petra raced home and found the front door unlocked. Was that how she left it? She hadn't expected to be gone long. Setting the deadbolt behind her and grumbling at her forgetfulness, she went to check Emil's condition. It was a relief he felt the same, knowing any change would be for the worse. On the off chance Gunndis lied, or was mistaken, she checked the St'Avgull. Already, it was brittle and dry, with two of the seven leaves gone. She watered it, praying she didn't in vain

Chapter 4

She knew she was too young for the decision she faced. It was time to involve an adult. With Atla gone and Gunndis compromised, Petra didn't have many she could call. Somewhere in the laundry swamp that was Atla's bedroom was a little black book, offering a lifeline in a sea of questions.

Emil hadn't had dinner so Petra set a kettle on a burner. Then, after a moment's hesitation, she headed up. Ideally, the book was under the floorboard, but there, she found only money and legal documents. Sighing, Petra closed the gap. Then she set about bringing order to Atla's chaos. Gritting her teeth, she breathed through her mouth, rather than endure the smell. Swearing, Petra wished the address book was any other color, her difficulties compounded by Atla's affinity for dark clothing. Unstained tops, she tossed in the hamper. Those faded, torn, or at one with the mildew floor, went in the trash. Her irritation mounted, the severity of the situation exacerbated by the faint, yet persistent, buzzing of the ceiling light. At least this bulb didn't flicker.

The kettle called and Petra returned to the kitchen. She regretted not accepting the treats from Gunndis. If Emil was already ensnared, maybe they'd buy him time. But for what? Moving the kettle off of the burner, she poured the steaming water into a pot, adding a broth packet and a handful of hard noodles. Quickly, she washed and chopped a head of lettuce, sprinkling in a handful. The rest she bagged and placed in the fridge, preparing the carrot next.

Retrieving a movie tray from the living room, she brought Emil his soup. He was asleep, so she set it on the floor beside his bed. Next, she carried in his juice. Then she woke him up. Once he'd wiped the blurriness from his eyes, she set the tray on his lap, telling him to call for her when he was done.

"Wait! Didn't you see the witch? What did she say?! Can she help?"

Petra took a steadying breath. Should she ask him? Was she sure of the truth? Should she tell him? He deserved to know his fate, to choose for himself. Right? But what if he chose wrong? She wasn't his mother. What right had she to say what was best for her brother, barely three years her junior? Except, three years is a lot when you're a kid.

"She won't help us. You eat up, okay? You need your strength."

"Where are you going?!"

"Look, Atla isn't coming back. The witch—Gundis, was clear on that. We can't stay here on our own or the government will split us up and put us in homes. I'm finding help."

"From who? We don't have any aunts or uncles. At least, none I've met."

"No, none, but do you remember Leif?"

Emil paused, the name pulling forth dim recollections of a musician with long dyed back hair and piercings. "Yeah. A little. You think he'll come?"

"I don't know who else to ask."

"Okay. Does—does this mean we aren't going to save Atla?"

"I don't know yet."

Emil may have been frightened or angry but he was too tired to show it. Defeated, he bowed over his bowl and began to eat. Petra's meal could wait. She resumed her hunt for the missing address book. Atla would be furious if she ever got out.

If.

There came a loud banging from out front.

"Coming!" Petra shouted.

Given Atla's attitude towards her last visitor, Petra grabbed the baseball bat from the hall closet. Then she swung the door open. A man with a goatee towered over her, oblivious to the cold evening air in his neon tank top and velvet sweatpants.

"How can I help you?" she asked, hoping she sounded more confident than she felt.

"Hey, kid. I'm looking for Atla. She ain't been to work and she ain't picking up the phone. Is she here?"

His gaze caught on the bat and he smirked.

"Atla's not home right now. She was having pains in her side so she's being treated at the medical center. My sitter just stepped out but should be back any minute."

"Your sitter? Sure kid. Sure," he said, laughing. "Any word on when your sister's coming home?"

"I don't know. It sounded like she might need physical therapy after her surgery. I don't know if she has to stay there for that."

"Alright. When you see her, tell her to give Jan a call."

"Okay. I will."

"Good. And kid?"

"Yeah?"

"Don't answer the door for strangers. A bat in little hands won't do nothing against a grown-up. You hear me?"

"I hear you."

"Good. Bye, kid."

"Bye."

Mildly chastised, Petra closed the door behind her, putting the bat back in the closet.

As she passed their room, Emil called out, "What was that?"

She shouted back, not slowing her step, "Atla's boss. He said not to answer the door for anyone."

"Then why'd he knock?"

Petra was fairly sure she'd bought them a few days but he would return. Next time, she planned to heed his advice. He was right. How could she protect Emil, or herself, from a grown man?

Petra's stomach rumbled but she prowled on, redirecting her focus to the gap under the bed. She'd nearly pulled all the CD binders out when a hand on her shoulder made her jump. Half under the bed, she lifted the frame with a solid thwack of her head.

"Oops. Sorry," whispered Emil.

Pushing herself out, she brushed a maelstrom of dust free from her pants and sleeves.

"I'm fine," she said, while anything but. Her crown felt like an egg dropped over a stairwell. "What's the matter?"

"I want to help. What can I do?"

Petra looked around. The wastebasket over-flowed with unsalvageable attire, ancient food wrappers, bundles of chewed gum, and any num-ber of other materials Petra couldn't begin to guess a use for. The bed bore laundry piles and Atla's music collection. Makeup, ranging from ex-pired samples to the overpriced and undersized, spanned the dresser top in front of a cracked and greying mirror. Were there room, she'd have thrown that out too. The purses she'd checked lined the wall. Otherwise, the floor was clear.

"Look for her address book. It's small and black. I went through her drawers already, but I haven't gotten to the closet yet. I'll go grab the stepladder and take the upper half, if you can handle the lower?"

"Okay."

Emil sat down roughly inside the closet, setting midnight blinds swaying, and faced the mound of shoes and debris. Immediately, he pulled free a matching pair, and set them aside. Satisfied he wasn't on the verge of fainting or other dramatics, Petra stepped out.

The stepladder wasn't in the hall closet, leaning against the wall beside the back door, nor in the space between the fridge and the cabinets. Having exhausted those few probable nooks, Petra opened the back door and stepped outside. The sky was clear but she didn't have time for stargazing. No aurora anyway. Ah, there—on the ground by the fence. Wrestling the awkward contraption out of the dirt, she carried it inside. Flakes of earth hit the floor as the door swung shut.

Petra grabbed a rag and brushed the stepladder off, revealing warped steps, greener than they were brown. Great. So she could either trust the ladder not to collapse and stab her with a tetanus nail *or* she could stand tippytoe on a kitchen chair and hopefully not fall onto her dying baby brother. What business did those stupid shelves have being so high anyway? Nobody in their family was above average height!

Inside she cursed. Outside, gripping a throw pillow to her face and inhaling her mother's lingering perfume, she screamed. She screamed until she cried. With the force of a burst dam, the deluge soaked the satin, until she feared she'd replaced her mother's essence with her own. Squeezing her doll calmed neither wind nor waves, and it was all she could do to wait out the storm.

When her eyes were as dry as her energy, spent, she closed them, breathed in, reminded herself that she had to hold it together for a mite bit longer, and breathed out. Just a tad longer and then—well, one thing at a time.

Maybe he didn't do it. Maybe he genuinely didn't eat the food. In the closet, Emil announced that he'd finished sorting the floor and was double checking the backs of the photographs in her albums. There was the off chance she'd jotted Leif's address on a picture of the two of them, or that he might recognise Leif's house.

"Good idea. Any luck?"

"No. Where were you?"

"The stepladder wasn't where it goes. Had to find it."

He nodded and resumed his hunt. Ignoring the softness underfoot and the telltale creak, Petra climbed the steps and took to pulling junk off the top shelf, including board games, a surprisingly heavy shoebox, magazines, and several Lucky Strike cigarette packs. The shoebox looked promising but all they found inside were first aid supplies, including syringes, pills, and the like. Medicine for her bug bites, Petra assumed.

"I'm going to keep looking but you should get back to bed. Why don't you go brush your teeth?" Emil opened his mouth as though to argue. Petra would have welcomed some fight from him, but he only yawned.

"Okay," he said, and left.

She had to ask, and then she'd have to tell. Emil didn't know what he'd done. If he'd even done it.

Could the address book be in the car? Petra checked, uncomfortable outside at night, after what Jan said. Locking herself in the vehicle, she thoroughly inspected the glove compartment and under the seats. Then she went through the trunk. Moving aside a blanket, flashlight, shovel, and a pile of reusable grocery bags. Petra was stumped.

What if her parents had Leif's number in their address book?

In the kitchen drawer, between number shaped candles, thrice used cookie cutters, and forgotten instruction manuals, lay a faux snakeskin-bound book. It was lined with cardstock alphabet tabs, peppered with cross-outs, white-out, and edits. Petra skimmed until she found an entry for Leif Laakkonen written in mum's delicate script. It was too late for calling around, so Petra perused those beaten pages for any other Leif characters. Finding none, she marked his page with a strip torn from a seafood menu.

If, come morning, she found this wasn't their Leif after all, she'd resume the previous search. Somehow. In the meantime, she was ready for bed. She'd missed dinner, but her stomach had quit complaining and she was asleep before she hit the pillow.

Petra awoke before her alarm. Turning it off, she dressed and showered. Calling too early would be rude. Petra had been fond of Leif when he and

Atla were together. It was unclear who'd ended things nor why, but soon after the accident, Leif stopped coming over. She recalled being upset by his absence. He'd been around so consistently in the months leading up, she'd come to think of him as a big brother. Regardless, after the sudden loss of their parents, what was another void? And there was always the chance he and Atla would make amends. Life's full of chances.

But that hadn't happened and now it never could. So it goes, she thought.

At half-past seven she dialed, holding her breath while the line *berrrranged* in her ear. A blissfully familiar voice choked off the inhuman serenade.

"Hello?"

"Hi. This is Petra, Atla's little sister. Am I speaking to Leif?"

"Hi, Petra! It's been—" His voice rose with alarm. "Is Atla okay? Are you alright?"

"Leif, Atla is gone and Emil isn't doing well. Can we come over? I'm sorry. I'm just—" She gasped and the tsunami arrived too suddenly to dodge. She tried to stifle the sound and speak normally. "I don't know what to do and we don't have any—"

"Petra—Petra, it's okay. It'll be okay. You guys didn't move, right?"

She coughed an affirmative.

"Where did she—Petra, it's okay. I'll be right there. Pack a bag for you and your brother. See you in twenty minutes."

"Thank you," she said, but his end clicked off.

She wiped her face on her shirt and then, disgusted, washed her hands in the sink and ran to change her top. Packing a bag, she grabbed the money, all of their documents, a favorite photo album, clean clothes, toothpaste, toothbrushes, the address book, etc. In fifteen minutes, she'd filled both of their school bags with the necessities, and tossed all of their textbooks into one of Atla's oversized purses. Remembering the pocket knife, Petra swiped it from under the mattress. The Leif she knew was trustworthy, but what of everyone else? Besides, a knife had many uses.

Their things prepped and ready, she woke Emil, urging him to get dressed.

"Leif should be here in a few minutes. We're going to his house."

"What about school?" he asked, half asleep.

What about school? Was it even a weekday? Petra didn't know. Had she just asked Leif to miss a day of work to come and pick them up?

"You're too sick for school."

Emil blinked, rubbing his eyes awake. Petra picked an outfit for him, dropped it on his bed, and left the room. Leif still hadn't arrived, so she heated up leftovers for breakfast and popped some bread in the toaster. While it was ticking, she dumped another of Atla's purses out and filled it with unspoiled food.

"There's no need to be wasteful," mum's fleeting voice said.

Leif pulled into the driveway as she was pouring soup into a bowl.

"Emil," she called, on her way to open the front door. "Breakfast is ready in the kitchen."

Petra held the door open for Leif before he'd raised a hand to knock.

"Wow. You got big," he said, offering a smile that didn't meet his eyes.

Leif looked more like a grownup than she remembered. He was tall, blonde now, pale with freckled cheeks, and high cheekbones. He wore a solid grey button-down shirt over skinny jeans. She spotted no band logos, nor pant chains. His tattoos were concealed, and he'd removed all of his facial piercings—but it was him.

"You too," she said, leading him inside. "Emil's just eating his breakfast. We don't have any more soup, but I can make you a sandwich before we go if you like."

Emil raised a shy hand in greeting and Leif waved in return.

"No. That's okay. Thank you."

He looked them over, then at the kitchen itself. Leif didn't say what he was looking for, but his lips thinned and his brows buckled.

"Where is Atla?" he finally asked, relaxing his features with what appeared to be effort.

Petra and Emil exchanged a look that to them said, "This grown man will not believe the tale of magic, and elves, that is all we have to offer," but which only read as *trepidation* to their guest-savior.

"I don't want to lie and you wouldn't believe me. What matters is she isn't coming back," Petra replied.

Leif's eyes lingered on their hard faces and he nodded. "Before we go, would you mind giving me a tour? While Emil finishes his breakfast."

"Sure," said Petra. "One sec." She rinsed her plate off, put it away, and turned back to Leif. In his absence, there had been changes. "Right this way."

"Okay so—kitchen." She indicated where they stood before moving on. Passing the couch, she waved a hand. "Living room."

"What happened to the TV?" Leif asked, pointing to the empty shelf at the center of the entertainment center.

"Atla got rid of it. It was broken anyway."

"How did it break?"

"No idea. One day we went to watch cartoons but there were only a few channels left. Just news and church, so we gave it up."

"I see."

She showed him the broom closet. "This is the broom closet. I guess I didn't put the broom back though. So—never mind. Here is the other-stuff closet."

Leif chuckled. "That sounds like most of my closets."

The bathroom was narrow, so she pointed from the doorway, before moving aside so he could peer in. "That's the bathroom."

He stepped inside, looked up, stepped right back out, and closed the door behind him.

"What's the matter?"

He shuddered. "Do you know what black mold is?"

"Mold that is black?"

"Yeah. It's very bad and your bathroom has a lot of it."

"Oh," Petra said. There wasn't anything she could do about that, so she shrugged, carrying on with the tour. "This is mine and Emil's room."

She'd moved their bags to the kitchen. All that was left were the beds, dressers, alarm clock, wastebasket, and a smattering of toys they'd outgrown.

"Should we bring our bedding?"

"Actually, yeah. That's probably a good idea. Do you have a duffle bag? I should've brought one but didn't think of it."

"Should be one in Atla's room."

Up the stairs they went, bypassing their parents' shrine to empty another of Atla's bags.

"It's cleaner than it used to be."

"Yeah, that was us yesterday. We were looking for her address book."

Petra selected a multicolored nylon bag and tipped it upside down. The contents fell with a soft clatter. There went a key, towels, sneakers, and an expired gym card.

"What's this?" came Leif's voice from behind her.

She turned, watching him lean into the closet. Stepping closer she recognized the shoebox in his hands.

"Medical supplies, probably for the bug bites."

"Bug bites?"

"Yeah. From work."

Leif lifted the box, opened it, examined the contents, and put it back, stone faced.

"Where has she been working?"

Oh. They must've broken up before all of that, Petra thought. "She works all over. Or she did. Atla's an exterminator." And then, when he still looked confused—"That's a person who kills bugs in people's houses."

Leif's lips thinned and he closed his eyes, rubbing his forehead like Atla did when she had a migraine.

"Are you okay? We have Aspirin."

"What? Oh. No, I'm fine. Thank you." He paused. "You said you kids found her address book. Would you mind showing it to me?"

"We wouldn't mind, but we didn't find it. I don't know where it could be but it's not in this room. Unless another floorboard comes up that she didn't tell me about."

"Atla hid things in the floor?"

"Just money for bills and food and stuff. And paperwork."

"You packed that stuff, right?"

"Yeah. It's all bagged up."

"Can you show me the floorboard now?"

She nodded and did so, prying it loose with her borrowed knife. He peered inside, felt around its edges. Coming up empty-handed, Leif returned the board to its slot. Then he stepped on top of it, tenderly, and again with more weight. It creaked both times.

"Petra, can you stand in the hall for a moment? I'm just going to check real quick that she doesn't have another hiding spot."

"Sure."

She stepped out of the room and sat down against the door frame. There, she watched as Leif tested the entire floor. He went so far as to move the furniture aside, then back.

Finally, in a stroke of inspiration, he stopped and knocked against the headboard. She didn't hear anything special, but he repeated this action on its other side. Satisfied, he poked a finger into a groove and pulled a panel forward. The musky odor that always accompanied visits to Atla's room billowed forth with renewed vigor.

"Ew," complained Petra, pinching her nostrils shut.

Leif examined the cavity, opting not to stick his fingers inside so boldly this time. The hole was wide and from her limited vantage point, Petra perceived that it was full but not what of. Slowly, Leif pulled free a small bag of flour and several film canisters, one of which was open and sprinkling plant matter onto the bed. These he lowered with distaste, shaking his head. Then he withdrew a familiar little black book. This he opened quickly, glanced inside, and pocketed. Before leaving the room, he returned Atla's secrets to their nook.

"Okay then," he said, coming to meet Petra in the doorway. "What haven't I seen?"

"Not a thing," Petra replied.

Her parents' room hadn't changed since before he'd gone away and so, as far as she could tell, the tour was over. He glanced at her folks' door as they passed by but didn't question the omission. Together, they rolled the thin blankets up and stuffed them in the gym bag. On second thought, she grabbed the St'Avgull as well. It wasn't looking well, but maybe she could nurse it to life. In the kitchen, they found Emil asleep, head propped on his hands at the table.

"You said he's been sick?"

"Yeah. He was supposed to get blood tests yesterday but we missed the appointment."

"Okay. Let's get your stuff dropped off at my place and then let's get him to a doctor. How long has he been like this?"

"About a month."

"And how long has Atla been gone?"

"Since yesterday morning."

She sensed Atla's disappearance angered Leif and Emil's illness compounded that hostility. Petra wanted to say it wasn't Atla's fault, but what evidence did she have to follow up?

Placing a hand on Emil's shoulder, she spoke softly, "It's time to go."

He didn't react, so she tapped him, repeating herself. This time he stirred. Giving him a moment to regain his senses, she gathered and washed his dishes.

"Ready?" Leif asked.

They were. The trio loaded up the trunk and piled into the car. Petra watched while their house shrank away. A turn later, it was gone.

Leif broke the silence. "I need to understand what's been going on—what your situation has been. It's nice to think I can just pick up where Atla left off, acting the parent, I guess, but there are rules. Laws, really. I need to have something to tell the authorities otherwise, legally, I'm pretty sure this is kidnapping. So I need you guys to talk to me. Even if it sounds unbelievable. Your sister—what you might think crazy, well, that might be *very* believable behavior for her."

Petra glanced at Emil in the rearview mirror.

Emil piped up from the back, "What happened to Atla wasn't her fault."

"Okay. Will you tell me what happened?"

Petra sighed. "We'll tell you the truth, but you're not going to like it."

Together they told their story, Petra reciting long swathes with Emil filling in any gaps. Only the occasional bump in the road disrupted their shared recollection. To his credit, Leif made no attempt to interrupt. He drove through the golden flower entrance, along the bleak tunnel of translucent eyelids, to the dais with its blood bowls, past a month of missed school, and finally to the dawn of one missing sister-guardian. Reaching her second visit to Gunndis' house, Petra left out any talk of fairy food. She wouldn't have lied, except she didn't want Emil learning his tragic future before an audience, even if that audience was the outsider taking them in. Neither noticed the gap, and she planned to clarify to Leif once Emil gave them a minute alone.

That was what she needed help with. Petra could have fed and clothed the two of them for quite some time with the funds Atla left. As long as they started going to school again, no one would have been the wiser.

Emil, though. Petra was too young to decide if a life in chains was better than none at all. She hardly knew what she'd have chosen for herself, let alone what was right for her baby brother. And if she couldn't have made that choice for herself, was it right to let him choose? The thought alone had her applying pressure to the doll, however subtly.

"So. Let me get this straight. Emil, you've missed a month of school?"

"Yes."

"And Gunndis, your neighbor. You're saying you spoke with her yesterday?"

"That's right."

"Would either of you happen to know her address or phone number?"

Petra pictured Gunndis' house and relayed the address to Leif. Gunndis wasn't coy. If Leif wanted to confirm their story, that was fine with Petra.

Finally, Emil asked, "Do you believe us?"

Leif didn't answer right away. Waiting, Petra became aware she was looking at the same quaint turf-covered church for the second time. They were going in circles. She guessed Leif was concerned a change in scenery might incite a retreat into furtiveness.

"It's a lot. But I don't believe you're lying," he finally said.

That was an awfully polite way to say they were either gullible or disturbed. As long as he was helping, for now, either mindset would do.

Leif ceased his roundabout wandering and headed to his place. In minutes they were pulling into the driveway of a pewter painted house with a tin roof. The grass was clean-cut and bushes billowed up against the siding, spanning a strip of mulch. They bore neither bud nor bloom. Leif parked. The trio unbuckled and carried their loads into the foyer.

"Home, sweet home," Leif said, shutting and locking the front door behind them. Leaving the bags where they were, he showed the kids around.

His flat was comparatively spartan, but tidy. Unlike their house, it was obvious nothing he owned was of a set. The two chairs in the kitchen weren't the same height, let alone make and color. In the living room, the couch was of patched viridian leather, while the loveseat may well have been corduroy. There was no entertainment center. Instead, a TV sat on a coffee table that was shoved against the far wall. There were blinds in the living room and Leif's bedroom, but no curtains beyond what wrapped the shower. Leif's bed was a long twin, and atop the dresser sat an antique alarm clock, a lamp, and a purple boombox. Across from his bed were two full bookcases. What few closets were full. There were no toys, beyond a few board games.

With only one bedroom, Leif showed them how to fold out the leather couch.

"Just don't try to put it back yourselves. It's heavier going in."

Their clothes didn't fit in the minuscule coffee table drawers, so they left them in their bags.

"That's fine. We can pick up a dresser this week," Leif said.

The kids dispersed their food throughout the kitchen while admiring how well stocked the cabinets and fridge were. Leif passed them pillows, and the TV remote, as Petra laid out their bedding.

"I've got to make a few calls. Why don't you guys watch cartoons for a bit? Just not too loud. These walls are paper thin and my neighbors are crotchety."

Happily, they obliged. They had to stand next to the set for the remote to work, but neither minded. Once they found a kids' channel, they didn't need to change it again. Petra could hear Leif talking but not what he said. Emil struggled to stay awake and was out cold before the credits ran. The third show was concluding when Leif muted it and sat on the loveseat.

"I called the police. They're coming over to take my report now. They'll want to ask you some questions. Maybe Emil, too. Be honest with them. They want to help. Tomorrow I'll call the school. You've missed too many days already and it's important we get you enrolled as soon as possible. I also made an appointment with a pediatrician for Emil. They didn't have any availability today."

"Okay. But the doctor won't be able to help, I'm pretty sure."

Petra looked at Emil. That snore was the real deal.

"Gunndis said if you eat *their* food—the star people's food—you have to keep eating it or you get sick and die. That's why we can't save Atla. It's too late for her. And Emil's been sick since we got back from Josalfar. He didn't say so and I didn't see it, but he must've eaten something. If I'm right and we don't send him back to be their worker, he's not gonna make it."

Leif looked from her to Emil and back, not speaking.

"I haven't told him yet. Not about the food. If he knows—"

If he knew then it was his prerogative to choose whether he wanted to return and be their pawn, or stay put with her while he shriveled up and died. She shook her head, unwilling to finish the statement. They sat quietly, thinking their separate thoughts, until Leif was spared from responding by a knock at the door. Rising, he let the officers inside. Petra woke Emil while the adults exchanged greetings.

"Hey. The police want to talk to us about Atla. You've got to stay awake for a little while. Want some juice?"

He sat up and nodded. She went to the fridge. The beverages consisted mostly of beer and milk, but there was a soda labeled *Orka* in the back. Snapping the top, she carried it out to him. The brand sounded familiar.

"Did he talk to my doctor?"

"He's going to take you tomorrow."

Emil nodded, pulling his blanket tight. The two officers, a portly man, and petite blonde women, entered the living room. Leif dragged the kitchen chairs in for them to use, opting for the couch himself.

"Hi. I'm Officer Helga, and this is my partner, Arnar."

Dutifully, the children introduced themselves although the officers must've been informed of their names prior.

"Leif was just telling us about your sister Atla," she said. "Would you kids mind telling us what you know about her situation right now?"

They'd already told Leif. What were two more adults? Reluctantly, Petra explained about looking for Foss and being caught on Gunndis' property. She emphasized Atla's shocked and dismayed response upon learning they had disobeyed her.

Emil must have been excited at the prospect of speaking with real-life police officers because he jumped into the verbal fray, taking up the story from there. Manic, with frantic eyes under a wave of sleep tousled hair, he exuded more energy than he had in many days. Rambling on, he braked only to acknowledge and respond to the officers' questions. Helga's face betrayed concern as she took notes.

They asked if Emil might have dreamed the flower blooming in the night. Then, apparently dissatisfied with his response, Helga adjusted her approach by inquiring as to whether the children were familiar with the concept of mass hallucinations, mass hypnosis? Petra was ready to defend Emil's testimony, but he didn't offer the opportunity.

"I know what hallucinations are. This was real. We were both awake. Wide awake. We didn't dream up a cave or being hungry or tired or sore."

Admonished, Helga gave a nod that, to Petra, said, "I hereby recognize these children are delusional and should be kept separate from the general public for their own well-being."

Undeterred, Emil carried on until Officer Arnar spoke up.

"And you don't know how long you were in the cave?"

"The watch wasn't working but about three days had passed when we got home."

"Does it work now?"

"Yes," Petra answered. "I had to reset the time after we got home, but it's working fine now."

Emil stood and raised his wrist for Arnar, to show him. Arnar looked at it and nodded. Emil sat back down.

The officers asked fewer questions about the fantastic elements of their story and instead zeroed in on Atla's parenting, career, and the children's home life. Did they have enough to eat? Was it normal for them to miss school? Were they keeping up with their makeup assignments? How many times had Emil been to the health clinic? Did they happen to know the name of their doctor? They planned to speak with him.

Judging by their faces, if Atla ever did come home, she was going to be in a world of trouble. What did Atla do for work? Did she ever bring men around the house? Petra pinched Emil under the blanket before he could bring up the noisy guy who'd attacked their door.

"No," he said, glaring at Petra as he rubbed the fresh bruise. "Men don't come over."

Did Atla ever act strangely? Did she become violent, have angry outbursts, or spend a lot of time crying? Did she leave them alone at home?

"Only for a few minutes sometimes, if she runs out for milk," Petra answered before Emil could.

"So at night, when Atla's working, you kids aren't home alone?"

"Nope. She hires sitters. Or she has neighbors come over."

"I'm glad to hear it. Can you name the sitters for our notes?"

Desperate, she listed common first names. Asked to elaborate, she replied that she didn't know their surnames, and two of the sitters had since moved away. No, she didn't know where the others lived. Helga's pen never stopped moving.

Then, like Foss, they got to the squeaker in the plush.

"So you woke up and she was gone."

"Yes. But the flower tunnel, the St'Avgull, was shrinking back. Just like how it sealed behind us. So we know where she went."

"And that was how many days ago?"

"The night before yesterday."

"Does Atla have enemies? Anyone who doesn't like her?"

Emil explained about the ladies at the supermarket who would frown at Atla and then whisper to each other and laugh. Or grimace. He told about the man who punched the side of their car last year and another much older man who'd tried to grab at Atla on the sidewalk, and then cursed at her when she yelled. Still sore from being pinched, he didn't bring up the guy banging on their door. It was one thing to tell the police strangers were rude when they went out, but another entirely to admit folks came to the house and threatened their safety there.

"Did Atla have any friends? A boyfriend, maybe? Coworkers? Anybody she talked to regularly?" Emil shrugged and looked to Petra.

"I met her boss." She detailed his appearance, giving his first name. "He came by looking for her when she didn't come to work. I told him she was in the hospital, but that we had a sitter, so he wouldn't try and come in. Atla wouldn't have left us alone if she had a choice, because she thought it was unsafe."

"Okay. Well, kids. Thank you for talking with us." Helga turned to Leif. "Can we speak alone with you for a minute?"

"Sure," he said, standing, then guiding the officers to his bedroom, shutting the door behind them.

"Do you think we got Atla in trouble?" Emil asked, fidgeting with a string he'd tugged from the couch.

"No. Not much anyway."

What trouble could she be in if the police couldn't reach her?

"What did the witch say? You said Atla isn't coming back. But we did. Maybe the witch lied."

Petra took a long breath, rubbing her forehead, and closing her eyes against the too-bright white kitchen light. The throbbing was beyond what Aspirin could quell.

"Did you eat the food?" she asked, opening her eyes.

"What?"

"When we were there, with the star people. Underground. Did you eat anything?"

"No."

"Really?"

"Really."

"Emil. This is important. Atla ate the food and now she can never come home. I repeat. Did you eat anything?"

"I—maybe. Yes. But just a berry! Only one. We hadn't eaten in—"

Petra swore. She'd known. It was her fault. What business did they have climbing into a giant flower hole in the first place? They could have died then and there. What if it had been full of lead, or arsenic sulfides, and they'd be breathing in poison the whole hike? Or they never found their way out? She was his big sister. It was her job to keep him from hurting himself. So what did she do? Lead the charge headfirst without bothering to consider the consequences. Now he would die. Or work in a mine, until he got too old. It wasn't fair.

"That's why Atla can't come home?!"

She could at least spare him the death detail while she decided what to do next. Maybe if she could talk to the fairy queen, they could come to an arrangement. He could work part-time. Weekends or something, like how divorced parents split custody. But to arrange that, she'd have to get back to Josalfar.

"I ate it, the food, but just a bite. What does that mean for me?"

She hadn't thought this out, telling him half of the truth. She wracked her brain, looking to the dark TV screen for ideas. What to say—what to tell him?

"You can't go back. If you do, you can never come home again."

"But—last time they let us go."

"The magic hadn't set in yet," she replied, untangling a lock of her hair. "It has now."

"That's what the witch told you?"

That and you're going to die. "Yup."

"I was just so hungry," he explained, squirming in his seat.

"I know."

"Do you want to watch some cartoons?"

Emil shook his head. "Not right now."

"Would you like to play a game?"

He looked up. "What kind of game?"

She'd packed his matchbox cars.

"We could play *Race Track?* How does that sound?"

"Okay."

Petra got his cars out while he pulled the couch cushions, slanting their faces, wedging them at each end of the blanket, setting slopes for the vehicles to slide down. The children made traffic sounds, taking turns dragging their toys around the track. Upon hearing the creak of a door, they stopped to say goodbye to the officers. Then Emil peered out the window as they pulled away, groaning when they rounded the corner.

"What's the matter?" Petra asked.

"They didn't put the lights on."

"They only do that when they're chasing a bad guy."

Emil nodded and let the blinds fall back into place. "Oh well."

The children directed their attention to Leif.

"They said it's fine for you to stay for now. They're going to be looking for Atla, so if you guys think of anything else that might be useful, let me know, and I'll give them a call. I gave them her address book, and they're going to be visiting her contacts to see if anyone has seen her."

"They're not going to find her," Emil said.

"They also suggested you both speak with a counselor, so we'll make arrangements for that."

"What's a counselor?" asked Emil.

"It's a nice person you can talk to about how you're feeling. You can tell them anything and they won't tell anybody your secrets."

"The officers think we have secrets?"

"They just want to make sure you're both feeling alright. Atla's disappearance has to have been a nasty shock. Talking about it might make you feel better."

"Did you have to miss work today?" Petra asked.

"Nah. I will this week, but it won't be a problem. I've known my boss a long time, and he understands. I'll be back at work when things are more settled here."

Leif whipped up a light supper of lamb soup. He tasked Petra with setting the table, and Emil with retrieving a folding chair from the bathroom closet. The ceiling light was fluorescent, without so much as a dimmer, and between the brightness and the sound of the bubbling, she was tense, so Petra donned a pair of Leif's glasses. They neither had earplugs, nor would she have worn them for long, the sensation of their weight in her ears likewise uncomfortable. Setting the food out, Leif asked after their interests, how they felt about school, and what their friends were like. Those weren't trick questions, but Petra pretended not to hear that last.

The kids, in turn, wanted to know about Leif's job, if he had a girlfriend, and where his parents were. Leif was a clerk at the post office. He was single for the most part.

"What do you mean? For the most part?" Emil inquired, loosing crumbs, his mouth full.

"I go on dates, but I'm not in a relationship with anybody."

There hadn't been a reason for Atla to bring his folks around the house, but she used to talk about them. They were strict, religious, and they hadn't liked her much. He explained that they'd since moved abroad.

"Why did they move so far away?"

"The winters became too much for them. They wanted a milder climate."

After dinner, Petra did the dishes while Emil dried. At his third yawn, she relieved him of dish duty, and he reclaimed his half of the couch.

"How often did Atla actually leave you kids home alone?" Leif asked.

"Most nights. She had to work. We don't need a sitter to make dinner and get to bed on time. Would have been a waste of money."

"So why lie to the police?"

"Grownups don't think kids can do anything for themselves. The second a parent gives their kid a little leeway, some responsibility, people give them a hard time."

"I don't know if I agree with that."

She shrugged, not engaging.

"You believe your story, don't you?"

Petra put the rag down and turned to face him.

"It's the truth."

"I told the officers about Gunndis. They're going to speak with her as well."

"It won't make any difference. Not for Atla." She looked past Leif, to Emil, who'd half disappeared under the blankets. "And a doctor won't be able to help him."

"Well, let's let the doctor determine that, okay?"

She nodded, changing the subject. "Do you have a library card?"

"Yes. Want to pick up some books?"

"Yeah. Can we go to the library tomorrow, please?"

"Sure. I'll take you both after Emil's appointment. Does he like reading too?"

"Sometimes."

Emil had never expressed an affinity for reading, but if a book had pictures of cops or cars, he'd look at it. Regardless, Petra intended to either learn how to cure him, or find her way back to Josalfar. The Queen would see to reason. Emil didn't belong to them.

"And you believe what you told me about your brother?"

Maybe Leif could read minds.

"Yes."

"Petra—he's not well. I can see that. And waking up one day, Atla not being home—I'm sure it must've been traumatic. For both of you. After what you went through when your parents—look. I don't blame you guys for needing to see the situation in a—a more magical light. This would be a lot for anybody to deal with, but Emil's going to be okay. He didn't poison himself with fairy food. Fairies don't exist. The doctor will tell us what's wrong with him and prescribe a treatment to make him better."

Petra shook her head. He couldn't believe the unbelievable without having experienced it. And if he didn't have the sight, that was that. The St'Avgull could've sprung up next to him, and if Gunndis was to be believed, it wouldn't have made a difference.

"I hope you're right," is all she said.

Letting the subject drop, Leif and Petra played Tic-Tac-Toe until he sent her to bed.

"Good night Leif."

"Good night Petra," he said, flicking off the kitchen light.

"Hey, Leif?"

"Yeah?"

"Thanks for taking us in."

"Anytime."

Chapter 5

The waiting room of Dr. Falk's office smelled like rubbing alcohol. The magazines were meant for homemakers and the only toy was marketed for children significantly younger than Petra—a fact she was grateful for as she watched a boy cough into his hands, then immediately grab hold of a bobble protruding from the plastic bead maze.

Leif and Emil had been gone long enough for Petra to have quit watching the clock and taken to perusing magazines. She had zero interest in the pie baking hacks of an autumn edition dating some three years prior, but the pile offered nothing better. She wished she'd insisted on going to the library first.

Petra awoke to a light shake of her shoulder. Must've dozed off, she thought.

"Sorry, we took so long."

"That's okay," she said, rising and following them to the car.

"How did it go?"

"They don't know what's wrong with me," Emil replied, glum.

Petra nodded. "Do you want the front seat?"

He shook his head. "I'll take the back. I don't feel like paying with the radio"

The ride to the library was quiet. Petras spent it bracing herself to be outgoing. Upon arriving, she strode up to the front counter and asked the clerk about applying for cards. She knew herself too old to ask Laks to handle strangers for her. Anyway, adults were easier to deal with than her peers. When in doubt, with few exceptions, grownups veered polite, professional, perhaps even stern. She could ask a question and get a straight answer. Kids, though. She could never guess how they'd respond. Leif helped Emil fill out his application while, with the exception of the lines denoting a physical address, Petra handled her own. The back of her form listed late fees, and the maximum number of books a patron could take out. Petra frowned, seeing the limit.

With her temporary card in hand, Petra inquired how to locate all of the books about any one subject. The clerk, a tall woman with curly brown hair, was happy to show Petra how to navigate the card catalog.

"What's the subject you want to learn about, dear?" she asked as Leif and Emil stood awkwardly to the side.

"I want to learn about the Alfarians, also known as the star people. They're a type of elf."

"Wonderful! Those will be in the 300s, in Nonfiction. Mythology. Here, I'll show you."

She led them past a rack of newspapers, areas labeled *Teen Fiction* and *Graphic Novels*, to shelves beneath a laminated placard that read *Nonfiction*.

"What you're looking for will be here. Fables and lore get mixed in with religion. Would you like a stepstool?"

"Yes please."

Leif offered his help reaching the top shelves as the woman ran off to find the stool.

"Thank you. Can I hand you books? It'll be faster if I don't have to climb down a lot."

"Ah. Yeah. Okay. Sure," he replied, leaning back against one of the chairs at an empty study table.

"Also, I'm going to need yours and Emil's library cards, I think. Will that be okay?"

"Wait. Am I not taking out any books?" asked Emil, who was gazing admirably an outdated comic book release poster. Petra didn't recognize the hero.

"Do you want to?"

He considered. "Maybe one or two. I'll go find the kids section. If nothing else, they'll have toys."

Leif winced as Emil stepped away. "This is all still new. Do kids normally split off in public?"

Petra considered, thinking out loud, "He should be fine. This place isn't very big."

The clerk returned, leaving the stepladder with Petra, who climbed, pulling books with promising titles and passing them to Leif. Confident she'd gathered everything even tangentially on topic, they carried their volumes to the children's area where Emil was tracing illustrations, in a book about a fast-talking Volkswagen, with his finger.

They successfully checked out his one book and her eleven.

Petra wasted no time sorting her volumes at Leif's house. Having spread them on the floor, she mulled over which to study first.

"Since when are you such a big reader?" Emil asked, putting his book aside and digging through the couch cushions for the remote. "One at a time, I get, but this? This is insane."

"What did the doctor say?" she replied, changing the subject.

"They're going to put me on a steroid, and I'm underweight, so I'm supposed to start drinking protein shakes. We go back next week."

There was z faint fizzling sound followed a metallic snap in the kitchen. The kids turned to see Leif holding a beer can to his mouth. He froze.

"I don't know. Is it okay if I drink a beer in front of you guys? Did your parents drink around you?"

The kids shrugged and Petra said, "I think so. Doesn't matter either way. I'm never going to drink."

"Yeah, me neither. Beer smells bad," added Emil.

Comforted, Leif and his beer claimed the love seat, where he too, peered curiously at Petra's hoard. Lifting one, he read the title out loud before placing it back where she'd had it.

"Kalevala. What's a Kalevala?"

"It's a book of Finnish folklore."

That's when it clicked.

"Is this so—are you going to try and get back there?" Emil asked, turning to stare at the brown and shriveled St'Avgull in the window.

"That's the plant?" Leif asked. "It doesn't look like much."

Petra rose and checked its soil. It was still moist from that morning's watering.

"Gunndis said the Alfarians would let it die now that they have Atla."

Leif sipped his beer, before speaking. "Gunndis again. Did Atla ever talk to her?"

"I don't think so. If she did, she didn't say so."

If Atla believed them about the gun, there may have been a chat, she thought.

Emil turned on the TV. Cartoons were too distracting for Petra, who asked if she could work somewhere quieter.

"Do you have a backyard?"

"Oh yeah. I guess I forgot to show you guys yesterday."

Leif opened the back door and stepped outside, barefoot. Concrete tiles trailed from the mat, disappearing into the unmowed grass bordering the woods.

"I don't know where this lot ends, technically. The woods go on for a ways. It's easy to get lost. You kids are fine to play up to the tree line, but no farther. I'll show you the trails another day. Oh! And stay behind my house. The neighbors can be touchy and they won't want you in their yards."

As far as quiet went, the backyard was that. There was the distant rush of moving water and the occasional bird call or car, sure, but those were magnitudes less distracting than whatever show Emil had on. Claiming a space of dry dirt, Petra laid out a garbage bag, weighing down the corners with the largest stones she could carry. Then, reasonably sure the books wouldn't get filthy, she brought them out.

Relying on indexes, Petra did not waste time reading beyond what she needed. Nothing and nowhere listed the Alfarians by name. One author mentioned star people, an elf sect cohabiting with Inuit shamans beneath mountains in Canada and Alaska, but offered no further details.

Undaunted, Petra focused on anyone similar sounding. She categorized her notes, building a table that spanned several pieces of paper. Column-A listed the names of fae species, while Row-1 listed their characteristics. Marking the relevant boxes, she found several creatures likely went by multiple titles. In a later, tidied copy, Petra condensed each batch of attribute sharing fairies into a single entry. For instance, the Welsh *brownie* and the Slavic *domovoy* shared an entry, both being wingless humanoid fairies who resided in and maintained the cleanliness of human dwellings.

She also jotted down methods for achieving contact. This sheet she taped to the inside cover of her notebook for easy access. Circles of mushrooms were portals to the fairy realm. That tip was mentioned enough to seem promising. Leprechauns could be found at the ends of rainbows. Some creatures could only be found in specific caves, mountains, or bodies of water. Petra highlighted the Icelandic locations.

Surely once she made contact, and explained the situation, the fae would help her return to Josalfar. It didn't sound like fairies hated humans. They were cunning tricksters or helpful gifters, but they weren't evil monsters. Not most anyway.

On another sheet, Petra listed fae strengths, weaknesses, and the like. Her gram's fairy lore saved her from her siblings' fate. There had to be more she could use. In her studies, she learned that a salt ring would protect her from enchantment. When facing a troll, she had to distract it until sunup, or be eaten. If a leprechaun asked what eye she saw them with, she was to remain silent, or lose that eye. Leprechauns didn't collect human slaves, but like most fae, they didn't appreciate humans with the second sight. As a rule, they were a private people. Regarding what superstitions might apply to Alfarians, she could only guess.

Petra also kept an eager eye out for a magical cure-all, but found nothing of practical use. Books mentioned the philosopher's stone, but there were no instructions on how to replicate, nor find, it. Likewise, for unicorn horns. That they could cure any ailment was great, except where was she supposed to find an unwed princess to summon one? And how was she supposed to remove the horn, assuming she was approached by a unicorn in the first place? Was she supposed to kill it? The texts were unclear.

Petra didn't know how to make mushrooms grow. Her fairy books didn't offer fungal gardening advice. When she asked Leif, he said she needed a wet log. Bonus points if it was rotten. Together, sticking to the trail and staying close to home so as not to wholly abandon couch ridden Emil, they came across the deteriorating top of a felled tree. Leif pulled loose a long strip, and borrowed her knife to cut what last few stubborn fibers. He shook the piece, pelting the ground with insects and debris. Then, together, they carried it back.

"Do I cover it with dirt?"

"You can? I've never grown mushrooms but some friends of mine—you want to keep it wet and dark. I think they'll grow if we lay it under the rowan tree. Just don't eat the mushrooms."

"I won't," she assured him.

Petra couldn't see the log from the back windows but made an effort to check it daily. Likewise, she kept watch for rainbows, but the rain came in sprinkles, and the sun was on vacation. She needed results. That weekend she knocked on so many trees, her knuckles bruised. When Petra thought Leif wouldn't notice, she ventured into the woods on the lookout for a stream, seeking bridges. Finding none, she made her way back, careful not to leave the trail.

Leif spotted her as she reached the yard, and he was not happy.

"I told you to stay here! You could have been hurt or lost."

"I didn't go very far in," she lied. "—and I stuck to the trail."

"There are lots of trails. Not all of them lead here. No more wandering off on your own. I mean it. If you want to play outside, you stay in the yard, or we can go to the park. If Emil's up to it."

That could work.

"Can we have a picnic? We passed a bridge on the way to the doctor's office. There was a park there.

Leif raised an eyebrow. "Why do I feel like this is part of your fairy hunt?"

She shrugged, noncommittal.

"What are you hoping to find under the bridge?"

"A troll," Petra mumbled.

He raised his hands and looked to the sky for guidance. "What's the myth?"

"Trolls live under bridges. If I leave a coin, the troll should come to take it. And if we wait underneath, we'll see him. Then we get him to talk."

"Petra, I'm not sure how healthy your interest in fairies is. I don't know what age you're supposed to stop believing in all of this stuff, and now you're sneaking around. I want to be supportive, but I also want you to be safe. We can go to the bridge. I'll give you some change. But no more sneaking out, or I'm bringing the books back to the library. And confiscating your notebook. Got it?"

"Yes."

"Okay. Get your brother dressed and we can go."

The bridge was a major hassle and a flop. They parked a hike away as there were no spaces nearby. Leif left a small pile of change over the central arch, before backtracking to the stairs leading to the park path lining the river below. From their picnic blanket, they watched the coins catch the light, unmoved, for over an hour, while ants swarmed their snacks. The toll was claimed by another child, who cheered at their good luck, their guardian looking curiously around. Petra wanted to try another bridge, but Emil wanted to go.

Monday morning, Leif asked Petra to wake her brother while he made breakfast. Nudging him proved ineffective, so she shook him harder, which also failed. Frightened, she yanked his blanket away and commanded him to "Wake Up!" He groaned and rolled over. Not dead. Emil was not dead. She closed her eyes and willed her heart to beat at a normal rate. Not letting on to her fear, she grabbed his shoulders and sat him up.

"Leif is making eggs."

"Alright! I'm up. Can I have the blanket back? I'm cold."

She obliged, laying a palm on his forehead. It was hot. It was always hot, and his voice wasn't losing its rasp. Emil just spoke less. She pretended not to notice the shaking of his hands, nor the brittle yellow of his nails. Clumps of hair peppered his pillow.

Monday was her first day at a new school. If not for Emil weighing on her mind, she would have been nervous. Instead, she was distracted. When the teacher called for her to introduce herself, she had to be summoned twice before she stood and spoke. A girl to her left asked her where she was from. Why had she moved? Petra answered vaguely and didn't pursue the conversation. At lunch, she sat alone, pouring over her chart, considering her next attempt. When the lunchroom attendants sent the children out for recess, she asked if she might be allowed to go to the library instead.

The attendant provided directions, warning Petra to head back to class at the next bell. Petra assured she would and left in search of knowledge.

She'd have to wait for picture day to have her Student ID made, so she couldn't take anything out, but was welcome to read within the library. Locating the nonfiction section, she found a single book of interest—*Myths and Monsters of the Old World*.

She didn't have long so she scanned the table of contents for the most promising chapters. Petra skipped to the blurb listing hobgoblin attributes, then turned the page. The following section was titled, *How to catch a hobgoblin*. Whipping out her notebook, she copied down the instructions, which required an unfinished article of clothing, salt, and a bell, but the steps were simple enough. Glancing at the clock, she saw that recess was nearly over, returned the book, and retraced her steps.

The teacher was again forced to repeat herself, asking Petra to read a passage in the text, and Petra expected a reprimand. When none came, she assumed the faculty had been informed of the bizarre circumstances preceding her enrollment.

Later, in confirmation, the teacher placed Emil's folder and textbooks wordlessly on one corner of Petra's desk, her homework on that, opposite, as the day wound to a close. When the final bell rang, and she was headed to the bus platform, Petra realized she hadn't learned anyone's name.

Spotting the main office, she detoured from the bus line.

"Hi, ma'am," Petra greeted a mousey woman with glasses too wide for her face.

The woman looked up from her paperwork.

"Hello. How can I help you?"

"Do you have a lost and found? I lost my scarf. It should be here, I hope. It's my favorite."

"I'll see if I can find it," the receptionist said, rising and stepping away.

From her limited viewpoint, Petra could see the women bend down and lift a cardboard box onto the desk. What Petra could not see was the contents therein.

Unhelpfully helpful, the receptionist called out, "What color is it?"

What were popular scarf colors? Didn't they usually have more than one?

"It has a bunch of colors."

"Ah. Is this it?" the woman asked, holding up a striped cashmere scarf.

"Yes! Thank you so much."

The receptionist handed it to Petra, who then raced to catch her bus. One of the last students on, she got an aisle seat in the front, next to a girl with no eyebrows, who wore a bandana. "Huh. I guess kids can wear hats in this school," Petra thought. She rolled up the scarf and stuffed it into her bag.

Her bus stop was shared by two boys who appeared to be Emil's age. He'd be happy to hear that, she thought, and he was when she told him. Petra did her homework, before helping Emil with his. Later, outside, she sliced through the knots tying off the scarf. Then, having painstakingly unraveled the ends, she admired her handiwork.

At dinner, Leif asked how her day had gone.

"It was school," she said, between bites. "—so fine, I guess."

"Did you make any friends?"

"No," she replied, when she'd swallowed her bite.

"Well, I'm sure you will. Were the kids nice?"

"Sure," she said, not having talked to them to know.

Emil didn't eat much, and nobody asked him to help clean after.

"Do you have a bell?" Petra asked, passing Leif a ladle to be hung from a wall hook, just beyond her reach.

"I have an alarm clock. And a wind chime. A piece fell off so I brought it in. Been meaning to fix it."

Petra requested the chime so Leif bent low, pulling soaps and sprays from under the sink. Shaking his head, he switched cabinets, removing a slew of ancient cooking oils, when tinkling announced his success.

"Would this work?" he asked, handing her a mobile of copper tubes.

"Yes! Thank you!"

"What's this for, anywho?"

"I'm going to hang it on the door."

She explained about the salt ring, that the bell was the alarm.

"Alright. Try not to use all my salt. It's warm tonight, so you can leave the back door open a smidge. I'm locking the front. Tomorrow though, go out to recess with the other kids. I'm going to call the school and check that you do. Read at home. You've got plenty of books here."

Petra promised to abide by those standards and they continued with their post-meal chores.

Chapter 6

The clock read after three when Petra awoke, gripping her favorite doll. It was the windchime. She was sure of it. Yes. There was a figure beside the now wide-open door. Grabbing the box of salt, she tossed it across the doorway and flicked on the light. The sudden brightness struck her like an open palm, but she ignored the pain. Emil murmured, turned, but didn't otherwise stir.

There, in her lopsided salt ring, stood a very tiny old man. His white hair and beard were long, wiry, divided into a multitude of tight braids and tucked into his belt. The little man's nose was remarkably broad, wide enough to draw attention away from his blatantly inhuman black eyes. Wrinkled as a bulldog, with brows drooping to either side of his face, the man's rubicund complexion contrasted sharply with his fitted burlap suit. On his back, he bore a backpack, not unlike the children's in shape, but also of burlap and equally *stainless*. Petra couldn't claim that of anything she owned whatsoever. Around his neck, and threaded into his beard, was a necklace of twine, on which hung a spiral charm.

"Harrumph. Well now. It seems you've caught me fair and square."

Petra nodded, too stunned to speak.

"I suppose you already know how this works, then? You clear this ring and I assume the position of your servant. The names' Iver. So new Mistress—unless you plan to keep me here forever?"

Petra shook her head.

"Alright then, what am I to call you?" His voice was soft, every syllable distinct. Brownies were the docile variety of hobgoblins in stories, but she'd seen many entries over the power of names.

"What does it mean for us if I tell you my name?" she asked in like volume.

"Why, it'll make talking to each other easier is all. You haven't met many of the people, I can see. If I know your name and you know my name, there is a balance. Not that it matters. You've caught me, and now I'm tied to you until you choose to free me, or until death do we part. If you let me out now, I can finish your scarf."

"Don't worry about the scarf. I nicked it from the lost and found and unwove it so you would come," she confessed. "Thanks, though. My name is Petra. Let me sweep this up."

"Pleased to meet you, Petra," Iver said, standing patiently while she located the broom, carried it back, and took care to brush the salt away, and more importantly—not at him.

"Well, Mistress Petra, how can I be of service? Would you like me to make you a late-night snack?"

"No. Thank you, Iver. I actually need your help with—I'll just show you."

Treading lightly to not wake anyone, she led him across the short distance to where Emil slept. The blanket blended with the couch, a leather mammoth pulling him in, his limp expression indicating he'd given up the fight legs and torso ago.

"This is my brother, Emil. He isn't doing very well."

Iver looked from Petra to her brother, and then cautiously, he placed his palm on the boy's forehead. Tutting, he pulled his hand away. Emil's bangs slipped forward, wet with sweat. Leaning forward, Iver gripped his pendant, bringing to Emil's forehead, while murmuring. As with the Alfarians, his native speech was animalistic. The charm flashed.

"Oh dear. Mistress Petra, I fear I have some terrible news. Your brother has partaken in a meal at her Majesty, Queen Siv's table. We must return him to her care at once, or he shall die."

"I know. That's why I've brought you here. I need your help getting to Josalfar. If I can just talk to the Queen, I'm sure she'll see to reason. He's just a little boy."

"Mistress Petra, with all due respect to yourself and her Majesty, that's not the way of our peoples. Her Majesty, Queen Siv, is not in the habit of releasing laborers. The peoples do not give away that which is rightfully ours. Not for free. Not anything. He ate of her table and thus owes his allegiance.

Her Majesty will assign him a caretaker, who will acquaint him with his new habits and home. Either he works and receives the enchanted sustenance that he needs, or he will die—and quickly. There are no exceptions."

"But he didn't know!"

"That is irrelevant. It is tradition and must be observed."

"But it's not fair."

"So little in life truly is. Would you like some hot cocoa? I can brew a pot. My last Master found my hot cocoa to be the best this side of the Atlantic. Or so he said. Trouble always seems less dire over chocolate."

"No. None for me, thanks. What is life like for the laborers?"

"It's not so bad, Mistress. The first thing the Alfarians will do is feed him nice and proper. His health will take a turn for the better, his recuperation, rapid, and his duties, minor, while he heals. Oh, he'll have to have his eye removed. Just the one, mind you, and the procedure is quite painless. Have no fear! His caretaker shall wear the eye himself to best guide young Emil. Once your brother has regained his strength, I expect he will be sent to the mines, where he will perform his life's work. It's very rare to lose a soul in the mines. Our peoples thrive in the dark, and with time, his eye shall adjust until he does as well. It's not a bad life, Mistress. He will want for nothing, and likely, this will be his final illness until he is retired, at which point his caretaker will grant him more freedoms in return for other, more sporadic services. By then, he shall be quite old, by human standards, that is."

So he'd be enslaved, but happy about it? Was that really better than dead?

"What about a deal? Emil is the Queen's and she won't give him up for free, but we could come to an arrangement."

"That's a dangerous game, Mistress. Deals amongst our own are fraught with peril. She will not give him up for anything of lesser value, and probably not of equal. Her Majesty is ancient and powerful. What, that she desires, could be beyond her possession? What, that you could lay claim over? Do you understand, Mistress? She will ask of you tasks that greatly outperform your abilities. Her Majesty, Queen Siv, will send you to your grave, and if she is merciful, she will then send for Emil before death becomes him. Unless, to raise the stakes, she includes a clause that should you fail, so then shall he. Her Majesty is not sentimental. She is practical, rational. And she's seen and spent too many lives to be touched by anyone, especially a human. Rather than marching off to suicide and martyrdom, why don't we return him to the Queen right this minute? It's for his own good, and yours. We can be back in time for sunup. Then I can bake you the most delightful molasses biscuits you've ever tasted."

The look on her face said it all. Iver's small shoulders slumped, creasing the armpits of his suit.

"Very well then, Mistress. I suppose you'd like to go now?"

She did. Iver explained that with him guiding, their route to Josalfar would be direct, which was a relief. She didn't wish to beg from nor challenge a Queen while hungry and exhausted. Petra also aimed not to return to Leif's flat without a cure, if she could help it. What would the Queen demand? What could she do that a Queen could not? Leave the kingdom was their mutual assumption. So it was for a great journey that they packed.

Iver meant well, but he didn't know where anything was, so Petra gathered supplies. For his part, he traipsed behind her, listing practical objects for an extended hike, these being water, food, a blanket and a knife. In addition, Petra collected a calculator, chalk, a sharpie, a can of salt, and a flashlight. The tunnel and Josalfar itself were of a comfortable temperature during her last journey, so at a guess, she sorted summerwear into her bag.

Before they slipped out the back, Petra left Leif a note explaining her next step as well as who she was with in the hopes that he would not worry. This was moot. Not believing in any of this magic stuff, he was going to reach the worst possible conclusions. Still, she had to do what she had to do. If she woke him up, made him acknowledge Iver, and then asked permission to take on the Queen, he'd still have said no. And that was if he could even see Iver, which she doubted. What did brownies look like to those without the sight? She didn't know. That was a question for later. Emil may well have been growing weaker by the hour. It was time to go.

Iver led the way across the yard and into the woods, disregarding any semblance of trails. The sky wasn't yet awake, but Petra swore there was a hint of tangerine on the horizon. Not that she had a clear view, what with the dense foliage. Tripping over a half-buried log, she flipped her flashlight on. When he stopped short, she collided with him, nearly toppling them both.

"Where are we?" She asked.

They'd wandered far, and the few stars she could see were giving way to a ruddy haze. The ground rose steeply before ahead, where a small cascade crashed into the stream.

"Behind the waterfall is a portal."

Warning her to step carefully, Iver slipped beneath and behind the rushing tumult. Far less sure-footed, Petra turned off the flashlight. She stuck it in her bag and crept on, sliding on the wet stone but swinging her fall into the rockface beside Iver.

"Are you okay, Mistress?"

"Yeah. Thanks. I don't see a door."

Not that she could see much of anything, between the falls and the rock merging to block what little day trickled in. The strip of ground where Iver stood and Petra crept was smooth, narrow, and slick with moisture. The duo was thoroughly wet by the spray.

"You wouldn't. I haven't awoken it yet, Mistress. I have to tell it which path we want."

That said, he held his charm to the stone, placing it in a polished crevice of like scale. Singing a guttural, then high pitched, tune, he lit his charm, and the escarp melted to either side, revealing the illuminated entryway of a tunnel. Petra tried to memorize the sound, to replicate it later. Those notes sounded attainable. Though, doubtless, without his amulet, the song wouldn't get her far.

"In you go, Mistress. I'll see to the portal behind us. The light fades fast, but the path is straight, so hurry right along. You need the light more than I."

Agreeable, Petra jogged ahead. As he'd said, the glow was dissipating. The walls felt identical to those of the St'Avgull, except, so far, there were no flesh hoops. When the light was gone, she'd have to rely on her handy dandy flashlight or else march blind. Petra assumed she would hear the prancing of tiny footsteps catching up, but Iver moved without sound, suddenly running at her side.

"Now, Mistress, how exactly did your brother end up at her Majesty's dais?"

Petra slowed to a brisk walk, and Iver followed suit, the better to talk. She reiterated the story, her telling succinct with experience. She concluded with where she'd learned to catch him.

When all was said, Iver shook his head. "Why didn't you punish the neighbor, Gunndis, for her treachery?"

Petra shrugged. "It sounds like she was a victim too. And anyway, it wouldn't do any good. It's not like hurting her will see Emil well or bring Atla home."

So saying, unable to explain her discomfort with the direction their discourse had taken, she ran ahead.

Then it was Iver's turn to shrug but he didn't, instead matching her step. Inwardly he admitted that regardless of the futility thereof, were he in Petra's shoes, he would have burnt that woman's house to the ground. Iver's capacity for revenge was as heightened as that of any slave who could only dream of the horrors they'd have wrought if not for their bonds—whose dark fantasies escalated with every insult.

"You'll want to step carefully, Mistress. We're nearly at the end and the drop will come as a nasty surprise at this speed."

Accordingly, she slowed. Moving sprightly ahead, a short time later, Iver announced that they'd reached their exit. Then he hopped out. Dawning on the hole, Petra peered beyond and let herself drop down. Landing softly, she straightened and looked around. In moments a swarm of Alfarians had converged on their spot, but Iver warned them off.

"She has business with her Majesty, Queen Siv," he said, speaking in Icelandic for her benefit. That claim was too outlandish to be fictional, and the Alafarians moved aside, letting them pass unmolested. He'd spoken with more confidence than his posture implied and Iver shivered like a soggy cat as they progressed.

Their walk was familiar. Petra spotted the dais, minus its cursed blood cups and berries. She watched as humans clad in linen dress uniforms marched past, their line unending as a cargo train. Her eyes scanned their faces for one she dearly missed, but Iver led her on. Between chiseled stalagmites and shaved stalactites, armed and unarmed Alafarians, and a slew of modest reflecting pools, they meandered seemingly without aim until they arrived at a golden arcade set into the stone wall. This, being the metallic variety, rather than the bioluminescence that Petra was fast becoming acquainted with. The hall was framed by guards, who crossed spears, blocking their passage. They barked at Iver who responded in their tongue. The guards looked to Petra like they might wield those weapons in offense but an unseen voice cried. Lowering their weapons, the guards exchanged a look Petra couldn't read, and returned to their prior stances. Iver moved between them, passing beyond sculptural torches, each flame cupped by a spiral cage that reminded Petra of his charm. He entered into the gilded abode. After a deep breath, Petra followed closely behind.

The chamber was domed, capped with an oculus. Instead of a mirror pool, every surface shone metallic. Peering down, Petra found her hands had all the vibrance of stained glass, painted by lit crystals. Ahead lay a raised platform, on which sat a white-winged Alfarian atop a curvilinear throne, her seat inlaid with precious gems, and flanked at either side by tall cohorts. Spanning the platform, their furs ranged from silver to sepia. They wore woven metallic gowns, and their foreheads gleamed red, though their aura was outmatched by her Majesty's ovular crown. She bore a mosaic, a byzantine halo, bathing those she faced in a sanguine aurora. Her wings, the only wings Petra had yet observed on any Alfarian, were as long as she, with veins stretching from shoulder to tip, paper flesh iridescent. With a start, Petra realized that the hair's-width gaps between stones were the Queen's fur. That was no crown she wore, but rather countless eyes turned rubies, inlaid around her skull.

The jewels were arranged so tightly that initially, there appeared no space between them at all.

Iver held a hand to Petra in the universal stop sign. Alone, he approached the Queen, who acknowledged him in their tongue, berating him by the sound of her snarls. Yet, on behalf of the stranger he'd met just hours prior, he spoke up, his barks comparatively mild. Petra knew not what was said, forced to trust that Iver was doing his best to see her brother cured. Let the books be right about brownies, she thought. Finally, assumedly having made their purpose clear, Iver stepped back to Petra's side and awaited the Queen's pronouncement. It came without pause.

"Human child, am I to understand that you wish for me to relinquish the hold citizen Roth has over your brother?"

Petra stood up straight and gave a sure nod. "Yes, your Majesty, Queen Siv. I do."

"And you are willing to pay any price to have him freed?"

"Yes. Any price."

"Before we discuss terms, would you like to see your sister? I want you to witness the standard you are so desperate to save your brother from."

"Atla? Yes. I would like to see Atla very much. Thank you."

The Queen growled a command at one of those backers who, in turn, left the room.

"What I will ask of you will not be easy. Nor will it be safe. You need not traverse such great perils. We are not a danger. The child will be happy here. We keep laborers well fed. They lead active, healthy lifestyles, not the sedentary arrangements so common in your homeland. They want for nothing. They experience no illness. And as a peaceful people, there is no danger that our laborers will ever be sent to fight in some ill-conceived war." Iver flinched at that, but if the Queen noticed, she didn't comment. "I doubt you could say the same of laborers in your home country."

Petra considered those baseless assumptions regarding Iceland, but decided not to argue that point. "It's a matter of choice, your Majesty. He's got his whole life ahead of him, but here, he'll never have one."

"And have you given him the choice? Is he aware that all of his symptoms would be cured if only you'd let him be reunited with your dear sister, the human Atla?"

So summoned, Atla appeared in the shimmering doorway, led by two Alafarians, one, a guard, the other, perhaps a lady in waiting, who seemed happy to rejoin the others on stage. Like the other humans, Atla wore a thin, colorless dress. Her skin was paler, no longer jaundiced, her remaining eye lacking its usual blood lightning. Gone too was the bruising of her lids, and the bug bites that long marred the apple whites of her arms. Her feet were bare, but appeared unhurt, if mightily calloused. Seeing Petra, Atla smiled, a smile of bliss.

"Consider yourself at leisure, human Atla," said the Queen. Released of whatever confines not being "at leisure" implied, Atla squealed, rushed forward, and pulled her little sister close.

"I've missed you and Emil so much! Where is he? Have you brought him too?"

"Atla! We've missed you too. He's not feeling well, so he's home right now. Leif is watching him."

"Leif? Well, as soon as he's better, you should both come to stay here. It's paradise. And only some people are welcome. Thankfully, we have the sight. We're the lucky ones!"

"So—you like working the mines then?"

"Of course. I mean, work is work, but I would've been working up there anyway. I didn't have a choice in that. No choices. It's the same everywhere. But up there, I had bills to worry about too. And you kids. Now though, there are no smelly men at the door. You know? No worrying if I'll have enough money to pay whatever the bank or Mr. Gunnarsson, says we owe. It's wonderful. I'm free. I feel so free."

"But Atla—don't you want us to grow up and be whatever we've always wanted? You said—you said we could be anything!"

"Petra, that's just something grownups tell little kids so they'll try in school. So they will follow the rules, vote, be productive, functional citizens. And it's hard—so very hard to grow up, and there are only ever more rules to follow! Not less. You're not free up there." She pointed through the skylight. "Not anywhere. I feel so much lighter here without everything weighing down on me. It's all provided. I just have to work a little. And work isn't so bad, you know? Me and the others—we're like a family." Atla's eyes rose to the Queen and traced the Alfarians spanning the width of the throne room. "Yeah. A family." The Queen motioned to a guard and purred. In response, the guard turned to Atla and gestured a signal she must have known.

"I've got to get back to my shift. And my shaft." Atla laughed, releasing Petra. "Can't let the team down! But I'm so happy to see you! Next time bring Emil. You'd both be so happy here!" she proclaimed, while led away. Petra called out her goodbye, eyes moist.

"Do you see now, human child Petra? Your brother will be well taken care of. You risk his health and your safety out of misplaced fear."

Atla's fanatic response to being enslaved did nothing but further cement Petra's opposition. The Queen had brainwashed Atla. That was all there was to it.

"What do I need to do to make Emil well again? What are your terms?"

"Very well then, human child Petra. Since you insist, there are three objects of great value that you must bring to me before the next full moon. Those treasures are as follows: the fleece of a golden ram, the saddle of a kelpie, and the talon of a griffon."

With every word, the rosy-hued flesh of Iver's plump face sagged, his mouth forming a silent O. Petra, however, had but the vaguest clue what those things were, so her reaction was milder. She'd read about kelpies and griffons, but as they weren't the sorts of fae one could summon home and ask for guidance, she'd disregarded them as soon as she'd gleaned their basic descriptions. As for why anyone would want those things, she hadn't the foggiest. The Queen had an entire golden throne room and throngs of slaves mining for more. What made the fleece so special? Couldn't the slaves just make her a saddle? And Alfarian claws looked plenty sharp already. What could be so great about a griffon's?

"In return, I will see to it that you receive a cure for the bonds ailing your brother. If he accepts the amulet, he will live free."

There was a pause Petra took as her place to accept.

"Okay," she said.

"Very well then. Golden rams graze on the frozen plains of Kolchus. Kelpies haunt the blood swamp of Postlov where the arteries meet. Griffons nest along the Borjan Mountains. Secrecy is paramount. Speak not of these tasks to any other."

Petra scanned the fuzzy faces of those figures lining the platform. Apparently, her quest wasn't that *secret*.

"I don't know where those places are. Can I have a map?"

The Queen's nose twitched. Was that the equivalent to a human raising their eyebrows? Or did that indicate humor? Petra wondered.

"My peoples have no need for maps. Brownie Iver shall guide you."

Petra looked to Iver, whose face was bereft of hope. She considered what she was asking of her new pal. All this because he'd been compelled to finish a scarf she'd intentionally left out. Then she pictured Emil, feverish, shivering, losing hair, and her resolve hardened.

"What happens if I fail?"

"We'll send for your brother should you die in your quest. Without our intervention, he shall perish by the next full moon. Should that be the case, we will inform the human Atla, who will mourn your folly," the Queen concluded.

Then, switching to their language, she barked, giving a half-wave. Petra opened her mouth to ask further questions, but Iver shook his head. He gave a low bow, Petra attempted her own, and they exited the way they'd come.

Ruby studded heads turned, their obsidian eyes following the odd couple as they made for the far wall. Petra pictured Atla hammering away at the side of a steep chasm, seeking gems, precious metals. At least she was happy, even if it wasn't of her choosing. But what was right, or at least not so terribly wrong, for Atla—wasn't best for Emil. Of that, Petra was confident.

"How many days are left until the next full moon?"

"An even fifteen, Mistress."

Would that be enough? It had to be. "In the event that I die, I need you to run back here and let the Queen know so she can send for him." At least he'd be with Atla.

"Of course, Mistress," he said, though they both knew that was only if he survived to do so. A big if, that.

Reaching the edge of Josalfar, Iver stopped.

"Now Mistress, shall we return to your home to better pack for our journey, or do you think a calculator and a knife will prove sufficient against a winged ram?"

Was that sarcasm? Were brownies sarcastic?

"We are going to be traveling through frozen planes, a swampland, and a mountainous desert," he added.

Petra had packed clothes, but not for freezing weather.

"I need winterwear, but I can't sneak in without Leif seeing me. He must be awake by now. Can you get in and out without being spotted?"

"That, Mistress, is a common skill of the peoples. Do you have any specific articles of clothing in mind?"

"I only have one bag of clothes. If you can get it to me, I can take out whatever we need and leave the rest. Oh. And can you ditch the calculator back inside? Emil needs it if I'm not gonna use it."

"Certainly. As for our venture, we should be armed. What weapons can I find in your home, and where?"

She shrugged. "I've got a pocket knife. Leif keeps knives in the kitchen, and he might have a hammer in his toolbox."

Iver shook his head. "If you don't know how to use a knife, Mistress, you're more like to accidentally stab yourself than to damage another. I have a slingshot and knives of my own. Have you ever killed anything with a hammer?"

Petra shook her head, startled by the question.

"Where would this Leif keep his tool kit?"

She considered. "It might be under the sink in the kitchen. Or in the bathroom closet. It's not a big apartment."

Petra hid beneath the waterfall while Iver left the tunnel and slunk off for supplies. She wrote the number, fifteen, on her side, fearing any other surface might be lost. Then she tried to nap, but struggled to get comfortable on the cold hard ground, waking with a start at Iver's return. He held the duffle bag and a hammer in tow.

"Were there police?" she asked.

"Yes."

"Did you hear what they were saying?"

"A non-officer human, that I took to be your Leif, was explaining your interest in the peoples. I also spotted some officers in the woods. If you leave your clothes outside, they will find them and reach their own conclusions."

"I want them to know I wasn't kidnapped. If they find my extra clothes, neatly folded, in the woods—what will they think?"

"I'm not certain I'm the best judge of human behavior, Mistress." Truthfully, neither was she, but she kept that to herself. "To my mind, a kidnapper wouldn't have slowed to let you write a goodbye note nor to pack your belongings. Leaving the excess laundry in an orderly fashion in the woods says you left of your own accord. However, unless you're an excellent swimmer, perhaps we shouldn't leave them by the stream. You don't want them to think you drowned. Or do you, Mistress?"

Petra did not. After she sorted out what warm weather clothes would just weigh them down, she had Iver leave them in a clearing. The hammer, she tucked into a sweater at the center of her bag. She'd be in a world of pain if it battered her back, but it was too long for her pocket.

Upon returning, Iver bade her step from the tunnel.

"I cannot redirect the path while it's open."

So saying, he closed the portal. Invisible bells sounded, audible even under the splash of the falls. Petra hoped nobody was searching for her nearby.

"Can you redirect the portals anywhere?"

Iver shook his head. "No, Mistress. A Master Pathmaker can forge paths where none rest, but I can only awaken existing paths, opening portals where they've opened before. The Alfarian you described, Temil, may well be a Master Pathmaker. The other, Roth, likely, is not."

"So, at one time, someone like Temil stood where we're standing and made a route to where the golden rams live?"

"Yes, Mistress. Although, perhaps Kolchus was not home to the rams then. Climates shift, peoples roam. Our peoples are far older than your own. Could be Temil himself forged the path."

Iver set his charm to the stone once more, his beastial tune low in pitch and volume. Chimes ricocheted, echoing as the duo stepped in, and he sealed the entrance behind them.

"The Pathmakers—they can make paths anywhere?"

"There are limitations. Portals can only be birthed within certain types of stone. Sedentary, for instance, wouldn't do. The stones should also be larger than the traveler who wishes to walk the golden path."

The entry glow lasted longer but so did their trek. Both of her arms were tired from turns carrying the light but she willed herself not to pass it off. Bad enough she'd taken a slave. Pushing unnecessary tasks onto him tainted her. After hours walking without passing a fleshy hoop, Petra asked about them.

"Those are natural portals to other worlds. The peoples did not create the St'Avgull, but once its properties were discovered, we toiled long and hard to master it. Left to grow naturally, portals can appear anywhere, in any world. And not every world is habitable for you nor us. Even with the advancements our peoples have made in guiding growths, there are always sprouts that bloom rebellious, leading elsewhere. My advice, Mistress? Don't reach through those branches. The main tunnel of any St'Avgull in this world, will eventually lead to Josalfar. The branches are a lottery, and not the fun kind."

"So these tunnels the people make—they're the roots of St'Avgulls?"

"Similar, Mistress. We prefer to travel through portal stones, as opposed to using the blooms, which mainly serve to ensnare unsuspecting humans in recent years. Our young practice pathmaking with St'Avgull sprouts, but that's the extent of our use for them. They were a wonderful teacher and now they are a tool at our disposal."

She had half a mind to tie the flashlight to her arm, but decided against slowing their trek. As much to distract from the growing soreness, as because information could prove valuable, she questioned further.

"This place we're going—Kolchus. Does Kolchus exist in my world, or yours?"

"Well, Mistress, brownies are more of your world than of the peoples', and so it has been for a great many years. As for Kolchus, I'd say it is a land between. There are places where worlds merge. You can reach Kolchus from your world as the Alfarians can from theirs."

The temperature dropped until they could see mushroom clouds emerging from their mouths and nostrils. Petra stopped to pull on a sweater.

"It'll be worse out there. Let's eat here where it's still dry," Iver suggested, taking a seat on the ground.

Petra joined him. From his sack, he retrieved jerky and two paper-wrapped salted eggs.

"Here you go," he said, splitting the food between them.

Jerky was a treat back home, being more expensive than the average grocery. Petra ate slowly, savoring every bite. The salted egg she examined before bringing to her mouth. It was larger than eggs usually were.

"Goose egg?"

"Indeed, Mistress."

Nodding, she ate. Eggs were eggs. Then she sipped from her water bottle and he from his canteen. Rising, they carried on.

Chapter 7

S hining tendrils reemerged and snowdrifts swirled at the mouth. Petra paused to put on her jacket, hat, half scarf, belt, and gloves, putting the flashlight away. Her mum had drilled the importance of layers when faced with cold. Grow over warm from being too bundled while active, and she would sweat, become complacent, and ditch the extra layers. Not bundled enough afterward, and she could catch a chill from the sudden cooling of said sweat. It was a balancing act, and

Petra's outfit was imbalanced. Her jacket was too tight, her belly only fully covered by her two shirts.

Stepping forth, Petra squinted, her lashes a dark gleam in her peripheries. She gave her eyes time to adjust to the glaring whiteness before progressing.

Iver made no adjustments to his attire. Lacking the dense fur of the Alfarians, Petra postulated his body heat was insulated by a thick layer of fatty tissue, as was the case for walruses and seals. Likewise, he didn't squint in the glare, as far as Petra could tell, and with the scale of his owl eyes, any lid movement would not have gone unnoticed.

"What do I need to know about golden rams?" she asked as they plodded through freshly fallen snow, occasionally slipping on concealed ice.

"Do you know what a ram looks like?"

"Like a goat?"

"Yes. Picture a goat the size of a bull, but with four large horns curling around the ears to frame the face. Those horns are sharp, hard. Nigh unbreakable. Like your goats, they live in herds, moving with surprising agility, given their size."

So each one was big, armed, protected by more of the same, and fast. While she was small, practically unarmed, had only a stubby old man for backup, and couldn't keep up with her eight year old brother. Petra tried not to think about her odds.

"I see. What can you tell me about the golden fleece?"

"That is important, isn't it? Indeed. Well, the mature golden ram is covered in thick golden wool, hence the name. This wool is not just gold in color—but curls of pure metal. I've never heard of anyone who got near a golden kid and lived to tell the tale, so their coat could be altogether different."

Well, Petra thought, that was about to change. She had no hope of subduing a full-grown adult, to shear it.

"Theoretically, you should be able to shear one if you can get a blade close to the ram's skin without crushing the wool. However, should the gold be subject to blunt force, it would be condensed, into a shield of sorts."

"Like chain mail?"

"Yes, Mistress. Like chain mail."

"And it's just gold? Because the Queen has tons. Why's this special?"

"I don't know, Mistress. Legend tells of a hero who proved his legitimacy, as ruler, by obtaining such a fleece. I imagine it was treasured then, as much for the hazards faced in acquiring it, as the inherent value of gold. The world's supply, your's and the Alfarians', is finite, while the element has many practical uses, beyond that of mere currency."

Huh. Petra thought. So the fleece wasn't even magic? Unless it was, but Iver didn't know how.

The longer they walked, the colder she became. Her ears were fast numbing, ice crystals clung to her hair, and snowdrifts chilled her ankles. Petra's socks were soaked to her skin.

"Did you not pack boots, Mistress?"

"No. I don't have any. I outgrew my old ones, and handed them down."

"Alright, Mistress. I know of a popular cave where we can make camp. It has a fire pit and a chimney hole chiseled out. When we arrive, you warm your feet by the fire, and I'll see what I can do about your shoes."

At this, Iver slung his bag forward, withdrew a slingshot, and a drawstring sack. Hooking these to his belt, he donned the backpack once more. They walked on, and Petra heard the thwack an instant before she spotted a rabbit crumple midjump. Iver retrieved his prize, stomping on its neck to finish the job. Petra told herself not to be too sensitive. Their food could last only so long.

Iver stuffed the rabbit in his bag, eyes peeled for more. By the time they reached the cave, Petra's pants were caked white to the knees, and he'd caught three more. He ran out of room in his bag so she had to make her peace with carrying the final corpse. It hadn't bled much, and as long as she wasn't staring at it, she could almost pretend it was sleeping. For better or worse, the freezing wind battering her face was plenty distracting, and there was only so much care to be dredged on behalf of the dead.

Had Iver not pulled her inside, Petra would have marched past the cave, assuming it a shadow in a snowbank. Bending low, they ducked under the icicle valance, entering the gloom beyond. Iver lit the meager woodpile another had left, with flint he carried. Petra left her shoes beside the firepit to dry. She'd anticipated resting but Iver suggested she help with the skinning.

"Mistress, this will go faster if we each take one."

She didn't want to. Everything to do with taking apart a dead animal *that still looked like an animal* made her uneasy, but she was asking a lot of Iver. And she knew it. She couldn't very well say no.

Step by step, he explained the process. First, Iver pinched the back below the neck, and cut off the head. The scent of rust filled the cave and Petra winced. Then turning the corpse to ease further access, Iver chopped off the tail and paws. Petra had seen rabbits' feet on key rings for years in just about every gas station she'd stepped foot in. Yet, until that very moment, it never occurred to her that a lucky rabbit's foot was an actual rabbit's foot. Heck, she'd had one herself at some point, linked to her house key, the toe beans black against its soft white fur. Real fur, apparently. That she'd possessed, held, and caressed part of a bunny, did not make watching one get butchered any easier to stomach. A side of guilt to flavor the nausea, thanks.

Iver stabbed the lower belly, and pulling tight at either side, slit a path to the neck, being careful not to pierce the muscle nor innards, which could spoil the meat. From there, it was a matter of tugging the skin from the body, like undressing an infant, he said. That imagery could not have been more unhelpful. Forgetting why not to, Petra breathed through her nose, which was a mistake. The fetor was murkier now and she fought to control her breathing. Fur stuck under the ribs and above the shoulders, but a snip here and there, had it free.

Petra succeeded in skinning her first rabbit without vomiting nor fainting. She didn't know if she could faint, but if so, today was the day. She took twice as long as Iver. The other rabbits were fully bare when she finished with hers. In fact, Iver was most of the way through prepping their dinner. He'd pulled ground herbs, a tin of lard, and a handful of mushrooms from his sack. When she was done, Iver explained which fungi were edible and how to tell them apart in the wild. Petra, whose hands remained bloody, retained none of this.

The furs, he placed skin side up beside the fire. To himself, he tutted, "Not ideal but it will do." Petra didn't inquire as to what he meant.

"We will need our strength. We must eat well," he continued, cutting the body into fourths, dabbing each with lard, followed by a smearing of herbs. These he stuffed into a pot, which he set by the fire, the handle leaning away from the flames. Dusting the mushrooms with spice as well, those too took a swim. Then he replaced the lid and moved on to prepping the rest of the meat. Once the bodies were quartered, they'd transitioned from rabbits to food.

As Iver worked, he chattered over which organs were worth using in a meal and which, for their purposes, were not.

"Had we rice and the time for proper curing, I'd save the intestines for sausages."

He did not throw away the heart, kidneys, nor liver. These organs he identified for her benefit and added to the pot. "They have the wrong texture for drying." The remaining meat was cut into thinner and thinner strips, thoroughly salted, and left to dry upon the stone ring around the fire. Then Iver rose to wash his hands in the snow, and gratefully, Petra followed suit.

"I thought brownies didn't like salt?"

"It burns, yes. But have you ever eaten a radish?"

"I don't think so."

"I suppose they've diminished in popularity, not being sweet. Everything has to be sweet now. Very well then, have you eaten chili? Made with peppers?"

"Yes, I've had chili."

"And I imagine it was rather spicy, yes?"

Petra nodded. "A little."

"Good. Spice is what makes a meal interesting. Memorable. A little salt here and there won't give me an ulcer. There *is* too much salt on these for my palate, but that's preferable to food poisoning. We need our supplies to last, and while we can trust the meat is safe to eat when it's fresh, with every day moist and unsalted, it will spoil. I can always dust the salt off my portions."

"We could eat the fresh meat raw and we wouldn't get sick?"

"That's right, Mistress. I can whip up some rabbit tartare if you want to give it a try? I haven't any tomatoes, and the flavor will be dissimilar to beef but—"

"No, thank you. Maybe another day."

The hot acid at the back of her throat burned a route to her stomach, and Petra would be satisfied just to get dinner down. He lifted the lid, adjusted the chunks, and closed it again.

"That smells good," Petra said.

It was true. The rust had been replaced by rosemary.

"The cave should contain the smell somewhat."

Petra cocked her head like a puppy, confused.

"We don't want any wildlife wandering in here. Golden rams aren't the only beasts in Kolchus."

"Are there bears?" she asked, imagining Greenland's polar variety.

"Not that I'm aware of, Mistress, but wolves aren't unheard of."

"Is there a way to keep them out? Can you seal us in?"

"Unfortunately not. This is not a golden path, but a natural cavern."

Petra sat beside Iver, who requested her shoes. She took them off, and soon he was hard at work stitching fur bootnecks where there had been none. She was soaked through and freezing, but the fire warmed, as her rubber doll leached anxiety from her grip. Things weren't so bad. She'd been colder than this after snowball fights with Emil, when he'd shoved handfuls down her back. The flakes were getting bigger outside, the banks camouflaging their hideaway.

"It appears we have a surplus of fur. I'm nearly done with your sneakers. If you would be so kind as to change out of your pants, I would like to add fur to those as well. The snow gets thicker farther on."

Petra ducked deeper into the cave, changed into dry clothes, and carried the soggy jeans to Iver.

"Place it so the ankles are near the fire, please, Mistress."

She did so. He finished with her shoes, and letting her pants dry, poured supper into shallow bowls.

"Anything you don't finish, I'll salt and cure. Try to eat it all though."

She complimented his cooking. The rabbit tasted like very rich chicken, or maybe like duck, although there was no fat. Petra's dad had loved duck, so that was a flavor she was well acquainted with. Iver drank from a second canteen. Petra could smell the alcohol from where she sat.

After dinner, she took the cooling pot outside, and wiped it clean with snow. Then she returned it to Iver, who set it aside while he finished with her pants.

"I have my pack organized so that everything fits," he explained. "I'll put it away when I'm done."

Petra poked and prodded the fire, adding sticks as the evening wore on. An unknown previous tenant had piled tinder high along the walls. Iver called her over to show her this or that knot, to explain why this sort of stitching was superior to that, while working with thicker materials such as furs and denim. When she began to doze, Petra wrapped herself in her nearly dried winter coat and Leif's throw blanket. She watched the flames dance through heavily lidded eyes until sleep drew the curtain on their performance.

"Time to wake up, Mistress. We've got a lot of ground to cover, and the weather will cut our trek short today."

She rose, stiff-backed, stiff-necked, stiff everywhere. Her knees cracked as she stretched. Thanking Iver, Petra changed into her new weatherproofed pants and footwear, before jotting the number, fourteen, on her side.

"There wasn't any fur left for your jacket, Mistress, but with luck, we'll catch something today."

Petra hadn't realized it was obvious she couldn't zip her coat, but of course. Why else would she leave it open in this weather? With what remained of their fire, he melted snow in her water bottle and his canteen. She accepted jerky, another salted egg, and a handful of familiar red berries. She watched as he dusted the salt from his meal.

"Did you find the rowan berries by Leif's house?"

"Yes, Mistress. I collected them as I made my way back to you, after leaving your clothes."

They were bitterer than blueberries and raspberries, but not inedibly so. They tucked their vessels into their bags. Her bottle was plastic, but his canteen was metal and he explained that if it froze against his skin, he'd have to tear it free. Then, certain they left nothing of use behind, they stepped out onto a blank page.

I spy something white, Petra thought, swallowing an insane giggle. The very air was opaque, foggy with flakes slipping beneath a grim sky, slowly at first, but the wind was gaining speed. The ground, where she could tell ground from heavens, was flat. What solitary trees interrupted the otherwise empty expanse, were skeletal, fragile, likely dead. Iver's narrow yet fortunately deep footsteps crushed a path for her to wade through. He'd been right. With every hour, the ferocity of the storm increased, and their visibility dwindled.

Gales struck their faces like a starlet offended in a black and white movie, and Petra's extremities were numb.

"Mistress," Iver said, as she rubbed heat back into her fingers, "Why not keep your hands inside your shirt, to warm against your belly? You'll be unable to catch yourself if you fall, but we're in a land of few obstacles and much snow to soften the blow."

Petra took his advice, withdrawing her hands and pressing them to her skin. She flinched as the icy contact made her stomach clench, but frostbite was a valid concern, so she kept her hands in place. It was a relief when the electric current shocked feeling back into her ligaments. A boy at her old school had lost his toes to frostbite. She didn't know the full story, but understood it could happen to her.

Heaving from the effort, she kept up. Twice she fell, and twice Iver turned back to help. The struggle was as constant as the gales, unyielding. The howling wind made conversation impossible. Iver charged ahead, cutting a track through the blustery uproar, oft disappearing in the waves of snow.

Petra spied smog on the horizon. The darkness rose over twinkling lights set into an undulating terrain, looking more like mammatus clouds than hills. Were those dwellings? Just as she observed the roiling black amassed over the starry milieu, Petra heard a clipped shout. Unable to discern the words, that she could identify the sound as verbal indicated the caller was either very near, or belting it. Petra couldn't stop to investigate without risking the loss of Iver's guidance, so quickly was the snow burying his steps, but she kept her eyes peeled. Iver hadn't slowed in the wake of the maelstrom.

Another shout erupted. Turning to look, she tripped and found herself at face level with the open-jawed muzzle of a wolf, her hands restricted by her jacket. In a panic, she slipped them free and threw herself backward, away from the beast.

"Don't eat me!" she cried.

"I said," it called over the roar, in Icelandic, "There are trolls ahead! You can't go that way. Come this way."

The wolf was shouting. The wolf could shout. And why not? Star people, brownies, magical tunnels—talking wolves and trolls made as much sense as anything.

"My friend is up ahead!" she yelled, pointing to Iver, a meandering lump, fading in and out of view.

"Stay here! I'll get them!"

So saying, the wolf raced on.

Moving kept Petra's blood pumping, her nerves a-tingle, so she could feel the cold's razor bite. Stagnation invited the ice to nest between her bones and pick at her muscles, so she shuffled her step, rubbing her belly, altering her bent posture. Spinning from side to side, she watched for incoming monsters. Unsure of the scale of real trolls, she hoped the famous rock formations she'd visited and learned of, were fictitiously titled. In the white-out, she imagined every rising hump and current to be an approaching monster, so it was with immense relief that Petra spotted the wavering shapes of Iver and the wolf hopping her way through towering drifts.

"Follow me!" said the wolf, when he was in hearing distance.

There was a browned copse of slanted firs far off to their right. The wolf turned and shot like an arrow at the trees. The pair was forced to assume their guide wouldn't deviate as the snow hid his path. Staying close, perhaps out of guilt that he'd been too far to protect her from the could-be attacker, Iver helped Petra balance while crossing a length of ice.

There was a dense line of smoke, staining the firs grey. Their canopy was so tightly intertwined, the smoke couldn't dissipate into tendrils of any identifiable thickness. Her eyes narrowed on the source. Concealed by shade and foliage, sat a cabin, or slumped rather, as if cowering from the incoming drifts.

The wolf waited beside the door as they shuffled down to the house. Before they could thank him or knock, the door swung open, and a young woman waved them in. Paler than Atla even after her time underground, with black eyes and brown hair, the petite woman wore a fur cap, and a dress of crude leather, over pants and moccasins. Her nails were

long, dirty, the natural hair of her ankles prominent. Startlingly, her forehead bore a diamond
shaped indent, but thankfully, no ruby.

Grateful for the offer of respite, Petra and Iver
entered the humble abode, thanking their hosts as
they shut the storm away. A hearth, if a hanging pot
over a fire pit could be called that, was arranged
at the center of the one-room hovel. Earthenware
dishes were stacked on the floor and rudimentary
cushions surrounded the pit. On one end lay a pile
of patched fur and leather quilts Petra took to be
a bed. Against the opposite wall were baskets of
produce, likely potatoes, although she couldn't tell
for sure. Rough-hewn wooden tools, utensils, and
a tin bucket hung from the wall above the food.
There were no books, nor anything else that might
indicate the residents enjoyed periods of leisure.

"Hey there. I am called Aslaug and you've already
met Orro. What do you call yourselves?"

Looking to Iver, Petra shared her real name after
witnessing him do the same. This was no time to
be shy.

"You look human," Aslaug commented.

"I am human," Petra responded.

"We don't get too many of our kind here. Come.
Take off your wet clothes to dry by the fire and

sit. Let's wait out this blizzard together. Orro mentioned you were headed towards Skrimslabesh. Fool's errand, that. Trolls eat people, you know."

That must have been the name of the twinkling village they'd avoided.

Petra plied off her hat, scarf, jacket, and gloves. Aslaug gestured to the cushions and her guests took the opportunity to rest their aching legs. Petra wasn't comfortable exactly, leaning forward, bending her feet from the flames, but she wasn't complaining. It was better than being outside. She spread her wet winterwear beside her seat, as Iver laid out his own.

The brownie was eyeing the produce, doubtless scouring his inner rolodex for recipes. Orro, his torso too long for the scant seating, flopped gracelessly down beside Aslaug.

"A human child and a brownie. You two are far from home. What brings you to Kolchus? Not our balmy autumn weather, I assume," Aslaug asked, chuckling.

"We're just cutting through," Iver replied, his gaze settling on her. "The paths have their limitations, after all."

"That they do."

Petra piped up, "And what about you? You're human. How long have you lived here? How did that come about?"

"I'm half-human, half-Alfarian. My father wears my mother's eye. Being neither nor, I could never live as the Alfarians, but being half that, I am impervious to the Queen's ways. The day I was old enough to feed myself, I was expelled from Josalfar. I believe I had six years when I left. Don't think the Alfarians cruel, however. They found Orro here, to keep me out of harm's way. Our journey wasn't direct, but after trying our luck here and there, this is where we made a home."

Petra wanted to know if Aslaug visited her mum and dad, but judged her inquiry too personal. Emil could have pried, but she was too old to feign ignorance of basic manners.

"Can all wolves talk here?"

"I'm not a wolf," said Orro. "I'm of the Wyvern. You won't find many of my kind in *your* world, but we are common in the middle lands and above Josalfar."

"Well, thank you for the warning. I'd heard of trolls, but not having met any, I doubted they were real."

"Yes. Thank you, Orro," Iver said. "I'd seen the lights, but I had no idea they had settlements this far north."

"With humans ever expanding the scope of their dominion and the Alfarians' more recent conquests, many such creatures have been forced to migrate. Times are desperate," Aslaug explained.

"How are the golden rams taking the impingement on their territory?" Iver asked, careful not to mention their quest.

"Not lying down, that's for sure. The trolls didn't ask for humans to take over every mountain and bridge south of the Orrick line. And the trolls aren't alone in their forced migration—not that the rams can do anything about the fog of will-o-wisps coming up from the east. Horns and hooves can't dent the unsubstantial."

Petra didn't dare ask about the scale of trolls compared to golden rams, but she didn't like the sound of that pity. As far as the mythos went, trolls were giant, so huge that when they mistakenly stayed up past curfew, their corpses formed mountains. Could a golden ram defeat a mountain-sized beast? If so, she had no hope at all.

The screaming intensified outside and the walls shook. Petra had no clue how long they'd walked, nor what time it was. Time moves differently when the very air attacks. The only window was shuttered, so Petra couldn't see white give way to grey, and then to black. Rising, Aslaug set about chopping and boiling the potatoes. Unlike Iver, she tossed in no additives beyond a dash of salt. Orro swaggered to a spot beside the door where he stretched and napped.

As Aslaug cooked, she sang a whistled and clipped diddy in the manner of her father's people. So she was right, humans could make those sounds, thought Petra. Or half-humans, anyway, she amended. Although, Aslaug looked more human than Alfarian. The only giveaways of her mixed heritage were the indent in her forehead, the lack of eye-whites, and the thick hair on her limbs. Though, the few women in Petra's life shaved their legs. Mayhaps adults were just as hairy, and Petra simply hadn't seen to know.

Announcing that it was supper time, Aslaug placed a brimming mug and a bowl of soup each, before their guests. Petra and Iver again gave thanks for the hospitality, as they nibbled at the flavorless stew. Orro, for his part, gnawed on a raw leg. Shredding it with his teeth, the meat stained his muzzle red, peppering the floor with small grey feathers. Petra took a swig from her mug and then tried to hide her surprised choking with an open hand. That was not water. Whatever it was, it stung her mouth and then her throat, going down.

"Vodka," succinctly explained Iver, before changing the subject. "Do you get many visitors here?"

His question was punctuated by the snapping of what was likely an unseen branch.

"Yes and no. Beast and brethren are migrating in droves. Few can and even less stop to chat. We've been finding their bodies on the days following storms like this one. That's why we invited you in. It's not every day a human girl passes by. I've always felt a kinship with my mother's people."

Petra didn't like the sound of that—not the kinship, which was well and good, but the mention of corpses strewn about following inclement weather. She'd learned to fear these golden rams she'd yet to face. Now, she had to worry about the elements as well. That was a first. Without the trappings of community, plows, and electric heating for instance, winter was perilous.

The conversation continued around her. Orro, for one, didn't mind the newfound popularity of their longtime home. Snow kept bodies fresh, so food was plentiful. Oh sure, sometimes he had to compete with visitors for scraps, but most of those trampling past weren't cut out to traverse a frozen wasteland, and those eating, were like to be eaten.

"You can dress up a sprite in all the layers you want, but underneath it all, they're still a sprite. You know where sprites thrive? Meadows, where rain comes as a mist, and sunshine is a given. You know where they don't do so well? Anywhere else. Here is about the farthest they can be from home without being on a different planet altogether. They've been driven to this. I understand. But their loss is my dinner."

"Why can't they stay where they're safe? Why do they have to move at all?" Petra asked.

Aslaug looked to Iver. "How long have you two known each other?"

It was best to lie as little as possible, lest they be marked untrustworthy. Untrustworthy house-guests wouldn't be welcome for long.

"Two days."

"My, my. For near-strangers, you've tied your fates together at great peril. Kolchus is where you've chosen to begin your exploration of the realms? Why here? Of all places—Kolchus is far from the most temperate of the midlands."

"It sounded the most like home," Petra lied, though the climate wasn't that extreme when she compared this storm to those of Iceland.

"Really? Where are you from?"

So, Petra described the long winters, the months of near-total darkness. She explained about the midnight sun, the auroras with their prominence in legends and tourism—not that tourists bothered with her neck of suburbia.

"Of course, I didn't consider how much I take the creature comforts of my homeland for granted, until I woke up in a cave with neither central heating, nor hot water, to combat the chill."

"Live and learn," Iver agreed.

"Live and learn," the four repeated, those so able, drinking from their lopsided cups. Petra, better prepared now for the sting, took an even sip and found she could get it down without coughing.

"Careful," Iver whispered. "Too much and you'll be sick tomorrow."

He didn't have to tell her twice.

Drinking less and eating all, Petra downed the potato water. Vodka was not what the body needed after a half day's hike in blizzard conditions. Not her body, anyway. Iver looked quite content drinking his and Aslaug may well have drunk nothing but.

"You two plan to travel deeper into Kolchus?"

"Yes. We've come this far. There'd be no sense in stopping now," Iver said.

"There was no sense in coming at all," Orro gravely admonished.

"What is the goal? How far must you go before you'll move on to the next midland?" Aslaug asked.

"She wants to see the golden rams. Then we'll leave."

"The nearest herd grazes a half day's hike from here. We will escort you. Orro finds it wasteful to spare a corpse, no matter how familiar, and I've forbidden the consumption of those who've slept under our roof. We will see that you reach the rams unharmed. Then, your folly is your own. Neither Orro nor I would dare scavenge within their borders."

Petra looked to the one window, as if she could see the rams beyond.

"They are a territorial lot, known for their vanity, " Aslaug added, continuing after a pause. "—Your best chance of getting close without being gored is to complement them profusely. Even then, proximity comes at great risk. Do not approach their young."

Aslaug did not elaborate further, which Petra found telling. She and Iver stammered thanks, silently mulling their private misgivings. The Queen had been explicit. None were to know of their quest. As for why, didn't matter. What the Queen said was, or Emil's freedom was forfeit.

Aslaug may have been genuine in why they were under her protection, but Iver suspected otherwise. Still, they'd fed at her hearth and had every intention of spending the night under her roof. They were, in point of fact, her guests. As such, if she insisted on journeying forth with them, for however long, they were honor-bound to accept her assistance. That was Iver's stock of the situation, anywho, honor holding no weight with his charge.

After relieving herself behind Aslaug's shack, Petra returned inside, stomping and shaking off snow in the doorway. She offered to clean the dishes, but Aslaug waved her off.

"No need. We ate them clean."

And so they had, finishing everything but Petra's vodka. Once Aslaug realized human children don't generally partake of liquor, she split it between herself and Iver. Then Aslaug introduced a tune, and he, recognizing it, joined in.

"There's no use talking to her when she gets like this," Orro muttered to Petra. "Those two will silly themselves out in time. You should rest. As will I."

Petra was content to take Orro's advice. Curling up beside his warm fur, she was asleep in minutes, and awoke refreshed before the others. Standing, she dusted fur from her pants and peered into the gloom. Aslaug lay on her stomach, head over the crook of her arm while Iver lay flat on his back by the hearth. She marked the day on her side, drawing the digits wide enough not to blur when smudged, but small enough where she had room for every morning until the next full moon. Then, on tip-toe so as not to rouse her hosts, Petra peeked out the front door. The wind had died down, and the sky was awash with grey. It had stopped snowing. Spying neither trolls nor will-o-wisps, she eased the door shut.

Turning, Petra saw that Aslaug was awake. Of course. If vodka was her water, that glass and a half wouldn't have cursed her with a heavy head and tilting stomach. Not knowing the drinking habits of a brownie, it was Iver, Petra was concerned about. A hangover might delay their trek. As much as Petra didn't want to die skewered by the head hook of ye giant gold puff, she also didn't want to agonize over the possibility for too long. Emil needed her to try and to try quickly. Unless she wanted to become an only child, they needed to get a move on.

Iver had gotten her this far, and it would have been poor thanks for his loyal efforts for her to shake him awake before he was ready. To busy her hands and still her mind, she asked Aslaug if there was anything she could help with. Together they set to peeling potatoes. These Aslaug sliced and tossed into a pot of snowmelt hanging over a fire that was more ash than flame. With a stick and the force of her breath, Aslaug coaxed life into the cinders until the pitiful pyre burned anew.

Petra hadn't found Aslaug to be particularly loud, but the slight commotion served to wake Orro and Iver. They rose, and Iver stretched the stiffness from his joints.

"How are you feeling?" Petra asked.

"Ah, never you fret over me, Mistress. Brownies don't suffer from lead heads as humans do."

"None of them, no matter the drink?"

"Not one. Be they wine or liquor, it's all the nectar of the gods to us."

Breakfast was a quiet affair. Petra reviewed what she knew about the rams, wondering why it was unwise to approach their young. Aslaug hadn't said, but Petra guessed that was akin to impeding upon their precious territory, and thus, bound to result in the aforementioned charge. And Petra, the kid-kabob, couldn't save anybody. Her initial plan to corner a baby didn't seem so great, anymore.

Their weaknesses? There wasn't much. If she, say, charged at them—a laughable idea—her body might crush their fleece into an armor which counted more as an advantage for the beasties, if Petra was any judge. So she couldn't come at them from the side unless she had a stabbing or piercing weapon. Blunt force would be useless unless she aimed for the face, legs, or tail. Complicating her ability to plan also, was her ignorance as to what these things actually looked like since—Fun Fact! She'd never actually seen one. Petra pictured bulky sheep with golden wool and swirly horns. She would have no way of gauging the accuracy of that image until she was face to face with Mister Stabby—or, rather, a flock of Mister Stabbies—and her imminent demise.

No death. She couldn't think about that. Focus, Petra, she commanded. Focus.

As for golden ram weaknesses, they were vain to the point of foolishness. Could she use that? Get one alone by appealing to its pride?

"Does being sheared hurt?"

"When it's done right, it shouldn't," Iver answered, looking pointedly away from Aslaug.

She'd spoken without thinking. Petra wished she had a tiny vacuum to suck in the words that ought never to have found ears. They still hadn't mentioned the Queen, so all was not lost. Fairies lived for technicalities and the Queen hadn't forbidden the asking of pertinent questions.

Aslaug was careful not to react, but she and Orro exchanged a look. For Orro, subtleties were complicated by the shape of his head. To look at somebody meant he could either side-eye or turn his entire face. In this case, he chose the latter, giving away their insight.

Chapter 8

After breakfast, they bundled up and set out. Iver gathered sticks en route, tying and hanging them from his sack. The bundle looked heavy to Petra, but he was insistent on lugging them along.

"We'll need these if we want a fire later."

A creeping breeze sifted surface flurries as they tread through the virgin snow. A proper guide, Aslaug pointed to unremarkable swathes of tundra, explaining what presently intangible factors set them apart.

"That's a field of wildflowers after the thaw. Last summer, a caravan of naiades made camp there. Their sort thrives along the banks of ponds and lakes, in temperate climates. They didn't last long," Aslaug gazed off into the distance. "This is our third summerless year in a row."

Iver inquired as to what flowers grew where, instructing Aslaug to use this plant for flavoring, or this plant as an antibiotic. Learning dandelions were plentiful come spring, he lapsed into a lecture on how to make dandelion wine.

Petra asked if the golden rams shed their fleece in hot weather like dogs did their fur.

"Oh, it never gets hot enough for that. And no. To my knowledge, the rams have never been known to shed," Aslaug answered.

Did that count as a weakness? Petra wondered. The inability to cool themselves in hot weather? She imagined tunneling beneath their field and building a giant kiln. Then she could swing by and offer to help them cool down by trimming their fleece. Her pleasure, she'd say. Not that she knew how to build a kiln, only that laymen could, as her art teacher had done so. That being her old art teacher now, what with her sudden district change and whatnot. Shame, that. Petra liked Mrs. Halonen.

If only she'd taught kiln building.

"If you walk a ways in that direction, you will come to a stream, now frozen. That's where Sten of old succumbed to his injuries, sustained from the unyielding Knud after the Battle of the Sky Shards. At the bend, you can still see the point of his—"

Normally Petra would have loved to hear the lore of this or any place, but right then, she was puzzling for a practical way to turn what few weaknesses against a single golden ram. The morning passed slowly, step by wetter step, Aslaug pointing out this feature or that, while Iver engaged, and Petra feigned attention. Orro kept to himself.

Lunch was brief, of salted eggs, jerky, and unpeeled potatoes. Any other day and Petra would have wondered how long Aslaug could survive on a diet consisting solely of potatoes and vodka, but an idea was coming together.

A couple of hours later, with the sun just visible, sandwiched between brief sheets of grey, Orro announced they'd reached their destination. His vision must have surpassed theirs, as he stated the rams were just ahead, while neither Petra nor

Iver could see the faintest speck of gold. Aslaug invited the pair to sup at her hearth again, if they survived their foolhardy jaunt. With that, Aslaug and Orro turned back, progressing rapidly, unhindered with the babysitting of foreign stragglers. It was no slow thing, their silhouettes shrinking and merging with the distant horizon. Petra watched their progress in parts, glancing back to escape the mighty glare of the naked sun on the ground, as the few clouds dissipated.

Squinting against the overbright expanse, it wasn't until Iver stopped short that she recognized motion amongst the glimmering mounds ahead. She gasped. The rams were so closely packed, what she'd taken for ground, moved in waves as they fed.

"Are you sure you want to do this, Mistress?"

"Yes."

The word came out hard and fast. What would come, would come, but no matter what, she wouldn't have to live with abandoning her baby brother. Maybe she'd see her mum and dad today.

"Do you have a plan, Mistress?"

"Sort of. Do you have scissors?"

"I have shears."

"Okay. That's probably better."

She didn't know the difference or if there even was one.

"What do you need me to do?"

"Your job was to get me here, and should I survive," She took a steadying breath. "—you'll get me to the swamplands, and the mountains, too. As for the rams, unless you have a plan, I'm going to handle this solo."

If the rams would feel threatened at a single intruder, they'd be doubly mad over two. Appealing to their vanity, she needed to be as unintimidating as possible.

"Can you make camp here?" she asked.

Iver considered their surroundings, running his hand across the powdery surface and letting the dry snow sprinkle from his outstretched fingers.

"I'll build a hut, with a flag on the roof, so it's visible from a greater distance."

On the off chance, I'm still in hiking order by tonight, she thought.

"Can they talk, the rams? Like Orro?"

Iver admitted he didn't know, while passing her the shears and some food. Petra didn't have a back-up if they couldn't and not much of a plan if they could. Thanking him for his efforts getting her thus far, she embraced Iver, who blushed claret.

"I await your return, Mistress."

Petra hoped that wouldn't be in vain, and turned to leave. The first step was the hardest, but her target was in view, and she fell into the rhythm of one foot crunching after the other. Getting closer, the roving masses gained definition. Their horns varied in scale, and Petra assumed those with smaller sets were female. For all their shine, they were more unnerving than beautiful. Shirley Temple coats failed to conceal the rippling muscles of their necks, shoulders, and legs, as they grazed, raced, leapt, and in the case of two larger males, bent their snouts low, before charging. They clashed with an audible crack, and upon disengaging, bore blood stained manes.

She flinched at the sound and again at their wounds, but maintained her course. Sooner than Petra was ready, she breached the ice shelf into ram territory, where the drifts had been crushed and maneuvered away, revealing frozen blades of grass. Petra would have known she'd trespassed even if not for the physical marker, as every ram abandoned their meal, leisure, and combat, to measure the fool who dared intrude on their land. For a moment, silence reigned. Even the wind died, as every pair of violet eyes gauged the threat.

She stood high up a slope, yet even with the boost, the rams towered over her. Without giving herself a moment to second guess, she took another step forward.

"Hello!" she called out, striding over grass that pierced and sliced through the rubber soles of her shoes.

In warning, rams opened their mouths, peeled their lips back, and growled, revealing flat teeth. She had a speech prepared, a story to convince one lucky ram that she was a world-renowned stylist, but she wasn't afforded the chance to attempt her ruse. As she'd been advised they might, the larger of the bloodied rams charged. Petra had just long enough to think, "This is it. This is how I die." One second, the monster was many meters back. The next, she had a mouth full of metallic strands, and was clenching with every muscle, as a roar sounded from above.

It was instinct. Pure instinct. The beast thrust its horns at her waist, then up to impale and toss her limp form away, but when he lunged, she'd ducked underneath. Gripping fistfuls of fleece, she squeezed, pressing the curls into handles. The ram paused, confounded. The intruder had been right there, yet there was no resistance to his upswing.

Where was the disemboweled corpse sprawled overtop the snowbank? With horror, the beast realized his mistake.

"Weg von mir! Get off me!" he thundered, livid.

Petra was preoccupied with carefully, non-instinctively, sculpting stirrup-esque pockets for her feet, not trusting herself to speak. It was plain what came next.

Wasting no time, the beast charged again, bucking and thrashing to knock her off. He rushed his flock, who dodged the assault. Then they were free, racing through an endless field of snow. Petra's hat came away as her head, hair, hood, and collar became one with the reckless plow. Snow wormed its way into her jacket, shirt, and pants. He cursed in more tongues than Petra knew, though she registered the Icelandic and English slurs, plus a few of the French, as she clung to his underside. If she lost her hold, she risked being trampled. The seemingly endless expanse of flat white came to an end, replaced by clumps of mummified firs, their branches shielding the earth from much of the previous night's snowfall, leaving stumps, field stones, frozen streams, and browned grass unburied. Heedless of the obstacles, the beast grazed rocks and boughs alike, smashing narrower ice drifts, every tremor threatening to shake her loose. She didn't know how long she hung on, but with her feet slipping, and her fingers losing their grip despite the adrenaline coursing through her veins, Petra changed tactics.

Catching sight of a frozen pond up ahead, she gripped her pocket knife. So much for relying on trickery, she thought. Then, before she could change her mind, she thrust the modest blade up and into his chest, pushing until the handle was flush against his skin. There was a scream, but they'd hit smooth ice, and his momentum carried them forward, despite his violent throes. Then swiftly, she slit a wide crescent, wherein she shoved her arm, blade still in hand. Making contact with something hard, she guessed a rib, she adjusted her angle. He bellowed wordlessly, swaying. Releasing a silent prayer, Petra retracted her gore stained arm, and let go.

She heard rather than saw the ram land with a muffled thump—having rolled out from beneath him, then to the side, before scurrying in the opposite direction. Reaching gravel, she ran, ducking behind trees, until the woods ended. At the tree-line, she stopped, and glanced back, but couldn't see him. Crouched between clumps of pine needles, she stood in wait. His moaning warned her off, until it ceased. Petra didn't rush to collect the fleece immediately, in case the lapse in noise proved temporary. The fading light wouldn't let her stay put for long.

Bracing herself, Petra set out, praying he was dead. She'd read enough about animals to know the dangers of approaching the injured and desperate. Returning to the ice as twilight dimmed her view, Petra stared out, looking for the massive hump. Instead, there was a painterly blood slick, leading back into the woods. Cursing silently, Petra glanced at the sky. Fearing the consequences of spending an entire night without shelter, she decided not to wait until morning.

Moving quickly, but as surreptitiously as could be managed in the dwindling visibility, Petra kept parallel to the trail. With few stars offering light, the ground was dark, the blood, black. Her fingers and toes were losing feeling as the temperature plunged. When trees hid the sky and she was unable to see, Petra located her victim by smell, the scent of rust heavy in the air.

Finally sighting the massive lump, she was too numb, both of mind and body, to shy from skinning him. Get the fleece, then back to camp, she told herself, closing the gap between them. He lay still and silent, so taking a deep breath, she pierced his back with her modest blade. To her shock, a pitiful wail erupted from his snout, followed by the determined twitching of his legs. He was attempting to rise. Cursing out loud, Petra fought the urge to jump away, and instead, lunging forward, sliced along his neck. The cry became a shriek turned gurgle, before fading into the death rattle she recognized from the final weeks of her gram's hospice stay.

Unlike the rabbit, Petra could not lift the ram, nor budge him beyond his hooves, so she cut where she could, ignoring where she could not. The body was warm, and Petra's disgust paled compared to her pleasure at the heat. Her fingers tingled until they didn't, and with renewed sensation came the knowledge she'd knicked them all over. Rather than pausing to consider her injuries, she stripped the wooly back, severing the skin just above the neck, limbs, and tail.

Exhausted, she pulled the golden fleece away, snipping the last stubborn strands of tissue. Holding her prize against her body, she told herself not to think about the sticky, grittiness, coating her gloves, and flaking off her jacket. Petra wanted to sit but the risk of hypothermia was too great. Stuffing her fabric laden hands into the wool for extra insulation, she hoped her hair was thick enough to protect her exposed ears. Petra had to keep moving. Leaning low, she found the pinpricks of dim starlight on the slick bloodied trail. Following the shine, she made her way back to the ice, then through the trees, and onto the plains once more.

The ram had charged a vast curve one way, and then another, before racing into the woods. Petra sighed, wishing he'd made a beeline. Keeping to his hoof prints, ram territory eventually came into focus, and rounding their field at a distance, she pushed on. With no clue as to the hour, face, ears, fingers, and feet numb, Petra came upon a break in the drifts, the width, that of her waist. This had to be her trail from earlier. With renewed vigor, she stumbled on, to where Iver was waiting. Where there was Iver, there would be fire. Wool in hand, and warmth on her mind, Petra progressed.

The clouds filled in, snuffing out the limited light. Blind, Petra felt exposed, her paranoia exacerbated by every gale that whispered her name. Casting futile glances into the night, she wondered if will-o-wisps could speak. Then, spotting a wavering flame ahead, Petra hurried with renewed vigor.

Bursting from the bank, into a circular clearing, she startled her friend from his perch beside the campfire. He cried out wordlessly, before rising to meet her.

"Iver!"

He turned, his shock amplified by the campfire's upward highlights.

"Mistress! You're alive! Where are you hurt?! Is that—is that the fleece?"

She nodded, before embracing him, passing the skin along, and moving to sit by the fire.

"I didn't shear it, but it's on there."

"But how? No, first, let me see to your injuries. Where did he get you?"

Petra stared up at him blankly, then down at her stained gloves, jacket, pants, and hair.

"Oh, that's not my blood," she replied, and it was true. Her hands were scratched, but their bleeding must have stopped by now.

Iver stared from her to the blood backed sheet in his grip, and nodded.

"Very well then. Let's get you cleaned up."

So saying, he pulled a cloth from his pack, and wetting it with snow melt, raised a hand to wipe her face, but she waved him off, accepting the rag.

"Thanks, but I can do it."

Absent-mindedly, Petra rubbed at the dried gore, examining instead, the igloo Iver built. The chimney hoisted the promised flag, really a shirt, waving over their heads. Iver accepted his shears and took to sniping wool from flesh. Already the fleece bore dents and wrinkles, although the Queen hadn't specified its condition, and a deal was a deal.

Once he'd finished, Iver held their prize up, admiring its gleam in the firelight. Petra realized she was famished, so after wiping her hands in the snow, she ate from their meager reserves. Once he'd finished shearing, Iver busied himself folding the metallic bundle until he was satisfied it wouldn't wrinkle in Petra's bag. Then he returned it to her, and she, carefully so as not to untuck any edges, put it away. She assumed her Majesty had the means to get it fluffed out.

Petra was thirsty and the remains of her water bottle, frozen, so Iver filled a pot with snow and placed it near the flames. He asked how she did it, and she gave a shorthand account, in monotone, while waiting. When she was done, warm water in one hand, rubber doll in the other, Iver shook his head.

"It's a miracle he didn't fall on you when you stabbed him."

"It's a miracle I wasn't shish-kabobed from the get-go."

It had to be getting late, and Iver admitted they didn't have enough wood for two fires, so he removed and repacked the flag. Lifting the small tray base with gloved fingers, they carefully carried the small pyre inside, placing it beneath the narrow chimney.

"How do we get to the—what were they called? Blood swamps?"

"We should be less than a day's trek from a portal stone. Come to think of it, if we backtrack to Aslaug and Orro's hut, it should be only a few hours farther out."

"They did want to know how our venture went."

"Is it wise to let on that we succeeded? We don't know them well and they suspect we're on a treasure hunt. Mightn't they have bade us return with the intent of stealing our spoils?"

"Maybe? I didn't meet you until this week, and you're trustworthy."

"I'm your slave, Mistress. You're kind, and I like you, but I didn't have a choice once you sealed the salt ring."

Petra couldn't argue with that. She needed Iver to guide her, or she would lose her brother. Afterward, sure, Iver would be free to go about his merry way, but she doubted telling him so then and there, would mean much.

"Okay. But it's rude not to say hi, isn't it? They fed us, and escorted us."

"And if they're thieves, they will rob us and perhaps kill us for good measure. If they mean us ill, at best we're delayed. At worst, we die. Will you gamble your brother's life for the sake of politeness?"

"I see your point. If we see them though—if they see us, we stop and say hi?"

"Yes, Mistress. Then manners win. Neither of us could outrun a Wyvern if we tried."

With that, they curled around either side of the fire, using their blankets as shields from the ground chill, nearly touching the walls of their small haven. Petra's sleep was uneasy, her dreams ghastly. The last fleeting image was that of a collapsed and emaciated Emil, asking where she'd been. Shaken awake before she could explain, Petra spent the morning wishing for one more minute of sleep. Just enough to make him understand.

Iver hadn't seen a rabbit since their first day in the tundra, and their egg-jerky meals wouldn't last them much longer at the rate they were eating. That's why, Iver explained, breakfast was smaller.

"Will there be food in the blood swamps?"

"Well, Mistress, I've never been to Polstov, so I don't know."

"Will we be lost then?"

"Our people do not lose our way. We have an innate sense of direction. What we can't do is summon wildlife, or create food from inedibles, so keep your eyes peeled for moss, berries, and animals. The portal stone is along the border where the weather trends milder."

They double-checked they weren't leaving anything behind, before moving on. Petra's legs were wet and cold in spite of the rabbit pelts. While the fur kept her lower legs from being completely soaked, they didn't stretch above her knees, unlike the drifts. Between the seeping freeze and the rumble in her belly, Petra was eager to leave Kolchus behind.

"Do you think Polstov will be cold?" she called ahead.

"I doubt it, Mistress. The swamplands are far south of here."

Then there was no point in lining the rest of her jeans, or expanding her jacket, before crossing the arteries—Which again, Petra *really* hoped was a mistranslation.

They didn't stop for lunch. Petra struggled to catch up as Iver jogged, deftly jumping over frozen snow banks. Were he not so far ahead, she'd have asked why he was running. Instead, she followed suit, keeping her eyes peeled for predators and food. What was that her dad said about polar bears that came ashore? "You don't have to outrun the bear, just your buddy." She didn't look back for polar bears, but tried to keep pace with Iver, just in case.

The wind picked up, threatening to pull her hood from her head, tugging at her scarf. Then came the snow. The flakes were small, the sky above, slate colored but darker to the west, and moving their way fast. Petra wasn't sure how much further they had to hike and soon the howling wind would make conversing impossible. Iver stopped, as if reading her mind, letting her catch up.

As she approached, panting, he spoke. "We've been spotted. It's Orro."

Petra looked where indicated but saw nothing beyond the weather. "Is he coming this way?"

"Not yet. I imagine he's gone to get Aslaug."

"So, what now?"

"We continue as if we hadn't seen him. When they suddenly appear, offering another night's hospitality, we feign surprise and accept their invitation. Otherwise would be insulting and they may yet prove to be friends."

"Okay. How do we explain bypassing them in the first place?"

"We're trying to beat the weather."

She nodded and they resumed their trek.

The flakes were larger and more abundant when Iver again stopped. This time, Petra could see he was flanked on either side by Aslaug and Orro. She jogged, or tripped rather, to where they stood and expressed an exuberance she did not feel.

"Aslaug! Orro! Thank goodness! I thought we'd miss you guys and wouldn't be able to say goodbye! But what are you doing out in the storm?!"

Aslaug laughed over the wind. "We live here. This is normal. It's sunshine that's an adjustment.

Come! Another night indoors will do you both good."

Following, Iver and Petra arrived at the familiar copse. Stomping their boots in the doorway, they stripped their outerwear on the way in.

Aslaug wanted to know if Petra had gone through with attempting to shear a golden ram.

"I did not. I tried to get close, and a big one, which is saying something since they were all huge, charged. I slipped or I'd be an earring right now. A horning? A hornament, for sure. When he backed up, I rolled into the snowbank, and crawled until I couldn't see the rams anymore. Then I ran back to Iver." Petra shuddered. "Did I mention how big they are?!" She fully extended her hands, in emphasis.

Aslaug laughed and Orro made a sound that could have implied humor.

"I'm just relieved to be moving on tomorrow. This land has been far too frigid for my liking," Iver commented before they could ask any follow-up questions.

"Well, you survived an encounter with a golden ram. That's remarkable. Was that adventure enough? Will you two be heading home?"

Petra shook her head. "We're going to travel a bit more. Not to get near any more monsters. Just to see what else is out there."

"I see. Which portal is next? Is your way set?"

"There's a portal southwest of here. That'll see us true," Iver replied.

"Ah. That's a full portal. Much farther out than the one to Nyja Adlandice. You'll be traveling far then? Perhaps to another midland?"

"Indeed, we are. I described Polstov to my Mistress, and she'd never heard of any place so strange. That's where we're off to next."

"Odd. I can't say I've ever met anyone who wanted to visit the arteries," mused Aslaug.

"We don't have anything like them where I'm from," explained Petra, hoping nobody would quiz her on what she thought they were like. "My world doesn't have many mysteries left," she added.

In truth, the nickname alone would have dissuaded her had she a choice, but she was playing the role of naive thrillseeker in accordance with her Majesty's orders. How would the Queen know? Petra could only guess magic would be involved, but she was positive her Majesty would. There it was again. Her Majesty. Even in her own head, she was thinking of the Queen like them. Like she was her Queen too. Maybe, having touched magic, she was.

Aslaug set Petra to peeling potatoes while Iver, who could keep silent no longer, insisted he spice the soup in thanks for their generous hospitality. While the stew boiled, Aslaug asked Petra about her family and how she'd met Iver.

"Humans in the middle realms are rarer than nymphs in winter."

"Ah, well. I'm an orphan. Have been for a while. My older sister was taking care of me, but she was recently enlisted as a laborer in Josalfar. I'm too young, so they sent me home. I tried to get her to leave with me but she wouldn't. Once the government realizes she's gone and I'm all alone, they'll claim my family's house and stick me in a home for orphans. That sounds like the opposite of fun, so I did some research, and figured out how to summon a brownie. Now we're traveling together and the county can keep the house for all I care."

"How was your sister enlisted?"

"The usual way, I gather. Our neighbor gave us a plant I thought was pretty. It bloomed into a tunnel and we went exploring. Once we were in the underground, she ate the food, and I didn't."

"No one warned her against eating from the Queen's dais?!" Aslaug exclaimed.

"Grown people, human people, think fairytales are make-believe. Gram told us stories, but we didn't know they were real. "

"What is full-grown to a human?"

"Eighteen years old. That's when we get to live on our own and do what we want."

Aslaug and Orro both turned to stare at Petra, apparently surprised.

"I see. And how old are you now?"

"Eleven," Petra answered. The walls creaked and the roof shuddered.

Aslaug nodded, explaining that Alfarians age more slowly. She'd suspected Petra was much older. Being half-human, she would have come up to Petra's shoulder at that age. She then distributed the drinks and potato stew. To Orro, she handed a dried meat chunk pulled from a box tucked into the floor.

"Wyvern don't eat potatoes, cabbage, nor radishes, not that we have much left in the way of vegetables, so the meat has to last while the caribou are down south."

"Is that all there is to hunt here? Just caribou and rabbits?" asked Iver.

"Well, there used to be more wildlife—bison, elk, wolves, and birds in the warmer months. Most wandered in from the human side. It's been years since we've seen any elk or bison, let alone wolves." Aslaug answered, wistful. "We still get the occasional tern or gull. Caught an owl a few moons back. While the frequent demise of ill-prepared travelers makes for decent scavenging, we can't rely on them when budgeting food for winter."

They ate and Orro tore at his meat chunk. Remembering human children don't drink vodka, Aslaug gave Petra a mug of water, while complimenting Iver's cooking prowess.

"Herbs are hard to come by here, so we've done without, but this is a treat!"

Iver thanked her, blushing scarlet. After dinner, Aslaug stacked the dishes by the entrance.

"Do you grow the potatoes yourself?" Iver asked.

"Oh, yes. You can't see them now, under all that snow, but the garden wraps around the house. The frost came quickly, so there is small chance of rot."

Petra moved to sit beside Orro, pointedly ignoring the red splashed along his muzzle.

"I'd never heard of Wyvern before meeting you. Do Wyvern visit my world?"

"Peoples with any sense stay out of the human realm. If they had the choice, hobgoblins would too."

"Because my people kill fae?"

"They have that tendency. Even when they aren't actively hunting us on behalf of some illusory deity or other, they're destroyers. Be it forests or the sea—they burn, poison, and corrupt everything they touch. I've seen them set fire to water. Water! There is no limit to the ruinous potential of man. Humans can't keep from killing. It's your nature. Not that the Alfarians are much better, mind you. That's why they're both given a wide berth. We don't want to be fodder, but we also don't want to end up like the brownies."

"Why? What happened to them?"

"That, human child Petra, is a question for your Iver."

Petra nodded, curious. She changed the subject. "Aslaug said the Alfarians gave you to her. Do the Alfarians raise Wyvern?"

"Wyvern are not pets like the dogs in your world." He spat out the word *dogs* like a slur. "And no, they do not raise us. I lived above Josalfar with my pack. As a pup, I was separated from my mother during a hunt. An Alfarian trapped me and brought me to Aslaug's father, who introduced us. From then on, we've lived together. When the Alfarians decided Aslaug was old enough to be cast out, I went too. I would have left anyway, with her gone, but we'd formed an attachment, so I chose to stay with her rather than seeking out and reuniting with my pack."

"Were you big then, when you left together?"

"Big enough."

Petra nodded, though she couldn't see casting out a child smaller than Emil as anything but cruel. Holding her tongue, she rose to check how dry her jacket was. Tucked into the pockets, her gloves were still so bloody she could have passed the color off as intentional, and she wondered if Orro could smell the lie. Her pants too, were crusty, but perhaps Orro couldn't tell the blood of rabbits from rams. Her outwear dry enough to pack, she stuffed the jacket into her bag. Aslaug and Iver spoke quietly amongst themselves. Petra wondered what about.

Later, blinking back sleep, Petra withdrew the blanket and sweater-wrapped hammer from her bag. Iver didn't trust their host, and she followed his lead. Concealing the weapon beneath her stomach, she used a folded shirt as a pillow. Pulling the blanket tight, Petra went to sleep.

In an instant, she was awake, alert, and tense. All was dark. The fire was freshly dead as the chill hadn't yet set in. She could hear a commotion, a muffled kerfuffle. Danger. Squinting, Petra let her eyes adjust. This was a gloom she could adapt to. There were burning cinders and the moon poked between cracked window shutters. Feigning sleep, she heard a low snarl, and saw the black shape of Orro snapping his fangs menacingly overtop a bundle—Iver!

Her view was eclipsed as a shadow leaned above, and controlling her breath, Petra's gaze caught on the glint of a point. The shadow bore a knife. Aslaug bent low over Petra, bringing the blade to her face, balancing on her haunches. Before the knife made contact, Petra gripped her hammer, swinging an arc as she turned onto her back, and slammed the head hard into Aslaug's shin. Then she threw herself forward, knocking the screeching woman off her feet. Reorienting, Petra threw herself at Orro, striking again with the hammer. In the dark, she couldn't see to aim, and it was the claw, not the head, lodged in the Wyvern's side. Orro snarled and roared, but he was backing away as Petra pulled at her friend. Iver rose. Iver lived. Grabbing two lumps she hoped were their bags, they ran for the door. Aslaug planted herself before the exit, arms stretched wide. Orro too, snarled, stalking at their backs, the hammer grip hanging just below his shoulder. Petra whipped out the pocket knife.

"Let us go," Iver commanded, a dagger in each hand.

Aslaug limped aside. "Fine. Freeze."

They strode past her, through the doorway, never taking their eyes off the threat. Aslaug slammed the door behind them. They couldn't walk fast enough as far as Petra was concerned. She kept turning to see if their hosts were moving in pursuit. She wiped at her brow, and her hand fell dark, wet. Sighing, she didn't bother cleaning away the blood before slipping her jacket and gloves on. They couldn't slow to clean it. Petra hoped it wouldn't get infected.

"All that for a fleece?" she asked.

"They don't know about the fleece, Mistress. That was for you."

"Me?!"

He pointed to her face. His hand was darker than the bleak night and sharp, the crook of his fingers not dissimilar to the curve of Aslaug's knife.

"With your eye, she could control you, tell you how to act, who to be."

So it wasn't just the Alfarians that enslaved her people. Half-Alfarians could too. Who else? She wondered. What a terrible superpower the second sight was. Petra's heart drummed wildly and her throat swelled.

"Did Orro hurt you?" she asked, when she could trust herself to speak.

"No Mistress. Not much."

She looked back. A paltry rectangle a football field away shone with a copper vibrance. They'd relit the fire.

"Come along then," Iver said. "—before they change their minds about letting us go."

The wind lacked its earlier force but Iver suspected the respite was temporary. They could see the moon, though the stars were largely hidden, blinking out as clouds passed overhead. Petra's teeth chattered and her ears desperately missed her hat, but her gloves kept the worst of the chill from her fingers. Without warning, Iver withdrew an object from his pocket, and with a snap and a cry, Petra saw a rabbit fall, its dark body land, unmoving.

"Do you ever miss?" she asked.

"No Mistress. Not anymore. When you've lived as long as I, you excel. It's not a matter of talent so much as persistence."

He retrieved the rabbit, snapped the neck, and stuffed the corpse into his bag. He slew another as they neared a shoulder height pyramidal field-stone. Petra filled their vessels with snow while he sought the spiral indentation. As before, he gripped his charm, and in his birth tongue, bade the portal open. Bells chimed but their tune was lost to the wind. Once they were safe within, Iver sealed the exit at their backs.

"Aslaug is only half Alfarian. I don't know if she's been trained to call upon paths, but the more kilometers between them and us, the better."

With that, they marched on, their eyes adjusting to the amber glow as it faded.

Chapter 9

They hadn't progressed far before the cave was uncomfortably hot.

"After we get the saddle, will we use this portal to get to the Borjans?"

"Yes, Mistress. There are only two full portals in Polstov, and the other is at the opposite end thereof. Unless we cross the entirety of the swamplands, this is our eventual route."

"Can we leave our winterwear here then?" Petra inquired, sweat pooling at her back and under her arms.

"I suppose so, Mistress, but we would be wise to wear long sleeves and pants. This being a swamp, I expect swarms of gnats and mosquitos."

"I didn't bring any bug spray."

"Nor did I, Mistress."

He was right about the mosquitos. They hadn't even reached the cave's mouth and already Petra was aware of a bug bite on her wrist. A prominent buzzing passed by her ear and she swung her hands wildly at incoming pests. Reaching the exit, she folded her jacket and stuck it against the wall. There too, she left her gloves. Iver folded and abandoned his coat beside hers.

Slapping at another mosquito, she asked Iver if he knew of any natural insect repellents.

"I'm not sure, Mistress. Mud? I doubt it'll keep them away, but the barrier should keep them off of our skin."

That would have to do. While Iver sealed their clothes inside, Petra grabbed handfuls of red clay, smearing a thick layer over her hands, face, and ears. She gritted her teeth at the texture, but she was thorough. Bloodborne illnesses could be debilitating, and she was on a tight schedule. Hoping Polstov's arteries were named after the cinnamon tinted ground, she kept close behind Iver.

A fist-sized mosquito flitting past his nose convinced him to don war paint as well. Then, shielded, they marched on, sinking into the mud with every step. Pulling their shoes free sounded with the squelch of a suction cup removed. Walking was an ordeal made more difficult by the thick foliage they resorted to slicing through, their slender blades growing duller with every slash. Full-bodied trees bearing vine curtains limited their view, and elevated root systems caught their already troubled steps. The air was humid, and the environment claustrophobic, after the vast emptiness of Kolchus.

Reeds propagated like grass, their leaves and stems razor sharp. One escaped a handful being snipped and swung back with enough momentum to leave a sizable scratch along Petra's cheek.

"Are you alright, Mistress?"

"Yeah. I just don't see any water clean enough for washing it."

Puddles burbled forth to fill the footprints they left, but the water was opaque. Petra's hand still bore a sliver of graphite from a classmate's trick two years prior. She worried shoving clay in an unclean wound would result in a currant-colored tattoo spanning half her face.

Iver backtracked to Petra and examined the scratch. Then, spitting, he moistened a cloth and wiped the grime away. From his bag, he pulled a paper bundle which, unwrapped, revealed tiny onion-shaped pods. Tearing the skin from one, he crushed and spread it along the cut.

"This will sting, but it'll keep your face from becoming infected."

"Smells like garlic."

"It is garlic, Mistress. Garlic is a mild antibiotic. That may leave a scar, but it won't make you sick."

Petra thanked him and they resumed their tedious trek. A scar was preferable to a crooked face tattoo.

"Iver, do we know where the kelpies are?"

"We do not, Mistress."

So they were wandering in the hopes that they might randomly stumble upon one? In that case, she needed to be prepared to tango without so much as a warm-up stretch.

"What can you tell me about kelpies?"

Iver pulled her from a particularly sticky mud patch and they continued.

"Well, Mistress, a kelpie can shift appearances between that of a black stallion with backward hooves, and a humanoid male. I say humanoid because kelpies feature some characteristics that help the discerning eyes to distinguish between the two. As a man, the kelpie has slitted ears, hooves, and his long black hair is wet. Wearing a necklace of banded leather, he reeks of swamp. His true form bears a saddle stitched from the flesh of his victims, the thread of fronds, and hair. They craft it themselves. The necklace and saddle are one and the same. When knights rode horses, a saddled and healthy stallion was an invitation. When that no longer proved tantalizing, the kelpies came to attract prey by other means. Nowadays, those other means are all that's keeping them alive. Humans don't rely on horses as they did when I was young."

Iver paused, reflecting on his great age and the unusual circumstances that led him here of all places, explaining monsters to a little human girl.

"Kelpies are musicians. Often they'll play a crude string instrument resembling a violin or a banjo they've made from found objects. The instrument may not look pretty, but the sound is, well—I've never heard it, or I wouldn't be here speaking with you, Mistress. It is said the kelpie plays an enchant-ing tune. Enchanting being the operative word, unfortunately. Listeners are pulled inextricably to the kelpie, man or horse. Once they lay their hand on the creature, it races to the depths and drowns the hanger-on, who is then eaten. It is impossible to remove oneself from the kelpie, until it chooses to remove you. And by that point, you can consider yourself drowned. The only way to defeat a kelpie is to remove the saddle or the necklace. Really, in any other case, you'd consider yourself fortunate to have been near one and lived to tell about it. Attempting to rob a kelpie is—" Iver paused, giving her a moment to contemplate her mortality and hopefully change her mind. When she didn't, he continued, shaking his head.

"—unwise. But, alas, you need the saddle. Since the kelpies drown their victims before eating them, they make their homes in the depths of ponds, lakes, and swamps. This being a swamp, the waters are generally shallow. That limits where they would thrive. I'm expecting the widest stretch of water to be the deepest, at a guess."

"So, if we hear music?"

"We drown."

"Could we make earplugs?"

Iver considered the suggestion. "When we make camp, I'll see what I can do. In the meantime, keep your eyes peeled for anything we can eat. Those rabbits won't last long."

"And water?"

"If we haven't gotten to one of the tributaries by the time we make camp, I'll collect from the puddles and boil the water to fill our vessels."

On and on they slogged, cracked mud raining from their filthy attire. Spotting the sun through the canopy, they broke for lunch, settling on a log. It sank into the earth under their combined weight. Surrounding sticks were too wet for a campfire, but there remained enough snow melt that there was no need for boiling, to drink, yet. Lunch consisted of a salted egg and a strip of jerky. It wouldn't keep the wambles at bay for long, but at least it wasn't potatoes.

They ate quickly and were off. Petra sweat through her crust and had to refresh the mask when the mosquitos returned en masse. In time they came upon a narrow stream. The water was crimson, smoky, and smelled. They stepped over the vein and ambled on. She had to ask.

"Iver, why is it called the blood swamp?"

"Mistress, our water won't last until sunset. We're going to have to drink this. Are you sure this is something you want to know?"

"Yes," she said, squeezing the doll in her pocket.

He sighed. "If you're certain. I've known humanity to have weak constitutions with regards to blood."

He checked her expression for any change at his warning and carried on at the lack.

"Once upon a time, a long time ago, there lived a fierce giant named Olst. He was insatiable. To quell his all-consuming hunger—" Iver lost his balance on a climbing root when a dragonfly swooped for his face, and Petra helped him to his feet.

"Thank you, Mistress. Now, where was I—oh yes. Hungry giant. So. To quell his all-consuming hunger, Olst ravaged the nearby homesteads, stealing and eating the humans' cattle. Their village was called Wieslesie. Its people suffered under Olst for years, until, at last, there were no cattle left. The long tormented villagers had no milk, no cheese, no butter, and little meat. Back then, this was all heavily wooded. There were no neighboring communities with whom they could barter for livestock. Trading occurred only during holidays and only after much travel—generally on the part of the merchant, not the villagers. Yet Olst came still."

Petra spotted a downed bird and was about to interrupt Iver, so he might hunt it, but it unfurled the damaged wing and flew. Her stomach rumbled at what to her, seemed a cruel prank.

"When he saw there was no livestock to be had, he demanded tribute. The village would send him a human sacrifice the next day, or he would slaughter them all. While Olst retreated to his cave in the woods, village elders gathered in their roundhouse to discuss how to proceed. Their choices were few. They could nominate a villager as sacrifice, but this would set a terrible precedent—For the beast would not stop at one, and they'd be forced to send neighbors, friends, and loved ones to their deaths from then on. They could leave, but the forest was inhospitable, neighboring lands infertile, and they knew of nowhere they could resettle with time to spare for growing and harvesting before the fast approaching winter. In effect, their choice was death by giant, or death by starvation come the chill. Furthermore, the beast was likely to follow should they flee, and kill them then and there. Thirdly, *they could fight*, but these were not a skilled warfaring people. They possessed no organized militia, and it was few among them who owned sword or stallion, not that the forest was suited for cavalry charges."

Iver paused while a cool breeze blew the sulphuric odor away. Silent, they both enjoyed the moment's respite, before the wind died down.

"As the elders debated, choosing the least terrible demise for their people, a young man swept in. Ulf, grandson to the eldest councilman, volunteered to go forth as tribute. He intended to slaughter the giant. Having won the midsummer wrestling match three years running, with a history of placing in the foot races, and as the keenest-eyed archer in their village, never returning from a hunt empty-handed, he decided he was their best chance. To his surprise and disappointment, Ulf's grandfather forbade him leave. Ulf was needed. With the livestock dead, they would be relying on their every able-bodied hunter."

Petra nearly walked into a spider's web, but caught herself just in time. Iver double checked that she was truly fine, before carrying on. The venom of tropical spiders was nothing to underestimate.

"So his great plea was denied. Ulf exited the council, but let it be known to all he passed that he wished to take on the monster. In his absence, the council voted to send another as tribute instead. There were no criminals in their midst. Several souls were suggested, from the lazy to the strange. In the end, they sent a widow, long suspected of being barren. The widow, Olga, had no relations to speak up and defend her from this awful fate. The people gathered, young and old, to watch her be paraded down their single street, etching her lined and somber face into their communal memory, as she was led away to the giant. And so she marched on, head high, not a tear shed."

Iver stopped short, and bent low, examining what Petra first took to be puddles, but she now recognized as footprints. He stood up, apparently disinterested, but she poked them and was surprised to find they were of stone. Fossilized footprints? But of what? She didn't dally longer, rushing to keep up with her friend as he launched back into his story.

"Ulf held his tongue at this travesty, enraged that his neighbor should die to feed the beast. The next morning Olst returned, and as the council feared, he demanded a second victim. Again Ulf offered his services and again he was denied. He watched in horror as the village fool was led to his end, for

Igor the Idiot hadn't known what way to go, not least what that direction entailed. Rollo, youngest of the three centurion members on the council, returned from escorting the fool to Olst's lair at sunset. He recounted the sight of the giant tossing poor innocent Igor into his gaping maw and gnashing him apart while he still breathed. Rollo claimed that it was only due to his lanky meatless figure that Olst did not eat him as well."

There was a great retching sound and Petra realized Iver was coughing. When he was done, he spat. She looked away. "Bug," he explained. She nodded. "Might have to cover your mouth while you talk?" In emphasis, she had her hand over hers. Nodding, Iver posed likewise. He took a deep breath, then continued.

"At this, Ulf could stand no more injustice. Two innocent, defenseless souls had been sacrificed to the monster that ruined their homestead and had all of Wieslesie quivering in fear. Again he burst into the council, but this time he asked for nothing, rather telling those in charge he was leaving to kill the beast—that they were welcome to send what assistance they may. Accepting that he would not be dissuaded, the council put forth his message to the village. That night every able-bodied man armed himself as best he could. Those with swords sharpened and sheathed them. The archers counted their arrows and oiled their bows. The rest pocketed knives, grabbed rakes, hoes, hammers, and cudgels."

There was a scream in the distance, but recalling Gunndis' pigs, Petra didn't assume a human source. She looked to Iver, who didn't glance back.

"Ulf's bravery had everyone shamed, and the community was sick with grief over the deaths of their own. As those who could fight gathered to do so, the mothers and elders packed the children. When the moon shone at its peak, the frail went one way and the warriors another. It just so happened the warriors came to the mouth of the cave as the giant was rising for the day. He had just stepped forth to stretch and drink before harassing the village anew when instead, he found himself peering down at a slew of tiny men with their feeble weaponry. The giant laughed at their folly as those armed for stabbing and battery, charged ahead. The archers reared back, letting their arrows fly. Olst swiped wildly downward, knocking villagers to either side. Then he stomped on those nearest, throwing his head back and letting loose a mighty roar. The archers were nestled against trees, and those otherwise armed, who'd dodged the deadly crush, hacked at his feet. Their efforts aggravated the monster who ducked low, swiping at the attackers. 'Now!' Screamed Ulf. As per his plan, the archers aimed for Olst's eyes. Then, at Ulf's signal, they loosed their arrows. The barrage flew true. Blinded, his face raining blood, and his body crossed with cuts at every height, Olst fell back."

The farther Iver got in his tale, the more Petra was sure she knew how it ended, and the less she wanted to be in Polstov, especially, without a vast supply of clean fresh water.

"His tumble crushed some poor few but missed the majority. Those remaining leapt up, climbing Olst's figure and setting upon him like a colony of fire ants."

Iver looked around them in the gloom, spinning slightly to Petra's left, then pointing in the direction from which the stream flowed.

"Out there in the depths, lay the once mighty giant, Olst. So large was he, and so many were his wounds, it is believed the blood swamps are fed by his still bleeding incisions, the currents pushed by his still pumping heart—for a giant's demise is no swift thing."

"By now, he should be dead, though, right? It's been a long time, you said."

Iver nodded. "A long time indeed. Yet, there aren't giants enough for me to say how long it takes one to die."

It was Petra's turn to nod. "And then the men chased down the women, and they all went home and lived happily ever after?"

"Oh, who knows? If they did, happily ever after didn't last long. You can't farm in a swamp, and there aren't any humans living this way now."

"So this," Petra pointed at the stream they'd been following. "—is blood? All of this is really blood?"

"That's what my people believe, Mistress. Of course, a variant of the legend is that Olst carried a titanic iron broadsword, which was too big and unwieldy to be of use against the tiny, agile humans. In that version, when he fell, so too did the sword, becoming lodged in the ground, revealing a spring, wherein it rusted, coloring all of the waters downstream red. That version is a tad more convoluted and hence, less popular."

"I like that version better," Petra said, wincing at their wine tinted surroundings.

"I don't know that I do, Mistress. Drinking rust can give you tetanus. Do you know what tetanus is?"

Petra did not.

"It's a serious illness."

"Oh well. I'd still rather drink rust than blood."

The opaque current widened as they followed it upstream. Squelching along, the duo reached a point where the water diverged into three tributaries leading back the way they'd come. Iver pulled a glass vial from his pack. Then, approaching a throng of cattails swaying beside the bank, he slid his knife into the base of the plant. With a vial, he caught the pale liquid issuing forth.

"What's that for?"

"It's a mild antiseptic. Garlic is useful, but we don't have much left and you won't want that scratch getting infected."

She nodded as he moved it back to his pocket. They walked on, with Iver pausing at every cattail until the ampule was full.

"If we stay along this line, we should reach the river that feeds into all of Polstov."

Petra, keeping her eyes peeled, spotted some mushrooms growing on a log.

"Do you think those are edible?"

He paused, bending down, pushing his face close to the fungi.

"I don't know, Mistress. I've never seen mushrooms like these. How about I pack them away? They're light, and it's unlikely, but maybe we'll meet someone we can ask."

Carefully, they cut the mushrooms from their mottled perch, and Iver wrapped them in paper. Later he stopped again, to pluck seeds from a flowering plant, its blooms similar to lupines.

"The seeds of the pickerelweed are edible. Keep an eye out for more."

She did, but perhaps that plant had experienced an untimely bloom as she found none of the same color, nor columnar shape. Hungry, she likewise kept her eyes peeled for low flying birds, or any mammals at all. Unfortunately, as far as she could tell, the birds were too high up, keeping the canopy between them and those who meant them harm.

"Could we make a fishing pole?" Petra asked, distracted by their limited food supply.

"I don't have anything to use as a hook, Mistress. I could carve one from wood, but it would soften once exposed to the water. We don't have the time nor resources to carve one from stone."

Petra nodded, wishing she'd thought to pack Atla's malleable hairpins.

"Well, let's do it anyway," he said after a moment. "Worse comes to worst, I'll make a new one every night. They don't take long to carve."

Petra didn't relish the idea of eating something that lived off of giant's blood, but that was too bad. Hunger meant weakness. They had to keep their strength up. As it was, Petra had nary two sips left before she was going to have to make *that* choice. She preserved the final splash of pristine snowmelt for as long as she was able, delaying the inevitable.

They plodded on, careful of the sharp reeds, their boots long since caked with clay. Now that she was better educated on the history of the place, everything took on a bloodier hue. Weren't reeds typically blonde? And what of the lily pads? Surely they ought to have been greener than that! Once she drank from the swamp, would she too turn red? Like the flamingo highlighted by its pink shrimp diet? My, my, Petra thought. A scarred face, and a ruddy complexion. How else would she be marked before all was said and done?

She paused, collecting more mushrooms. These too, Iver wrapped and bagged, in case they proved useful. Or, in case *they* proved desperate.

By sundown, Petra missed Kolchus. Polstov was awful. Everything was sticky and wet and made walking hard. She was the dirtiest she'd ever been, and only some of the muck was her mosquito shield. To top it all off, her face reeked of garlic. Her clothes and boots were casualties of the swamp. She couldn't tell where the mud ended, and the cloth or leather or fur began. Petra tried finger-brushing her hair, but kept getting snagged. She'd have to get it cut when she got home.

To make matters worse, she was finally out of water.

"As am I, Mistress. It is time."

They made a simple fire where the ground was dry, cracked, and flat, and Iver filled a pot, setting it to boil. While the water—or what Petra insisted on calling water for her mental well-being—perched over the heat, they skinned the rabbits. Iver then cut them into strips, rubbed them with an herb blend, and laid them by the fire. Neither wanted stew made with the red water. For supper, they ate old jerky, the last of the eggs, and roasted pickerelweed seeds. The last wasn't filling, but it broke up the monotony. Petra hoped to find more such stalks the next day.

A film with a sheen like an oil slick bloomed atop the water. This, Petra scooped out and tossed to the side. Iver retrieved his funnel and filled their vessels, leaving rouge sediments in the pot. Either the thirstier, or the braver of the two, he took the first swig. Iver failed to hide his grimace behind his hand.

"Well?"

"It's not that bad."

Petra sighed and followed suit. The taste was between metallic and savory, not unlike under-cooked steak, but with a hint of fish. It was *that bad* and Petra held her mouth shut so she wouldn't vomit. If she couldn't take it going down she didn't want to know the more acidic version.

"And now I drink blood," she thought. "May as well be a swamp monster myself."

As for their earplugs, Petra volunteered a T-shirt, from which Iver cut four small strips. These he sewed into tiny pillows. Then they tried them out.

"Can you hear me?" he asked.

She could, as if from far away. The volume was reduced but his words were clear. Would that be enough to protect them from the kelpie's song?

"What if we made earmuffs?"

"To be worn over our earplugs, Mistress?"

"Yes. So we can't hear at all. I mean—what if hearing it at all, means it can eat us? We can't risk it."

"Very well. I'll see what can be done."

Iver traced the edges of their ears onto the remains of the scrap fabric, cut them out, pinched the edges, and sewed. Finishing the first, he handed it to Petra to try. She had to push in the upper edge of her ear for it to fit, but the wrap wasn't painful. That wasn't the real test, though. With the plugs in, she covered her other ear with her hand and asked Iver to speak.

"What should I say, Mistress?"

His voice was quieter, but she could still make out his words. Petra shook her head and took the wrap off.

"It works but not well enough. What if we make it thicker? Add another layer of fabric? The T-shirt has plenty left."

Iver did so and they tried the wraps again.

"Okay. Can you hear me now?"

Petra could, but barely. She sensed that were he a couple of meters back, she might not hear him at all. Furthermore, all background noise was gone. There were no birds, no bugs, no rustle of reeds on reeds, and no running water.

"I think this will work," she said. "Unless he's standing right next to us or using a megaphone, we won't hear him."

"Then, we'd best wear these from now on. We can't afford to be separated. Footprints fade and yelling won't work from afar. Keep me in sight tomorrow and I'll keep you in mine."

They rubbed fresh mud onto their hands, faces, and arms, tossed on what meager coverings they had, and curled up by the fire. The silence was eerie. Petra was used to bone rattle winds, walls that settled in the night, passerby traffic, and a sister who came and went at all hours. What she was not used to was quiet, but with her muff-plugs, she had to adjust, until finally, exhaustion won.

Iver was up early, carving the fish hook. She wrote the day on her side, where the marks from those prior were already fading. They breakfasted on what remained of the older jerky, and Iver packed the rabbit strips in the hopes they would dry more in his bag. Petra smeared the cattail fluid over her scratches and they reapplied their mud masks. Before leaving camp, Iver tied the rudimentary hook to a length of twine, and the other end to a stick. It was fragile but *should* work, he said.

If there were any fish, there would be many fish. Such was a land without people.

"When we get to the next tributary, I'll see what I can catch."

They'd been hiking a while when Petra asked, "Why do you think there are so few animals here?"

"Might be the water is toxic, though I feel fine. Could be acidic, perhaps. Did it taste like acid to you?"

She shook her head.

"Might be it's only toxic for freshwater fish. There are plenty of bugs, birds, and I heard frogs before we put these on," he gestured to their ears. "—so they're getting on. Could be that when people left, the kelpies resorted to eating fish. A kelpie can live a long time. If there are many, they could eat a swamp empty. Or, maybe we aren't looking hard enough."

At that, Petra more carefully observed her surroundings. She examined the sludge puddles for movement beyond the burping push and pull of her sneakers. Her eyes scanned the waifish catkins up to the branches and down the bark of willows. So too, she gazed into the calm surface of the stream, its ripples relatively uniform.

There was life. The swarms of mosquitoes, face slashing reeds, and trees were life. But why wasn't Polstov bustling with fauna? For wildlife to not have taken over in humanity's absence, something had to be damming the wave. Was that *something* kelpies? The Queen would not have sent them if she hadn't reason to believe there was a saddle to be had, so they were in the right region. But were kelpies decimating the ecosystem? Or was it something else?

That night, the ground shook. They forgot their hunger, clamoring from beneath swaying branches, racing to a clearing. They fell asleep waiting for aftershocks. As for where the wildlife had gone, that question was answered the next day.

Iver was giving his rod another chance. Petra sat at his side so they could comfortably talk.

"Third time is the charm after all," he announced with a cheer he did not feel.

The growl in his middle mocked the sentiment. Petra was watching for submerged shadows when she saw the surface ahead, rise, shift, and lay back down. She blinked, confused.

"Iver?"

"Yes, Mistress?"

"There's something wrong with the water."

"Wrong, Mistress?"

"Yeah, wrong. As in—the water might be a monster, wrong. I think it just stood, upstream, but on stubby legs, and then laid back down. Are there giant water monsters?"

Iver looked up and ahead to where she was pointing. As if on cue, a well-camouflaged tail swung outward, flicking at a fog of gnats, before slapping down with a splash.

"I don't think it likes bugs," she guessed.

"Let us walk around it, slowly and carefully," Iver advised, before continuing. "We don't want it to see us."

Petra nodded. Slowly, Iver pulled his useless rod from the stream, and they crept from the tributary. Although crept is the wrong word. They hopped and dragged themselves through the mud that alternated between sucking them in and cushioning their steps with sponge-like soil that threw off their balance, all while dodging a cloud of what she suspected was an ancient and long-forgotten breed of super mosquitoes. The farther they stepped from the portal stone, the larger insects appeared. At this rate, they'd soon be encountering bugs the length of Petra's arms. With their ears stuffed and covered, they couldn't tell how much noise they were making, but both assumed it was decibels over *none*.

From a great distance, to not draw its ire, they plodded around to the front. From their new vantage point, they watched the wave raise its round head, revealing a perfectly spherical gaping mouth. This it dunked half into the river, snapping up fish caught in its seemingly liquid jaws. With black beady eyes at either side of its bulbous face, the monster was the unfortunate crossover of a ven diagram labeled blobfish and giant salamander—emphasis on the *giant*.

"What is it?" she asked.

"That's a nuppeppo, Mistress, and I'd wager that's where all of the fish have gone. If we keep heading upstream, there should be fuller waters. Nuppeppos are sedentary creatures. If that's where he's chosen to hunt, not much will get past him. But he won't migrate until he runs out of food."

"I don't think my books mentioned those. Should we stop and ask him about the mushrooms?"

Ivers' head swung to face her with alarm. "No. We do not want that thing to know we are here. I should have said they are *generally* sedentary. If it thinks it has to compete with us for food, it will strike, and quickly. By strike, I mean it will do its favorite thing, Mistress. And that's swallowing us whole and letting its stomach juices do the rest. So, let's go before it sees us."

"Are they always red?"

"No Mistress. That's camouflage. They take on the colors of their ecosystem, much like chameleons. No more questions now. We need to move."

Petra nodded, letting Iver lead. Hours later, when he was sure they'd left the monster behind, he attempted fishing again. This time he caught three fish, back to back, in an hour. Petra thought they looked like salmon, if a leaner and redder offshoot.

They were gathering firewood when Petra hit a mud patch that wouldn't release her legs. Adjusting her posture, she discovered she could not lift either leg. What was worse, she wasn't merely stuck, although she was that. She was sinking. Instinctively she pictured the nuppeppo stationed below, sucking her in with his enormous mouth, the image propelling her heart into her throat.

"But wait!" she thought.

It couldn't be him. From what Iver said, he wouldn't have left his perch, and there was unlikely to be a second nuppeppo in the area. They'd have fought to the death, surely, one eating the other. She'd watched this predicament unfold before, in movies, and it wasn't caused by monsters then. No, it was quicksand.

Adjusting her feet, seeking a ledge with which she might push herself out, Petra slipped farther down. While she wasn't sinking rapidly, and if she refrained from moving, not at all—she was trapped. What if there was another earthquake? Her legs would be crushed!

"Iver," she yelled. "Help!"

Looking from tree to tree, her pupils like a pinball, she sought mud stained braids, a clay mask, and ruined suit. Oh no! He wouldn't be able to hear her. The stupid earmuffs!

"Okay," Petra thought. "How can I get out of this?"

Continuing to scream, she ceased scanning for Iver, and instead, looked for anything she could use to pull herself up. There was a branch just ahead and to her right. Stretching, her legs and arms unnaturally taut, she lunged for the end, only just grabbing at its splintered point with her thumb and forefinger. Cursing, she wiggled the length of it across her palm until she could close her fist around the damp wood. Pulling it forward, she kept the length slightly aloft.

The branch wasn't light and she wasn't strong, but she inched it along. Petra tried not to panic as her waist slipped to ground level, and again when her chest followed suit. The quicksand didn't look different from the surrounding clay, other than the acute bend of the reeds, so she moved the branch until it passed the flattened flora. Then, she rested her elbows overtop and pulled herself up. The branch rolled and her heart lurched, but she clamored on. All but her legs from the knees down were freed when a wrinkled hand gripped her arm and yanked her out.

Crumpling beside a clump of tall, scratchy weeds, Petra caught her breath, waiting for her pulse to return to normal.

"Quicksand," she warned, rising, then stretching her strained limbs.

"Are you okay, Mistress?" Iver asked, brows high, and eyes wider than his norm.

"I will be," she said, tiring as her adrenaline dissipated. She swatted mud from her pants and top, and checked that she still had her doll. Finding it, she allowed herself a relieved sigh.

"I'm sorry. I hadn't realized you'd fallen behind."

"I know. It's not your fault. We'll just have to keep a closer eye on each other, and watch out for trouble. See how the plants look like somebody stepped on them?" She pointed.

"I do, yes."

"We dodge downed plants. Okay?"

"That sounds wise, Mistress."

They trekked on, more alert than before, skirting crumpled flora. Iver moved slowly so Petra could keep pace. Had their roles been reversed, Petra wasn't confident she could have found him again, let alone pulled him up and out.

That evening, Iver roasted fish and seeds both. What remained, he salted and left to dry beside the fire. Petra preferred land or sky meats, but she was grateful for the break from rabbit jerky. That night they slept well, on full stomachs. It was dark when Petra awoke. Iver, in his haste, had kicked her. Thinking there had been another earthquake, she grabbed her bag, to dart for a clearing, but Iver spoke.

"Do you hear it?" he asked, striding forward without waiting for a response.

She didn't hear anything beyond him. Then she saw it—a small cloth not far from their fire. His muff must have come loose! Petra lunged for it, then at him. Colliding, they went sprawling. Using the momentum of their tumble, she swung herself onto his chest and, ignoring his protests, pulled the fabric over his ear. Iver immediately ceased struggling.

"Oh, dear," he said.

"Do you know which way the sound was?"

He shook his head. "No Mistress. I'm sorry. It was as though—as though I were dreaming."

Drat. Well, more importantly, Iver didn't sound enchanted, so Petra got off of him, and pulled him to his feet. She could feel what would be a nasty bruise smarting above her shin bone. Still, the kelpie was near. They had no time to lose.

"Maybe we can still catch him."

She raced to their camp, tossed her loose belongings into her bag, which she donned as Iver did the same. Then she charged into the wetlands, scoping where Iver appeared to have been heading. He followed after, warning her to slow down and let him catch up. They couldn't afford to lose each other out here, "Remember?" More to the point, she could not afford to lose him. Petra slowed to a jog, hopping over a jagged rock. Arriving at the riverbank, she saw no sign of horse nor man. It was just her and Iver in the night. Petra let out a curse and Iver pet her shoulder.

"Let's find a dryer patch of land, light a new fire, and go back to bed. We've covered a lot of land tonight, Mistress. That's still progress."

Crestfallen, Petra agreed. They found a square of mud where their feet didn't sink in. There, Iver laid a pan, within which he piled paper, before adding a scant selection of sticks to the mix. Using his flint, he sparked another flame. If nothing else, it would dry the ground some. Then, having cozied close to their modest fire, the duo covered themselves and went back to sleep.

The sun was high when next they rose. Iver woke first, fishing while Petra slept. She sat upright as he was retrieving the third fish from his hook. Over breakfast, they discussed whether to maintain the current campsite as a home base or to trek onward, settling in a new location every night.

"You heard the music. He had to be nearby. Do kelpies migrate?"

"They will if they have to but we weren't moving quietly last night. He won't leave now that there is prey worth hunting. You and I, we're far more filling than fish or frogs."

They were agreed.

"So this is camp," Petra said, peering at the length of hard ground they'd claimed.

Iver confided his supposition that kelpies, like other predatory fae, would hunt at night, so they spent the morning improving their living standard since, for the foreseeable future, this was home. After applying new layers of mud to their faces and exposed limbs, Iver fished and Petra manned the growing blaze. At Iver's prodding, she pulled the mushrooms from his bag and strung them, hanging the garland from a head-height branch. It was far enough that neither feared them catching fire, but near enough where the flames might contest the humidity. Dried mushrooms could last for years, Iver claimed, not that they had years. Heck, they still weren't sure the mushrooms were safe to eat.

Petra wanted to make a tent, but short of stitching their blankets together, they didn't have the spare material to patch a tarp—Not that she would have known how to frame and mount it, had they the supplies.

That afternoon, Petra suggested they supper early and get to bed. She wanted them awake when the song sounded.

"But Mistress—" Iver spoke up. "How will we know the music is playing if our ears are covered?"

He had a point. The answer to which was inconvenient, the implication uncomfortable.

"You're right. One of us has to leave a muff off. And the other can return it once we're in sight of the kelpie."

"That's risky business, Mistress. Timing will be crucial. If the unenchanted isn't fast enough, the enchanted will die. Horribly."

"All of this is risky business. The Queen—the Queen is unkind. Unfortunately. But it has to be done. We'll take precautions though. Let's race. The winner will keep their muffs on and tackle the other. The loser will be barefoot, to slow them further. Also, we won't be waking up to magic music tonight. You and I will be wide awake, waiting for the summons. We won't be caught unawares."

"I suppose, Mistress. Where should we race?"

Petra looked around. "See the big tree with the bald patch, that's leaning over?"

"Yes."

"Let's line up by the water and run for that. Whoever touches it first, wins."

"Very well, then."

With that, they stood and walked to the water's edge. Petra counted down to *one,* and then they ran as though their lives depended on it, because they did. It was a straight shot with few bladed reeds. A root nearly caught Petra's foot, but she saw it in time to hop over, not that it mattered. She'd known who was faster before she made the suggestion. Iver hit the bark with a thump of his fist.

"Okay. So after our afternoon nap, I'll pass the muff to you. Keep it safe for me?"

"Will do, Mistress."

After their race, they covered up and went to sleep. Petra had assumed nerves and daylight would prevent her from getting any rest, but the humidity made her drowsy.

She awoke to Iver squeezing her shoulder.

"It's dark. We should stay alert, Mistress."

She rose, yawned, and sat beside him at the campfire. Once she'd rubbed the remaining sleep from her eyes, Petra removed her muff and passed it to Iver. Then she took off her shoes. The better to slow me with, my dear, she thought. It had been a long time since she'd read a picture book but the Three Little Pigs had been a mainstay.

"I'm ready," Petra said.

Iver pocketed the muff. "Now, we wait."

"Should we put out the fire? So our eyes can adjust?"

"Good thinking, Mistress."

At that, he filled a pot and spilled the contents over the flame, killing it with a hiss. Then he resumed his post, the cool night air immediately filling the fire's void. Iver could see in the dark, but Petra suffered the loss.

Shapes gradually gained definition. The stars were hidden by trees, but moonlight rippled along the waterway, illuminating the undersides of canopies. Mosquitoes batted their masks, straw mouths pricking harmlessly. There was a malevolence to the constant buzzing around her uncovered ear. Above, she heard a squeaking that may have been bats. There was no talking. Iver couldn't afford to lose focus, lest Petra be lost.

They waited.

There was a distant splash and then there was only music. The melody filled Petra with joy. This song, without words nor vocables, spoke to her core, and it said everything was going to be okay. She didn't have to try so hard. There was no strife, nothing to fear. If she could just meet the musician, he would take her where she would never hurt again.

Iver followed, only a step behind, ready to pull her back at the first sign of man or horse. So intent was he on Petra, and what lay ahead, Iver didn't realize he was falling until he hit the ground. There hadn't been time to outstretch his arms to soften the blow, and the impact shook his jaw. Was that a rock? He rose dizzy, sore. Tripped now—of all the times?!

Where was Petra? Where was she?! No! She was almost to the water! And there, just ahead, was a stallion, legs submerged from the knees down. Its mouth hung open, bellowing its terrible, glorious, summons.

Iver ran, and upon reaching Petra, grabbed her, pulling her back, but it was no use. His gaze traced her arm to the kelpie. There, just beside the saddle, her hand lay flush against its hide. The instant he realized what needed to be done, the music must have stopped. Petra let loose a harrowing scream, cutting straight through his muffs, and the creature began to descend into the murky depths.

"Oh no, you don't!"

Iver sliced the cord, yanking the primitive saddle from the beast and tossing it onto the land. In that same motion, before Petra or the creature could react, Iver slashed through her wrist. In any case, the screaming did not stop, but the bleeding had to. Iver pulled her back, and her voice died abruptly at the sight of her dismembered hand still stuck to the kelpie's side.

"So sorry, Mistress. Now run to camp! I'll be right behind you."

Petra obeyed, retreating to the meager safety of the blankets and fire.

Turning back, Iver saw the kelpie sinking into the water. Only, no. That was wrong. He wasn't sinking. He was shifting. Shrinking? What next swam, then crawled to the edge, was somehow horse and man, yet neither, an abomination with the features of each. The kelpie rose, revealing more fully its mutations.

Quivering, he shook the sopping mane from his face, over his shoulders, to his back. The parting of his overlong hair revealed wide set eyes, a horse's snout, and a mouth stretched across the width of his face, which hung open, as if the beast knew not how to close it. Therein were fangs, three concentric rows of teeth wrapping the cavity from which a serpentine tongue flit out. The figure twitched, the hooves capping too-human limbs, slipping, sliding on the wet banks. Bowlegged, he lunged, tail splashing wildly, and falling, he landed on all fours.

"Where is it?!" the beast cried, as he attempted to gallop for the saddle, on a body better built for the hominid's short step.

He swayed clumsily, determination all that held him aloft. Changing directions, the kelpie rushed Iver, who jumped aside with a deftness the devolving monster couldn't match.

"What do you want?" the beast demanded in the old tongue, tone mellowed by the muffs. Reaching for Iver and toppling again, he begged. "Give it back! I'll give you whatever you want! Please! I—I'm coming apart!"

Iver took a step back. Petra's hand hung from the monster's side, warning of the remaining threat.

"We came for the saddle. We can't give it back."

Iver said this evenly. He did not pity the beast. The kelpie would have eaten him, given the chance.

"But what will you do with it?! If it's destroyed, I'll die. I'll do anything! Just give it to me! *Give it!*"

Desperate, the kelpie charged again, and again he fell short of his intended victim, collapsing in a heap. Iver watched the kelpie's shoulders shake with sobs.

"We aren't destroying the saddle. Get back in the water."

The beast lifted its head, choked back a cry, and sinking, it receded. The kelpie didn't stop begging as he descended, but Iver didn't care to listen. He watched until the wretch was fully submerged. Then he too ran in the direction the saddle had been thrown. Not seeing it, he continued to camp.

Arriving, he found Petra with their prize on her lap, her filthy shirt wrapped around her stump. Her feet remained bare of protection, layered instead with muck. Iver couldn't tell what was blood and what was mud, but he knew Petra needed help.

"Thanks, Iver," she said, dully.

"We need to get you to a healer," he replied.

Likewise, they needed to get her wrist clean. Iver closed his eyes and focused on the location he most needed. Josalfar. When that proved too far, he recalibrated his intent. What about a hospital? It didn't matter which or where. Any hospital would take one look at a child holding a bloody stump and take her in. He spread his arms wide and spun until he felt a connection. Then he opened his eyes and stared in the direction his pointer indicated. The vibration was potent. It wasn't a full portal, but the stone wasn't far. Afterward, they could find another.

"Let me see," Iver said to Petra.

Wordless, she released the pressure below her elbow. Iver examined the stump which seemed to be trying to regrow its lost digits. The crimson current was so steady, Iver had the fleeting impression her fingers were trying to regrow. Shaking his head at the fancy, he tore a long strip from her shirt, knotting it above the stump. She winced from the pressure, but the tourniquet had to be tight or she'd bleed out. Wetting a cloth, he wiped away the clay. He did not clean the blood from the stump. Clotting, even thinly, might buy her time until they could find help. Iver had lived a long time, a *very* long time by Petra's standards, but he'd never before had reason to cauterize a wound. That was a task best left to medical professionals, which he was not.

From his bag, he retrieved the last of the cat-tail liquid. This he slathered along the nub. She winced, but did not cry out. Shock. His Mistress was in shock. Reaching into her bag, he pulled out a cleaner shirt, rinsed it with *water* from his canteen, and used it to bandage her arm.

"Keep pressure here," he said, holding her remaining hand around the makeshift bandage. Then he gathered their few scattered belongings, and gestured to her feet.

"Do they hurt?" he asked, locating her shoes,

Petra looked down, flexing her toes and gauging the pain.

"Not much."

He blinked at her. She looked so vulnerable, cradling her loss.

"I'm going to wash some of this off," Iver said, motioning for her feet.

Petra nodded. Iver wiped away the clay caked onto the soles. A brownie's night vision is superior to that of any man, but even he couldn't see which of those dark lines were slivers of missing flesh, and which were stains. They sure looked wet, though. Her feet cleaner, he helped her to pull on socks and then shoes.

"I know how to get to a hospital," he said.

Then he shouldered his pack, and on second thought, looped her bag over his arms so it hung over top of his chest.

"Mistress, can you carry the saddle?"

She nodded, and he helped her hoist it while maintaining pressure on her wound. Their prize was sizable but surprisingly lightweight, the leather thin and pale. Laying it over her arms, it hung off her shoulder. Iver did a last sweep of their camp and they were off.

With a keen eye on his Mistress, he led them from the stream. Iver wanted to rush. He wanted his Mistress to receive professional medical attention as soon as possible, but her steps were slow, steady, labored. He feared she'd lost too much blood. He feared infection. He feared he knew too little about first aid to have been helping at all. The cattail syrup would slow any infections, but would it stymie the clotting?

Dawn blushed as Iver spotted a stone ledge he supposed to be the portal. Closing his eyes, he raised his hand in confirmation.

"This is it," he said.

Then, grasping his spiral amulet, he pressed it to the indentation and bade the pathway reveal itself. A ringing sounded. When he next opened his eyes, the amber light of the entryway glimmered in welcome. Petra stepped inside and Iver sealed the entrance behind them. Safe, they removed their muffs.

Petra didn't bother with the flashlight and they walked on in blackness. The ground was comparatively flat. There were no lofty roots here to snag their legs. Iver's stomach bemoaned his hunger, but he didn't slow to pull food from his sack. Mistress Petra was silent.

When the first light trickled in from without, Iver picked up the pace. Humans needed light, and Mistress Petra was no exception.

"The hospital will be close now," he said.

Petra increased her pace, which he took to be a positive sign. The path delivered them to a meadow of human design. A park, judging by the benches. Iver glanced to the tunnel they were leaving, laying the path to rest. Then spinning once more, he clarified their course, and ignoring startled passersby, hurried on. Two humans mid-embrace, a man and a woman, may have witnessed a girl and her cat—or a girl and a little old man, if they were so gifted—stride from a solid rock wall, beneath a memorial plaque. Iver chose not to make eye contact in either case, and Petra may not have seen them at all.

Stepping past pruned flowerbeds and trimmed branches, the pair strode from the park. They were in a city, a real metropolitan area at that. Cutting through bustling traffic, and crowds racing to their next obligation, the pair only slowed at gawking tourist blockades. Vacationers mobbed sidewalk corners, snapping pictures of landmarks that looked wholly unremarkable to Iver and went ignored by Petra, marking the locale safe. They wouldn't be all dressed up to spend large sums of foreign currency in this neighborhood, were it permeated by criminal activity.

Iver wrapped his hand around Petra's good arm, at the elbow. It wouldn't do to lose her now. Watching the crowd, he crossed what he assumed to be the main boulevard, given the slew of neon billboards flashing overhead. Then they turned. A man took notice of Petra and, gesturing at her arm, spoke words of concern. Did she need help? Did she need him to call someone? Petra just shook her head, not caring nor comprehending what he said. Of course. Humans were rarely polyglots. At her age, he doubted she could speak more than two languages. Iver listened to pinpoint what nation they were in as he shuffled her forward. It was as they reached the hospital that he narrowed it down. The language was French, so this was likely France. The age of colonies was past, and there were only so many places left with a majority French fluency. She'd be well taken care of.

The French demanded a high living standard. This would be a hospital of quality.

"Petra, I'm going to walk you inside, but then I'm going to leave."

"What?"

"To those without the sight, I'm a pet. A cat. They won't let me in. And anyway, we aren't going to be able to carry all of this through the Borjan Mountains. If you can pass me the saddle and the fleece, now, I'll deliver them to her Majesty. Don't fret. I'll be back by tomorrow, at noon. If they discharge you before then, wait for me in the waiting room at the front. Not the park. Stay inside. I'll come to you."

Petra had proven herself to be a tough kid, sure, but he didn't want her alone outside. Especially at night, but even during the day. Not all humans were decent. A park, after dark, was no place for unescorted children, even in the most affluent of humanity's cities.

"Okay," she said, complying. Then she hefted her bag anew, while Iver sorted the treasures into his pack.

"Tomorrow. This waiting room."

"I'll be here."

True to his word, he walked her to the counter, past rows of adults bent over paperwork, some leaning on their peers in visible discomfort. Then, after squeezing her remaining hand, he left.

Chapter 10

Petra watched while Iver walked away. As he stepped outside, leaving in the direction they'd come, she turned to the woman at the counter. Petra had a golf ball-sized lump in her throat, and her eyes grew wet with her friend gone. Iver had come to feel like more than a guide. He was her protector. Except now she was in immense pain, more pain than she'd ever experienced, and alone.

"Hello," she said, or rather rasped, in English.

Everybody spoke English. The receptionist was busy jotting notes down, a blabbering headset hooked over her one ear. Petra waited a moment, distracted by the fireworks sizzling against a palm that wasn't, as the woman ended the call.

Then Petra tried again. "Hello, ma'am. I need a doctor."

The woman glanced from her forms to Petra, who waved her stump over the counter. Despite the wrappings, the motion peppered the desk and its glass overhang with blood.

"Mon Dieu!" cried the woman, eyes wide. "Un moment!"

The woman opened a door behind her, rushing beyond. Petra could hear her calling for a doctor. She hadn't learned much French in school, but she caught some of the more distinguishable words, such as sang, main, and manque. The woman reappeared with two men.

"Ce qui s'a passé?!" inquired the first.

Petra didn't recognize those words, not when spoken so rapidly, but the meaning was clear.

"There was an accident. Please, it's burning! Can you make it stop?!"

The receptionist, who may have been a nurse herself, followed the doctors as they escorted Petra to another wing of the hospital. Switching to English, she asked Petra for her name, her guardian's contact information, and an explanation of what happened. Petra was too tired for lying, and she needed to know how Emil was doing. All but the last, she answered with a frankness she knew she'd miss come her adventure's end. The kelpie was beyond belief, so she kept him to herself, stating only that there was an accident and her hand could not be saved.

The doctors, meanwhile, conversed in French, fast reaching a consensus. The receptionist made it clear she would contact Leif right away, but the doctors couldn't wait for his response. They needed to address the area of amputation immediately. For that, they needed Petra to change into a hospital gown. Her clothes were too soiled. They would sedate her, clean the nub, shape it for future prosthetics, and seal it. Normally they'd have had her guardian sign off on the procedure, but there wasn't time.

The medical personnel stepped out to provide Petra with privacy so she could change. She avoided looking at the source of her agony, her pain amplified with every shift and shuffle. Donning the gown, she kicked her mud and blood covered clothes to the edge of the room, next to her bag. When decent, Petra let the adults back in, and the nurse collected Petra's things. Petra asked her not to throw anything out, explaining she didn't have replacements. Before the nurse could respond, the doctors led Petra down the hall to a set of double doors, through another hallway, and into a larger numbered room framed by metal trays of cutting tools, a wall of sinks, and machinery. At the center was a bed.

"Lie down. Don't move," commanded a doctor.

Petra complied. The nurse attached a breathing mask to her face, counting her down. A doctor said that once they reached twenty, she would be asleep.

Well, Petra counted along silently. Anything to distract from the burning. By eight, the room had blurred, and by twelve, Petra wasn't listening to anything anymore.

When she awoke, the nurse was leaning over her bed. Petra looked from the familiar face to her arm, remembering what transpired to land her in a French hospital. Sure enough, her arm from the elbow up was swathed in a tight white bandage. There was no hand to be seen.

So it was real. It really happened.

This wasn't the room where the procedure had taken place. It was smaller, with two beds and two doors. The other bed was empty, but there was a rod circling each, bearing a curtain should she require privacy. The nurse, seeing Petra was awake, introduced herself, offering aftercare instructions. Petra barely listened. None of it mattered. *"Keep it clean."* Well, that was as obvious as it was futile. The Borjans were next, and she doubted there would be baths, showers, and soap in the desert mountains. One detail she caught was her good fortune in how smooth her wound was. Nerve damage would be limited, and the risk of infection, diminished.

Was she supposed to be grateful? She'd lost her hand! What was lucky about that? Already she felt crooked and uneven—damaged goods. Not that she voiced her lamentations. It wasn't this lady's fault she'd decided she could take on a damn kelpie.

There was a knock on the door, interrupting the nurse, who turned to open it, speaking with the visitor in French.

"Petra, Madame Boucher is here to speak with you. She helps children and she is going to ask you questions. Goodbye for now."

With that, the adults swapped out, and Petra sat herself up, watching Madame Boucher pull a chair from the wall, to Petra's bed. This wasn't her first meeting with a social worker. Atla taught her how to handle these people.

This woman too, introduced herself in English. Petra assumed not many Frenchmen spoke Icelandic.

"Hello. As Nurse Renoir said, my name is Judith Boucher. You may call me Judith. I am here to get to know you. Your forms say your name is Petra Kristjandottir."

Petra confirmed the accuracy of the details listed on her chart. Then Judith pushed on to the focus of her visit.

"So when was the last time you spoke with Leif Laakkonen?"

She pronounced *Leif* like the English word, *leaf*. Petra thought back to the last number written on her belly, subtracting that from the initial twenty.

"I left a little over a week ago, eight days I think. Was I out through the night? What time is it?"

Judith shook her head.

"No. You came in today. You weren't out for long." She glanced at her watch. "It is fourteen hours, thirty-two minutes."

Petra breathed a sigh of relief. She hadn't missed Iver.

"Why did you leave Leif's house?"

"You won't believe me. I told the police when Atla disappeared, and they didn't believe me. I don't know what you want me to tell you, but it's not the truth."

She took note of Petra's response.

"How long were you living with Leif?"

"Not long. I guess a little over a week."

"And how did you end up there?"

"Atla was gone. She wasn't coming back so I called him. Leif was like family when he and Atla dated. If anybody would help us, he would."

"And did he?"

"Yes. Leif is a good guy. He showed up straight away, packed us up, and brought us to his place."

"Yet, you ran away?"

Instinctively, she wanted to grab the doll, and could have, with her nondominant hand, but there would have been a very visible awkward reaching for the opposite pocket. Then she remembered she was in a hospital gown, and, come to think of it, the doll might have been lost in the recent struggle.

"I didn't run away. I left. I had important things to do. I'll see him when I'm done."

"And these important things cost you your hand?"

"I don't want to talk about that."

"But it was an accident? That is what it says on your forms."

"Yup. An accident. Look. My hand still really hurts. Or my arm. I guess," Petra paused, considering the best course of action, before continuing, "Can I call Leif?"

"Yes, if you want. There is a phone in the lobby. May I escort you? Doctor Renoir will be upset if I let you wander without supervision."

"You can come. It's just really important that I talk to him."

"Very well. The hospital notified him you are here. We said we would call as soon as you were awake. I just wanted some answers first. He wanted to fly here and bring you home. We told him to wait for an update on your condition."

"And what is my condition?"

"Well," The social worker cleared her throat, visibly uncomfortable with Petra's directness, "—aside from the amputation, you have a big scratch on your face, and more on your feet and ankles. Judging by your blood work, you are malnourished. When you arrived, you were covered from head to toe in mud, and well—blood. Which was probably your own. You are unwell. And having run away, you might be a danger to yourself or—"

"I am not dangerous. I haven't hurt anybody, and as for my hand—it wasn't like I did this to myself. Hey! My things. What did they do with them?"

At this, Judith poked her head out. After a conversation with someone unseen, in French, she closed it once more.

"They're coming."

Petra waited, unspeaking. Then came a knock. Judith opened it, accepted an overflowing plastic bag, and shut it again. She passed the bag to Petra, who emptied the contents onto the floor, assuring nothing was amiss. The doll remained.

"Okay. We can make the call now," Petra said, satisfied.

Judith led her past the three adults waiting in the hall, one of whom was an officer, judging by the uniform. Judith let them know where they were going. Then she and Petra continued to the lift, down to the lobby, where the payphones were.

"I don't have any money. Can I use the office phone?" Petra asked.

Shrugging, Judith inserted the necessary change into the slot. Being an international call, it was a lot. Petra held the phone to her ear. Leif answered on the second ring.

"How is she?! Is she awake? Did she say what happened? Where has she been?!" he cried out, in English.

"Hey, Leif. I'm okay. I'm sorry I left. Is Emil okay? How is he?" Petra responded in Icelandic, to Judith's obvious annoyance.

"Petra?! What happened?! We just woke up and you were gone! The back door was open. I thought someone took you. Did someone take you?! Where did you go?"

"Nobody took me. The trap just worked is all. How's Emil? Have there been any changes?"

"Petra—damnit. Yes, there have been changes. He's—he lapsed into a coma two days ago. The doctors don't know—they just don't know what is causing it. And you've been gone. I've been at my wit's end! I'm coming to get you. Sit tight. I'll be there tomorrow to pick you up."

Petra's heart took a dive, and her throat grew tight. "Emil is in a coma?"

"I'm sorry, kiddo. You should be here. You should see him."

"Leif, don't fly here tomorrow. The doctors said they want me to recuperate for a few days. And Emil needs you. When I'm done here, I'll come home. I'm sorry to have worried you."

"I know. You're not a bad kid. Just, how did this happen? How does an eleven year old lose a hand? How does an eleven year old get to France? You can't have done this alone."

"I've got to go, Leif. But I miss you. And I love you. And Emil, too. I'm just really tired, after my procedure."

"Alright. I have the number to the hospital. I'm calling tomorrow. And feel free to call me as often as you want. Just get better, and then we'll get you home. I can come there and get you, or we can fly you here. I don't care how we have to do it. Just get better and be here. Okay?"

"Okay. Take care, Leif."

"You too, Petra."

She hung up and looked at Judith.

"Did you know my brother is in a coma?" Petra asked, switching back to English.

Judith nodded.

"Why didn't you tell me?" she demanded, sounding forlorn even to herself.

"You needed to hear it from someone you know and trust. Will you be calling Leif tomorrow?"

"Probably. Will you?"

"Yes."

Petra raised her chin. "I'd like to go back to my room now."

Judith nodded, and they retraced their steps upstairs, past the crowd at her door. After watching Petra climb onto the bed, she stepped out. Petra could hear her social worker going off in French, doubtless lecturing the lot. Likely she was sharing notes with the officer to spare Petra the *trauma* of two interrogations in one day.

The nurse entered, following a knock. The door was open, so that was a courtesy. Petra was offered pain relievers and something to help her sleep through the night. She declined both. Her dominant arm throbbed, but she could bear it. The fireworks were gone for now.

Despite the pain, or perhaps from it, Petra was exhausted. She fell asleep wishing she was home. Come morning, her eyes shot wide open, and Petra hopped from the bed. Misjudging the height, she fell farther than she'd expected. Stumbling forward, she caught herself on the wall, whacking her nub in the process. What erupted was an agony of the likes she'd only experienced two nights previous. Sitting and cradling her stump, Petra focused on her breath until the pain was manageable.

A nurse entered.

"Ça va?"

The meaning was clear.

"I'm okay. I just fell off the bed."

The nurse tsked. "You must be careful. You are sure you are not hurt?"

Petra nodded.

"Okay. Want breakfast, yes?"

"Yes, please."

"Good. I bring it now."

Petra retrieved the sharpie to mark the day on her belly. Then she climbed back into bed, and scanning the walls, found a clock. It was still early. Too early to have missed Iver, but the longer she stayed, the more likely for Judith or Leif to show up. The nurse returned, carrying a tray of food and plasticware.

"I put this on lap now. Yes?"

Petra nodded, moving her arms out of the way, as the standing tray was set over her middle.

"Thank you," Petra said.

The nurse left and Petra dug into her meal, or attempted to. She was not left-handed. Lifting a fork full of scrambled eggs to her mouth had become an awkward endeavor. She found herself angling her jaw forward to bring her mouth to the fork rather than the other way around.

May the mountains be not steep, she thought.

The bacon, Petra didn't even attempt to cut. Between the soft plastic and her limited motor skills, it wasn't worth the trouble. She folded the first strip, shoved it into her mouth and chewed it thoroughly before taking a swig of orange juice to wash it down. The rest she handled in the same fashion. Drinking the orange juice was easy, and when the nurse returned for her tray, she requested a second drink and an apple.

After her second orange juice, Petra stowed the apple and asked a hallway nurse where the restroom was. The nurse indicated a second door within her room. Petra looked at the door in question and shook her head.

"That one is too small and I saw a spider in there."

Neither was true. She simply hadn't guessed it led to a bathroom, thinking it a supply closet.

"A spider?" the nurse asked, in disbelief.

Then she shrugged, giving precise directions to the visitor's bathroom. These Petra followed, more to plan an escape route than because she had to go.

Conveniently, she passed the lift when turning into the hallway featuring bathroom signs. On her way back, she looked for another exit. Unfortunately, the stairwell was too far off, all the way at the end of the hall.

Back in her room, she considered her next step. Petra had a choice. She could either leave the hospital early and return to the waiting room when Iver was set to arrive, or she could descend to the lobby just before noon. A cat couldn't remain in the lobby of a hospital for long without being chased away or apprehended by some well-intentioned bystander.

Mostly, Petra aimed to limit the risk of bumping into Madame Boucher on her way out. That the social worker hadn't given a time Petra could expect her by, was problematic. However, the hospital would contact the social worker, the police, and Leif, the second she stepped foot beyond the lobby. Authority figures, both alert and roving the perimeter, could impede on the upcoming rendezvous, especially if they were looking for her.

There were too many variables, her arm hurt, and the hand she had left was no good. Sitting around was only making her more anxious. She'd go, find a place with a clock, wait, and meet Iver on his way into the lobby. He hadn't considered the delays authorities would cause when he opted to meet inside. That, or he was counting on them. Slave or not, Petra was pretty sure Iver genuinely cared, which meant that like any grownup, he thought he knew best.

She closed the door and sorted cleaner clothes from her bag. Donning her least soiled top, over pants so stained with red mud, as to pass for dyed pleather at a distance, Petra pocketed her knife. Peering out, she watched nurses ducking into the rooms of other patients', their meal carts sounding with squeaky wheels. Before the turn, was an inset with a desk. There gathered several nurses, who appeared preoccupied, discussing a chart, but not so distracted they wouldn't notice a little girl sneak by. Then again, she'd told the social worker she might call Leif today.

Petra strode into the hall, but not too quickly. Nobody would stop her if they thought she was going to the bathroom. One step, two step, three step, four. Passing the nurses' station, she pretended she wasn't watching them but none looked up. Her finger was raised to press the down button when a nurse erupted from a patient's room, pushing a cart. She bustled past, without a word. Letting out a sigh of relief, Petra hit the button, which lit up, just as a voice called from behind her.

"Où allez-vous?"

Drat. Petra turned. She'd been so close. "I'm supposed to call my guardian. The payphones are in the lobby."

The nurse gestured to her bag. "Why do you carry this?"

"I've got my address book and money in there."

The nurse's lips thinned but she nodded. "Very well. I am calling down, so they know to watch you. We do not want you lost."

A chime sounded and the wide metallic doors slid open. Petra stepped inside, tapping the closed-doors icon, and hitting *0* for the lobby.

"Thanks I guess? Bye."

Atmospheric jazz mocked the tension while she readied to run, and she was out before the arrival ding. Ignoring shouts from behind, Petra flew through the lobby and out the door. Nobody wanted to be held responsible for a missing child, especially one in recovery after being grievously wounded, so they would follow.

Well aware that she was alone in a country where she barely spoke the language, this was not a *zigzagging, left, right, left,* kind of run. This was a *charge forward for as long as she could until she was sure nobody was following her anymore,* and then a *hide in some bushes until the coast's cleared for sneaking back,* kind of run.

Her arm hurt, but she pushed through the pain. The crowds were thick, only a touch faster than the stand-still roadway traffic for anyone too polite to shove through, but she wasn't so hindered. Those pursuing on foot, would lose her rather than knock passersby aside. Unfortunately, the police could already have climbed into their vehicles, set their sirens on, and taken to combing crowds for anyone matching her description. And speaking of her description, her clothes were an issue. The French weren't dirty and she needed to blend in.

The hospital was large, and knowing the street name, she could find it again. Petra turned, without crossing away from the row of buildings that led back to the rendezvous point. Keeping a wary eye out for officers, she sought a storefront. It was early, but she only had until noon. Spotting mannequins in a window, she headed in. The weather was pleasant, and the door, open. No welcome bell rang.

Petra observed the racks. Women's clothes took up half the front and teen girls, the other half. The shopkeeper was tidying up, not having noticed her only customer. Petra wasn't quite up to the juniors' sizes, but venturing further in only increased her odds of getting caught. Spotting a thick hooded jacket, Petra slipped it off the rack, pulled it on, and stepped quickly from the store, picking up her pace. Without examining her find, she ripped glossy tags from the sleeves, leaving their plastic cords in place.

It was too warm for a jacket but it covered her bandaged arm. There wasn't much she could do about her pants. Petra was loath to push her luck, but suspected food would be hard to come by in a dessert, and so knicked oranges from a bodega while the shopkeeper had his back turned. Tucking those away, she searched for a clock. Blocks later, finding none, Petra tapped a man to inquire about the time. Naturally, she asked in the wrong language, only correcting herself when she saw their confusion.

"Bonjour. Quel est l'heure?"

The pedestrian responded, also in French, before moving on. She knew numbers one through twenty, so she understood the hour, which was eleven. The minutes, however, were lost to her. Did she have enough time to get back?

Concerned, Petra took a right, turning the way she'd come. Popping her hood, she broke into a jog, sweating through her clothes. Distrustful of police officers, she kept other pedestrians between the street and her. Why did France have so many cops? An adult spat contempt, probably at her, but she ignored them, elbowing on.

Thoroughly winded and thirsty, she caught sight of the hospital. Petra stopped another watch-wearing passerby for the time. The Frenchmen responded. She still couldn't quite translate the minutes, but the hour was not yet twelve. Good. She wasn't too late.

Heartened, Petra crossed the street, continuing until she was a mere crosswalk from the lobby entrance. Two men, seated atop blankets on the sidewalk, belted pleas at those walking by. Pedestrians dodged them, averting their eyes and ears. Hoping to borrow the men's invisibility, Petra took a seat beside them. One noticed, speaking kindly to her just as she spotted a familiar figure headed towards the hospital's automatic glass doors.

"Bonjour. Désolé! Au revoir!" she replied, jumping up and racing across the street as the crossing lights allowed.

"Iver!" she cried! "Iver," she called.

He turned, steps from the door. "Mistress Petra? You were supposed to wait inside!" he huffed, rushing up to her, clutching the saddle to his chest.

Did he have the fleece too? Had the Queen refused his visit? The push-door to the hospital spun outward.

"We've got to go," Petra responded, as the security guard crossed the lobby, and headed for the exit.

Iver took her at her word. "Very well, then. After me!" he replied, weaving through the crowd.

This time Petra kept up, elbowing a route through the languid and oblivious masses. She was moving fast until she wasn't. Swung backward, caught by a force unseen, a stone dropped in her belly. Looking up, she peered into the eyes of a towering officer. Her shoulder was in his grasp. With his free hand, he brought a radio to his mouth.

After giving his call sign and location, the officer continued, "J'ai la petite fille. Elle était avec un petit vieil homme en costume sale."

Petra peered into the roving crowd. The officer had the sight. He'd seen Iver. Could she see Iver? Had he realized she'd fallen behind? There he was, rushing her way, squeezing at a crab walk between two bickering old ladies.

"Iver! He can see you!"

Then, hoping to catch the officer by surprise, Petra pulled her knees up from under her, letting herself fall to the ground, a dead weight. The ploy worked. The officer relinquished his grip, and she shot from him before he could reclaim her. If she'd been rude before, that was nothing to the way she hurdled over sidewalks now. Wordless, she rammed past the ancient woman at Iver's left, and spinning him by the arm, yanked him along. The park could wait. They had to lose the cop.

Petra's lungs heaved, her side throbbed, and her feet stung, every discomfort a welcome distraction from the electricity riddling her damaged arm. The next intersection sported a public transport sign, an arrow indicating subway stairs.

"Down!" she ordered, releasing her grip, and they descended.

At the base, she paused, scanning the platform. A mechanical roar announced a train. Were the incoming breeze condensed to a liquid essence, bottled and sold, the label would have read, "Eau de la Gouttière." The tainted wind blew a tangle of curls across her face, blocking her view. Brushing the knots aside, Petra pulled Iver into the sardine-packed carriage.

They had no ticket, but as they weren't aiming for anywhere in particular, that didn't concern her. A toddler pointed and waved, from his mother's hold, to where Iver stood. Meanwhile, the underground streamed past, alternating between fluorescent graffiti and smog stained concrete. Petra steadied herself as they decelerated, positioning her sore feet apart, not unlike how she imagined a skier might, to slow. When the motion ceased, a crossroads was announced, and the doors slid open.

It didn't matter if they got out now or later, so they hopped off. Locating another stairwell, they went up. They slowed to a walk, to blend with commuters. Ascending, they saw no police.

"Okay. I think we lost him. Now let's get to the Borjan Mountains."

"But Mistress, are we not returning to Polstov for our things?"

Petra shook her head, continuing to scan for anyone in uniform. "No time. Emil's in a coma. If you've left anything important, we can go back after we save him."

"Very well, then. I require a safe, quiet space, to locate the appropriate portal."

"Would another park work?"

"Yes, Mistress. A park will do us fine."

Petra nodded. "Lead the way then."

This would be easy. Cities were littered with synthetic oases. Iver cracked his shoulders, closed his eyes, and massaged the air.

"That way," he said, pointing.

Petra kept her hood high as they kept to the middle of the walkway, maintaining a wall of pedestrians between themselves and the tortoise race roads. Upon arriving at a park, this one larger than the last, Iver raised a hand, suggesting they pause and observe their surroundings. His eyes flicked to a dark gap between berry-laden shrubs, at the crushed cans and cigarette butts strewn underneath. Then he spotted the neon sneakers.

"There are humans hiding there, likely full grown. Know where your hammer is. Be ready to grab it," he whispered.

"I left the hammer in Orro, but I've got my knife," Petra whispered back, patting her pocket.

"That'll work better as a threat than a weapon. Don't use it unless you have no choice."

They were not pursued into the park, where the chirping of birds, buzz of insects, and rustle of leaves replaced the dull roar of chatter and traffic. Twice, Iver stopped to make Petra aware of adults watching her from the shadows. Twice, Petra tapped her pocket to make sure the knife was in place.

Then, all at once, he stopped short. Petra half expected another warning.

"This is a good spot. Watch for trouble while I search."

What good she'd be against a full-grown ne'er-do-well was anyone's guess, but Petra acquiesced. Iver closed his eyes and spun. First this way, then that, he let his arms sway, fingers spread, feeling. His orbit shrank with every loop until he'd narrowed the location to a single point. Blinking his eyes open, Iver's arm remained raised, taut, with one finger pointing ahead.

"This way. Let's go."

And they would have, had not another, rougher voice erupted from behind.

"Coucou petite fille!"

The pair spun around. The catcaller's eye was blacked, brow swollen, bloody, as he stepped confidently forward, a manic grin plastered across his face. Reeking of a sickly sweetness, reminiscent of rotten apples and acetone, his stench preceded him from meters away. They didn't see a weapon, but looks could be deceiving. Petra's gaze flicked to Iver for guidance, as she backed away. Should they run? This guy couldn't see Iver, but just as clearly, he meant to do her harm.

"Viens ici, petit! Je ne vais pas te blesser!" the man shouted in a sing-song voice.

His stride was faster than her backpedal, and Petra righted herself to flee.

"Run," Iver said.

On his word, she did. Ditching the path, she could hear the man calling after her.

"Attends, reviens! Reviens ici, petite—"

Petra broke into a sprint, racing from cover to cover, even after his yell choked off. That was when she realized Iver hadn't fled with her. Arriving at a central fountain, she crawled under a guano covered, patina striped horse. Catching her breath, she waited, watching the few evening stragglers for threats, and keeping her eyes peeled for her little friend.

Iver was staring down, his body crouched low to the ground when he came into view. Then he stood, and steps later, bent down again. Was he hurt?! Abandoning the bronze stallion, Petra clamored out and ran to him. So focused was he on the ground at his feet, he didn't look up until she was nearly upon him. He straightened, his hands splotchy, crimson.

"Oh, good, Mistress. I've found you. It's best we leave now."

"Are you okay?!"

"What? Oh, yes. I'm fine. That fellow won't be following you anymore."

Spotting the fountain, he stepped to, scrubbing his hands therein.

"How'd you find me?"

"I tracked your footprints."

She nodded. Returning to their route, they followed the dirt path until it diverged from the direction Iver'd indicated. Breaking off, they emptied and filled their vessels at a drinking fountain. Then they walked straight for as long as straight was an option, which wasn't long at all. Leaving the park, Petra kept her hood up. Spotting police, she pulled Iver into a department store. Letting the officers pass, they then merged with the sidewalk throngs, strolling from the crowded shopping district to residential neighborhoods with mailboxes and street parking.

Traffic came less frequently and more quickly. Petra stopped worrying about officers, and her gaze swept for busybody parents. It only took one well-meaning mother to see her, assume the worst, and call the authorities—for Petra to be apprehended and delayed. Her skin crawled when she saw a face in a window here, a woman parking, getting out of her vehicle, there. If they could just mind their own business, she'd be okay. Petra was about to ask how much farther they had to go when Iver, turning for the umpteenth time, gestured to a neglected path between the fencing of two squat apartment buildings.

"This way," he said.

The walkway traced the fence, under creeping branches that drooped into their headspace, threatening to knock even their short selves flat. At the dead-end were overgrown flower beds circling a mossy fountain bereft of water. Beyond sat the remains of a playground, a rusted swing set, and a lopsided carousel. There were no boulders large enough for a child to fit inside, and Petra nearly said so, but the words died in her mouth as she saw it. Nearly flat to the ground was a stone. It was polished, black, and longer than they were tall.

"Is that it?"

"Yes."

Perched overtop, Iver leaned low and pressed his charm to the nook. Petra watched while he closed his eyes and sang the bestial melody she was coming to recognize. Leaning on his haunches, Iver waited while invisible bells clamored. The polished center crept outward, taking on an amber glow as it curled. With the halo, neither Petra nor Iver could see the bottom, to gauge the depth. Petra spoke first.

"How far do you think—" Unsure how to word her concern, she tried again. "I mean, with my hand—is this the best way?"

"Unfortunately, this is the only direct route I can sense from the city. The peoples do not intentionally create dangerous portals. However, those left to rest for ages have been known to shift."

"Okay."

Petra took off her backpack with difficulty and they threw their bags inside.

"Alley-oop," Iver shouted, moving too quickly to hear Petra's protest, dropping in, and hitting the ground without a sound escaping. Petra stuck her head through the circular entryway, leaning to see her friend below, and finding the perspective distorted. He lifted his hand to her, yet the distance between them appeared in flux.

Despite her uncertainties, Iver appeared unharmed. She watched him carry their goods farther inside, leaving a space for her. Knees bent, and arms prepared to soften the blow, Petra steeled herself and leapt. Unable to judge the distance, she hit the ground hard, smacking the unyielding surface with her nub despite efforts otherwise. And, being so focused on protecting the one limb, she hadn't tried to roll. Her forearms, elbows, open palm, and knees were scraped and bruised alike. Yet all of those pains were a sigh compared to the screaming of her severed wrist, ricocheting up her shoulder and back.

The agony was all-consuming until it wasn't. Petra breathed, and pushing herself up, spoke.

"Okay. I can do this now."

Iver, who'd been leaning over her, drew back.

"Very well, then." Glancing at the entrance above their heads, he sighed. "I can't seal this. I'll report it to the Queen when we're next in Josalfar."

Hopefully, nobody would fall in during the interim. The park had been modest, old, and beset by trees and housing, perhaps forgotten. Comforted, Petra removed her jacket, and laid it over her good arm for quick access.

"What happened with the Queen? Did she refuse to see you?" she asked, as they'd resumed their journey.

"What? Oh."

Iver examined the saddle in his grip, as if only just taking note of what he held. Then his eyes lingered on the bandages, poking free from her sleeve.

"No Mistress. Her Majesty, Queen Siv, honored us by granting me another audience. During which, I updated her Majesty on our progress, and offered what treasures we've thus obtained. Her response was not what I anticipated."

"How did she respond?"

"Well, Mistress, with humor and criticism. You see, her Majesty, to her immense credit, did not arbitrarily set the order of our three tasks."

Petra considered him blankly.

"What I mean is, these treasures are useful. We were supposed to weave a net from the golden fleece, and with it, catch a kelpie. Utilizing even a paltry section of fleece, even an amateur weaver can create a functional net. And I am not an amateur weaver. At the risk of sounding vain, I come from a long line of exemplary artisans. My technique is impeccable."

He paused, twiddled with his beard, and continued, "What I was not aware of, and what you could not have known, is the golden fleece is an incredibly versatile material. Any product crafted from the fleece powerfully meets the intent of the maker. A net made from the fleece would have been a vital tool in capturing the kelpie. Then, as a condition for his freedom, we could have demanded the saddle."

He broke off his explanation, giving Petra time to reach her own conclusions, which she did. Because her Majesty hadn't bothered to explain why she wanted what, they'd gone up against two monsters now, woefully unprepared for the second. Petra glared accusatorily at her throbbing nub. Would she have lost her hand had they made and used a golden net? Maybe. They still had to hear its song to find and trap it in the first place, and that was where their plan had gone awry.

"Okay. Fine." I lost a hand, but whatever, Petra scoffed inwardly. "We haven't deviated from the order. You have the saddle. How's it going to help with the griffon?"

"Latch a kelpie's saddle over the back of any beast and it will be tame to you."

"And will the beast remain tame after the saddle is removed?"

Iver paused in his step.

"Huh. Well, Mistress, I don't rightly know. Her Majesty didn't specify."

So no, then. "And the talon?"

"Ah yes. As for the talon—it is an essential ingredient in the making of the charm to free your brother."

Now it was Petra's turn to pause. "So how were we supposed to defeat the golden rams, then?

Iver tilted his head, thinking. "Her Majesty didn't say, but Alfarians are unable to approach the rams with any force short of an army backing them. Bad blood, you understand? Perhaps exploiting their vanity would have come easier to you, given your race and youth. Your initial plan may have been hers all along."

Or maybe she had no plan in mind for the rams, Petra thought. Perhaps the first task was the real test, and every challenge thereafter should have amounted to a comparatively simple, if exhausting game, had they only known the rules.

"Why would the Queen send us out to play monster dominoes? What is the point of all this?!" Petra snapped, the sting of her stump leaving her susceptible to frustration.

"Oh, we wouldn't have needed much fleece to make a net, Mistress. She'll expect us to take that saddle back from the griffon, once it's defeated, and weaker by a talon. And if we kill the subdued griffon, that would leave its hoard unguarded."

"Meaning?" Petra asked, treading softly in the mounting darkness.

"Griffons collect treasure, building their nests with precious stones and metals."

The Queen wasn't great or good. She wasn't majestic. She was greedy and selfish. Queen Siv didn't value the lives of others at all, let alone freedom.

"Iver? Why do brownies accept—" What was that word? Not enslavement. That's what it was, sure, but it shamed her to say it. Oh. "—subservience. Especially to humans, but in general. Why let me tell you what to do?"

Iver stopped short so suddenly, Petra bumped into him. She offered a muffled apology, stepping back.

"Let us make camp here. We could use a meal and some rest. Why don't you get out your flashlight, Mistress? It must be dark for you."

Petra nodded, taking a seat and fiddling with her bag for the light. She heard rather than saw him settling across from her. Iver divvied meal portions out while she propped the flashlight on the floor. Her jacket cushioned the rod at an angle allowing her to see comfortably.

Remembering the oranges, she passed one to Iver, who thanked her. They ate, skinning their fruit, and tearing apart the jerky. Iver took a long swig of his whiskey and wished out loud for a fire.

"Some tales should only be told over a hearth," he said, "—but no matter." He heaved a throaty sigh. "We didn't choose to be servants. We disobeyed the Queen. This is the consequence."

Iver's voice was flat. Emotionless. Petra waited for him to continue. When next he spoke, his hands were animated, casting shadows on the varicosed walls.

"Long ago, before you or any living human can remember—my people had a civilization of our own. We were artisans and merchants. Our capital city was considered a marvel by all who visited, but amongst the peoples, few did. When we founded our capital, Adlandice, it was a port city. Not to be confused with Nyja Adlandice, which is a midland the Alfarians pacified much more recently."

Petra raised her hand and Iver paused. "What is it, Mistress?"

"Your home city is Atlantis?"

Iver nodded. "I believe the legend of Atlantis refers to the history of my people, yes. Perhaps the human philosopher, Plato, had access to records pertaining to my people's heritage. Or mayhaps, our tale was passed down as an oral tradition, until he set his interpretation to papyrus."

Petra didn't know who Plato was but nodded for Iver to continue.

"Anyway, as trade increased, our homestead flourished and urbanized, so too did the waters rise, finally cutting us off from the mainland completely. By this time, mankind was fanning out, their population increasing at a rate that intimidated the peoples. Even at our height, we fae, have never been capable of breeding as rapidly or in such quantities as humanity. And unlike our own, humans made no attempt at maintaining harmony with the natural boundaries of the earth. Our values were not man's values. Mankind hunted in excess, eroded their soil, salted their enemies' fields, and burned down what woodlands slowed their endlessly conflicting paths. Entire wildlife populations were being wiped out, their corpses barely used, wasted. Mankind was brutal, acting shamefully but without the sense to know they did wrong. The peoples were beset on all sides by humanity's destructive reach. Man was a problem that needed solving. The peoples came to a consensus that the time to act was nigh, after man decimated the Eurasian nymph population during one unseasonably hot autumn. That they hadn't even meant to was the worst of it. In claiming land for themselves, they'd ruined acres upon acres for others, until the nymphs' habitat dried up. They, our gossamer-winged brothers and sisters, became ill and died."

He paused to breathe and Petra waited, one hand in her lap, her nub resting on it.

"And so it was that her Majesty, Queen Engyl, may she rest in peace and glory, held a counsel with the heads of our brethren. At this time, each of the peoples followed a counselor of their choosing. In great matters that would affect all of the peoples, those counselors would congregate to reach an accord regarding the issue at hand. Their conclusion would then be shared with her Majesty, who could either affirm their word or officially disregard it. Then, like now, her Majesty's word was law. Ideally, every people would be represented in this manner. In practice, less prominent peoples found their councilors excluded from many such lawmaking sessions, and despite being an economic powerhouse, brownies held less prestige than many others in the eyes of our peers. This may be because we long cooperated with those among mankind with the sight, but could also have been due, in part, to the distaste the peoples held towards seafarers in general. But I digress. The council gathered to answer a question. What was to be done about mankind?"

A part of Petra had to wonder if humans deserved such hate. Surely, they could have been reasoned with?

"The council took seven days to reach a verdict. A separation was enacted between the peoples and man. An embargo was set, cutting off all trade with humanity. Adlandice took two counts of offense at this proclamation. Firstly, my people were informed of the policy afterward, by messenger. Our democratically elected counselor had not even been alerted that the congregation was taking place until after it had concluded. That we were excluded from this decision was a slight against our pride. Secondly, and exacerbated by that initial point, was the fact that our economy, of all the peoples, would be the most undermined by this affront. The Alfarians did not trade with humans! Nymphs were not cultivating lucrative ports teeming with taverns and spice shops for man! We were! This policy, that we hadn't any say in, would hurt *us*! Not them."

There, now, was a rancor to Iver she'd not before witnessed. This story needed no campfire. His words gave off the heat of passion long suppressed.

"The other peoples had been deemed worthy of consideration by a Queen who could not be bothered to step foot on our tiny island, despite the increasing convenience of the golden path. May she rest in peace and glory," he said, grimacing at his restraint.

"In hindsight, it's clear her Majesty hoped such severe embargos might limit humanity's growth. Perhaps starve them out, altogether. In and of itself, that wasn't an unworthy goal behind which to unite the peoples. Had our counselor been included, the history of brownies may have been very different."

He stared wistfully at an earthen wall, gathering his thoughts.

"Unfortunately, my people had grown accustomed to a certain lifestyle, a high standard of living, and Adlandice was shielded on all sides by the vast sea. When it comes to water, you have to understand the peoples are culturally averse to crossing the world's barriers. Unlike humanity, we spread only as far as the first natural border, before settling down. Sailing, for instance, was as foreign to the Alfarians as manipulating the golden path is for man. Only the uppermost echelons crossed the tumultuous seas and anxious rivers with any regularity. So paranoid were they, it was tradition to cleanse oneself thoroughly after every such journey."

"Secluded, we felt secure. Which is to say, the embargo we were ordered to abide by, via messenger, of course—" Iver scowled at the memory.

"—went ignored. Our human neighbors brought with them wine, spices, silk, marble, and parchment from their travels. Goods that my people would not traditionally have come by on our own. We were comfortable and grievously overconfident. Things had gone well for us for a long while and we did not foresee a future where such bounty could be undone. Our secret was short-lived. Word got back to her Majesty. Upon discovering our treason, Queen Engyl sent a tsunami to submerge my home beneath the waves that had been our guardian and friend. As we had betrayed her, so too, our ally was made to betray us."

Petra imagined a mighty storm drowning Iceland, her people running to high ground, to no avail.

"Our few survivors sailed to human ports. We called for aid. Humanity was superstitious then. If the gods brought about our destruction, then to stand with us, was suicide. So said many a king and warlord, disregarding ancient alliances overnight. Tales of an unruly Queen and foreign politics fell on deaf ears. Any Queen that could corrupt the sea was either a goddess, or had the favor thereof. Humanity feared heavenly retribution. The armies we requested would not come. The legions we begged for were ordered away. In the end, some few individuals, men with more loyalty than sense, joined ud in our march against her Majesty. In battle, men and brownies alike fell like newborn foals under an onslaught of hail. We were seafarers, a proud but peaceful people. Soft. The Alfarians, trolls, giants—they were warriors, skilled in hand to hand combat, archery, and swordplay. My people never stood a chance."

Petra'd butt was numb, so she adjusted her posture, careful not to brush against her nub.

"We could have left it at that. Accepted our defeat, gathered the last of us together, and re-built along the coast, but we did not. Vengeance weighed heavy on our shoulders. We would not rest until we'd honored our fallen. A few brownies convened their own privy council post-defeat, to determine our response. At dawn the following day, my people attacked anew, an act as futile as it was fatal."

Iver took a swig from his canteen, blinked, and continued.

"The purpose of the battle was not to defeat our enemy. No, those fighting were not in denial at the sight of trained armies that outnumbered and out-skilled them. Our tiny band of survivors was being swallowed up by an interminable deluge of hacking, slashing, and marching soldiers, seasoned by more battles than we had brownies left to fight. No, combat fwas a distraction. Most of us would die that day, but—but! If the plan was successful, those who lived would bear witness to the triumphant rebirth of our valiant people."

But you didn't win, Petra thought. Or you wouldn't be here, with me, now.

"So it was that five of our best warriors and two human mercenaries slunk down a golden pathway, through to Josalfar, and onward into the Queen's private dwelling. They crept deliberately, seeking treasure. Not treasure like you might think. Not gold nor diamonds. Certainly not a fleece, saddle, nor claw. We lost more than our wealth when our home was drowned. We lost everything, or so we thought. What we sought, was power. Wield enough, and not only would we be impervious to future attacks—we would dominate over the other peoples. Brownies would never again find themselves forgotten, neglected, nor controlled. What we sought was a weapon so terrible, we need never fire it. Fear of us, from then on, would be our shield."

"Her Majesty, Queen Engyl, then had in her possession two precious stones. Precious, not because of the way they sparkled nor due to their purity of color. Although yes, it is said they were magnificent to behold, the one radiating gold, the other silver. But no, they were precious in that they served to amplify one's magic. The one stone was named *Sol* and the other, *Luun*, and they were so named for the sun and moon, from which it has long been theorized they originated. In the centuries that followed their discovery, every decade, a pair of Alfarians would be sacrificed—their essence fed to the stones until such a time when they could be filled no more."

So her Majesty didn't just find human lives worthless? Petra grumbled, inwardly.

"These stones were infamous for pacifying unruly peoples. Her Majesty never announced their use, but there were rumors of Alfarians disappearing directly after each rebellion surrendered. Twins, a rarity, made a habit of leaving Josalfar, following uprisings and natural disasters, so common was this belief."

In that case, Petra couldn't understand parents letting their twins live there at all, and surely adult sets could find a safer home.

"During this final battle, a battle we fought to lose, five of ours and two of yours snuck into the Queen's private chambers where they were caught. In the ensuing struggle, Bon, hero to all brownies everywhere, fought against his captor. He freed himself just long enough to shatter *Luun*, the moonstone, with his hammer. Never forget—of all of the peoples in all of the lands, it was the brownies, who succeeded in halving the Queen's might."

Iver smiled, but Petra'd heard the regret coloring his every word.

"Afterwards, her Majesty summarily executed all seven intruders and the Sol stone was hidden away. Now when disaster strikes, Josalfar needs to anticipate only the disappearance of a single citizen. Thus twins flee no more. As for why my people were enslaved—"

He took another swig from his canteen. Then on second thought, a third too.

"We lamented Bon's death but worst came after. In punishment, to teach us the value of obedience, my people were given a choice. We, less than a hundred survivors of a civilization that had numbered in the tens of thousands, could follow her Majesty Engyl, and work in the mines, or we could live as slaves to mankind."

Oh, Petra thought. He could have ended there, having answered her question, but legends merit a conclusion.

"Our pain was fresh, and to her Majesty's surprise, we chose the ally that had largely abandoned us over the enemy, by whose hand we had been mercilessly culled. Utilizing Sol, publicly for the first and last time, her Majesty laid out the curse. Doubtless, some forgotten Alfarian's life was ended to refill the stone's energy basin later that night, and the rest is history. You'd be hard-pressed to find one amongst our women willing to wed now. We are dying. We've been dying ever since. Some believe that her Majesty, Queen Siv, will lift the curse one day, decreeing an official end to our penance. I'm not holding my breath."

They were quiet as both reflected on who had driven them to this point.

"Do you hate it? Having to listen to me?"

"No, Mistress, I don't. That's the problem. Servitude is comfortable. There is peace in not needing to think for myself. Never having to ask myself—what do I want? Who should I be? In between Masters, I find myself overwhelmed with anxiety and self-doubt. Those questions, now distant, return with a vengeance during periods of freedom. I like being led, but I don't like liking it. Finding peace in servitude is unnatural, and I would give anything to relinquish her Majesty's hold over us."

Petra didn't know what to say to that. After dinner, she pulled her blanket tight and went to bed. Even with the electric pain of her severed wrist, she was asleep in minutes.

There is no sunrise in a cave and Petra awoke to the sound of Iver rustling through his pack. She'd been dreaming, but the figments evaporated as she sat up. Reaching for her flashlight, she recalled only that she had been whole. A lump rose to her throat and she felt her eyes grow wet. She squeezed her favorite doll with her remaining hand. Releasing it, she grasped the flashlight, and flicked it on. There would be no tears this morning.

So she was crippled. So what? Emil was in a coma. Atla was a slave. Iver was a slave—her slave, sure, but still. At least Petra was free.

Iver looked into the shifting light. "Ah good, Mistress. You're awake. Here."

She looked down at her hand, identifying the shrunken mushrooms they'd dried in Polstov. "So they're safe then? You asked?"

"Yes, Mistress. These won't cause ill effects."

Petra nodded. "Any idea what food we can expect in the mountains?"

"Unfortunately not."

"Were you able to eat anything in Josalfar?"

"Yes. I am welcome to eat amongst the Alfarians when I visit."

"But they didn't give you anything for the road?"

"Nothing was offered that you could safely consume, Mistress."

The unhelpfulness of the Queen was wearing. "If you ate from the Queen's dais, would you have to work in the mines?"

"I don't know. Such a thing isn't done. The humans eat what they've been given, but only amongst themselves. Her Majesty blesses their food. As I am not human myself, I don't know the extent to which her Majesty's charm would affect me. Especially as my people are already enthralled by her, just to a different effect."

The mushrooms felt deceptively hard in Petra's hand, but when chewed, proved soft. Iver'd spiced but the umami was overwhelmed by salt. After more than a week of dried meals, she would have been happy to taste the last of salt forever. They split the apple. Breakfast left her thirsty, but with her bottle less than half full, she made do with a small sip. Then they packed and were off.

Absentmindedly, Petra imagined Emil with them, jogging just ahead, asking, "Are we there yet?" She pictured him slowing to keep pace with her, making shadow puppets with the light, giving his invented animals names and voices, breathing life into their adventure. His tale would have been vaster, and fraught with stranger perils, than their own.

The temperature dropped to warrant donning her jacket and she asked Iver to slow so she could put it on. Once simple motions were difficult. Her left hand, bulkier than it looked, pried her nub from its strap, and carefully pulled the bag down. She winced when the strap bumped her bandages. Then, with her backpack on the floor, she pulled on her coat. Starting with the nub, she pulled that sleeve up, before reaching for the left armscye, and shoving her hand through, which took two tries. Pulling the bag onto her back again proved an ordeal. A less stubborn child would have asked for help. Petra suspected that in the time it took her to get ready, they could have reached the exit, which they did some minutes later.

Chapter 11

Stepping from the glow, Petra scanned the heavens before realizing, what she'd taken for sky was a mountain, and one of many. The ground was steep. If they fell, they'd fall far. Weather-stripped boughs stood vertically a ways ahead, dotting the land in a linear manner trees did not. Did they set a boundary?

Petra bent low and examined the pebbles at her sneakers, ignoring the sting of her feet. They were every shade of periwinkle and grey, but there wasn't a blade of grass in sight. Standing, her eyes traced their mountain upward until it faded into oblivion. Turning, she scanned for peaks, an act that made her dizzy. Several split into jagged points that pierced the fog, rising so steeply and to such impossibly narrow points that Petra disregarded them immediately. How could a griffon make a home on those? Moreover, how could a one-handed little girl make any headway climbing one?

So much for scaling the smallest mountain. Neither she nor Iver could tell which was shortest. This would have been a great time for a topographic map of the area, Petra thought bitterly. She could just make out pinprick birds swooping up through the clouds before disappearing. Their song was too distant. The only sounds were the wind and that of their shoes displacing gravel.

Birds were a good sign. Petra hadn't seen Iver shoot any down, but he'd had no trouble with rabbits. If they flew low, he could get them.

There were no swatches of green quilting the far off slopes, nor even the auburn hues of autumnal foliage. As above, so below, all was awash with grey. Even the sky was bereft of a more saturated azure. So this was a desert. She'd assumed, from what pictures she'd seen of the Sahara, that they were brighter, defined during daylight by a saturated cerulean sky over golden sand. Meanwhile what negligible streaks of color were so thin as to miss at a head turn.

Below lay a valley, spanning the unending mountain range. If they planned on ever drinking water again, the base was their best chance. Water ran downhill and with clouds up above, it stood to reason this wasn't the dry season. Precipitation meant water. Actual water too. Not blood or liqui-fied rust.

Worryingly, Petra couldn't make out any streams. Maybe they were too high up, she thought. Or perhaps the water was reflecting the sky and so camouflaged.

"Should we close it?" she asked, gesturing to the cave.

Iver shook his head.

"You might need to get back without me, Mis-tress. Also, the way remains open in France. The only thing crueler than a passerby falling in and climbing out into the wilderness, is not finding their way out at all. It must remain open."

"Okay," Petra said, hoping neither scenario oc-curred.

Given the other end opened into a playground, the next one in would be a kid too, maybe younger than herself. With luck, the park was abandoned. Iver moved downhill with the same swift grace he'd possessed on even ground. Petra, well, she didn't lose her other hand. That was something.

Initially, she tried to match his speed, but after skidding and sanding her shins, she'd given that up. They were headed in the same direction, however—down. So it didn't matter if she kept pace. There weren't any woods to lose each other in. She'd reach him when she reached the bottom and that was that.

Petra's meandering followed a pattern of rush, stop, rush. Where the ground sloped sharply, she took quick little steps. Then the earth swung upwards, briefly flattening out, she'd use the solidity to reorient herself. A soreness bloomed in her quadriceps, but that paled to the billowing ache of her feet, while the fireworks of her nub came and went. Half a step from falling, Petra grabbed at an odd pole, for balance. If alive, they offered no sign, covered only in a barely perceptible moss. Had they roots, none crept above the pebbles.

Iver's path was more or less a straight shot to the valley below. Petra followed along the least steep route she could manage. Bruised and out of breath, she caught up. The soil was gritty, coarse, and she'd passed no shrubbery, not even low lying. Lichens and wisps of grass poked from cracks in the earth. She had the distant sensation that this wasn't earth at all, but another planet entirely.

Near to, then at ground level, the wind came hard and fast. Opening her mouth to speak, Petra kept her hand up to block debris. She was reminded of the trips her family used to take to the black beach, how she'd hated sand, and the beach by extension. Back then though, they'd had a cooler of sugary beverages and restaurants offered hot meals back in town. What she wouldn't have given to go back and relive those days.

As for their food situation—there were birds. Lichens and grass weren't exactly appetizing, but they were proof this desolate land could provide nutrients for life. There were soups made from lichens, back home. She'd never tried them but supposed Iver would know a recipe. Perhaps by watching the birds, they'd learn what produce made up their diet, unless they were living off of insects. If it came to that—Her stomach clenched and she winced her eyes shut. She was being stupid. After a few days of drinking blood, was she really above eating a cockroach?

Anyway, it might not matter. They weren't out of food yet, and a human could go without for days. It was water they needed and water they'd best seek. Petra thought back to what she knew of camels, and by extension, their environment. In desert regions, oases, centering around natural springs, were hubs of life, a gathering point for diverse flora and fauna.

"Are you alright, Mistress?"

"Yeah. Thanks. Any sign of water?"

She was thirsty. He had to be, too.

"Not yet, but the valley drops again a ways ahead."

Not as far as she could tell but she took his word.

"Can your magic find some?"

He shook his head. "No Mistress. I can seek out a river or a body of water by name but not by subject. The issue is water isn't a place. It's everywhere, in us, the air we breathe, and in the ground."

She nodded, having assumed if the solution were so simple, he'd have been the one to suggest it, but she'd had to ask.

"You know Mistress," Iver said, interrupting her thoughts. "—this trip has included several firsts for me. A first time seeing a golden ram, first time in Polstov, first time encountering a kelpie, and now I'm visiting the Borjans. Most of my Masters were content with having me prepare their suppers and clean the dishes. Brownies have generally stayed within your world since long before your homeland existed under its current title."

Petra considered this, listening to and smelling the wind for traces of water.

"How old is Iceland?"

Iver shrugged. "I don't know. But to my knowledge, there isn't a government in your world that predates the downfall of my people."

"Oh. And that Queen—"

"Her Majesty, Queen Engyl, may she rest in peace and glory."

The words rang hollow.

"Yeah. Her. Is that Siv's great great great grandmother? How many greats is she?"

"Her Majesty, Queen Engyl, is the mother of her Majesty, Queen Siv. May she reign infinite."

"Her mother?"

"Yes."

"So is Queen Siv just really old?"

Iver laughed. "You can't imagine how old she is. And I am."

"Were your parents born before the downfall?"

At this, he offered a sad smile. "Mistress, I fought alongside my mother and father during the rebellion."

A part of her wanted to know if they'd survived the short-lived war. Tact prevented the question. Besides, talking would only make her thirstier.

Against her better judgment, Petra downed another sip. If they didn't find water soon, they would have to turn back. How long could a person go without water? Not long, Petra thought, fighting the urge to cough. Just don't think about it, she thought. Don't think about your cotton mouth. In fact, she commanded silently, don't think about your mouth at all.

If only it were that simple.

There was a trench nestled at a midpoint between two rows of ridges, but it was dry. Petra had never been one for measuring distances. Frustrated, Iver raised a hand for her to stop. Petra complied, listening hard for the burble of a stream or a creek. Iver stepped to the ledge and lowered himself down to the cracked floor below. There, he pushed his fingers into the dirt. Petra watched as he raised his soiled digits, rubbing them together at eye level.

"What are you doing?"

"I'm checking for moisture," he said.

Then he put a finger to his lips, reminding her to be silent. She watched while he laid himself flat, pressing his ear to the ground. Iver remained in that position long enough for Petra to become uncomfortable with her stationary pose. She shifted her weight, to not lock her knees. Then he stood, shaking his head.

"I'm sorry, Mistress. If there's water in the ground, it's too far down to hear. I think we should return to the cavern and better prepare ourselves for the Borjans. We can't save your brother if we succumb to dehydration."

Petra frowned, thinking. The sky was thick with clouds that could fall at any minute. There was water. It just wasn't accessible.

Did Iver want for them to leave so they needn't face a griffon? They only had five days left. If he ran out the clock on Emil's livelihood, they'd never finish their quest. If so, was he preserving his life, or both of theirs? Iver had to hate the Queen after what her mother did to his people. Was he purposefully keeping Petra from giving her Majesty tools that would empower her? Had he truly met with Queen Siv and given over the fleece while she,

Petra, was being operated on? Or had that been a lie? Did he carry it still?

Iver didn't want to be there. He didn't even know Emil. He wanted to be warm and safe, baking, and tidying.

"It's going to rain. Not right now but soon. Look at the sky."

Iver did and nodded.

"We just need to last until it does," she said. "The ground might be too porous to hold water at its surface but we can catch it. There are flat stone ledges above. We passed them coming down. The rain won't seep through those. Could be some hold water already."

"With all due respect Mistress, that's a big gamble to take. You're risking our lives."

Petra straightened her posture, meeting his eyes. "I know. But we don't have time to dilly-dally. Emil needs us now."

"Very well then, Mistress. We're about," Iver paused, taking in their immediate surroundings. "—equidistant between these three mountains." To the three, he pointed, turning. "Which will we be climbing?"

Petra spun, contemplating their ascent. "Is there any way to tell where the griffons live?"

Iver shrugged. "I doubt any of them have more than a single griffon, given their mating season just ended. Other than spotting them circling the peak, they won't have left much of a footprint this low to the ground. Doubtless, griffons have adapted to breathing the thin air of those higher elevations. They hunt close to home."

"What do they hunt?"

"Treasure hunters, if you believe the legends. I expect we'll see carcasses picked clean nearer to their nests. You'd be surprised at how many fools are willing to take on a griffon to steal their trove. Although, in their defense, I suppose that's less dangerous than going against a dragon."

"And the treasure hunters probably come better prepared than us."

"You can bet they bring more water."

"Okay. Well—" Petra coughed, dislodging sand. "I don't see any bones, so let's just make for the mountain we came out of. We know it's a way out if we get desperate, and if we haven't found water by tomorrow night, we'll use it to backtrack and resupply."

"Very well, Mistress."

They trudged from the empty ditch, up from the valley, Petra's legs aching as they ascended. Something dark moved across the ground, catching her eye, and she stopped.

"Wait!" she called to Iver who was already yards ahead, the weight of the saddle not having slowed his steps at all.

The insect changed course as Petra bent for a better look, darting beneath a wide stone bearing imprints similar to those of ammonites, but far larger. She debated lifting the rock, but it would have been heavy even had she two fully functional hands.

"I think it's a scorpion. Except it's covered in hair. Have you ever heard of a furry scorpion?"

"No Mistress. I have not," Iver said, returning to her side.

"Think it can lead us to water?"

"No Mistress. I can't imagine a scorpion would drink much."

Petra nodded. "Bye little guy," she whispered, grateful she hadn't seen its underbelly. Rodents were cute. Bugs were disgusting and she'd been raised not to tolerate them.

The duo stood, resuming their hike. The sky hadn't lightened since they'd arrived. Nor had the chill lessened despite the slowing wind speed. Petra kept her hand gloved and her nub tucked in its sleeve.

The sun, without having shown its face all day, was setting as they reached the golden path again. Petra refused to dwell inside, the temptation to turn tail and find water too strong. They continued to climb. When next she looked up, the sky was ashen, bleak. Rising, they were swept by a dense fog. A freezing damp set in, the moisture infuriatingly useless.

"Can we catch it?"

"You want us to catch the fog, Mistress?"

"Yes. If we can."

Iver nodded, thinking out loud, "Let's make camp here. I won't be able to start a fire, but we can use those sticks anyway."

Petra wandered off in search of wood. There weren't many mossy poles this high up but they'd passed a few just above the cave. There, around the bend, a blunt end jutted out.

"Found one!" she called, stepping carefully onto the narrow ledge towards her prize.

Hugging the shear wall, she eased herself step by precarious step to the wider ridge beyond, loosening pebbles underfoot. The sound of them clattering far below set her heart racing. One more step. Then another. With a deep breath, she threw herself over the final gap, an intimidating break in the shelf she hadn't spotted before, thanks to the mist.

"Still alive," said the pain in her palm, knees, and shins, after her rough landing. Standing, she dusted herself off, and looked down, away from where she'd come. Even without seeing the ground below, the distance made her dizzy and she sat back.

"Are you okay, Mistress?" Iver called out.

"Yeah. I'm fine," she replied, that last syllable a squeak, as she reflected on her near end.

Again Petra stood, and turning, walked the negligible distance to the stick. A blasted stick. Sure, there were three more beyond she hadn't initially seen and could now reach. But still. Stinking sticks. She could have kicked herself, nearly falling off a cliff over something so insignificant. She wasn't just risking herself.

With a firm grip on the first pole, her back to the wall, she gave it a yank, to no avail. Widening her stance, she pulled once more, but harder. Zero give. Curious, she attempted to pull forth another. Then again with the third and fourth.

How far down did they go? The sounds of dislodged gravel caught her attention. It was Iver. He'd jumped to the thin overpass, no worse for the wear.

"I can't pull them up," Petra confessed. "Either they're dug too deeply into the ground or—"

"Or they have their own root systems," Iver finished for her.

They exchanged a nod and took to digging. The soil was moist and cold, less gritty than the sand in the valley, yet sprinkled with frequent rocks that required removal. Iver confirmed the root system first.

"You're right, Mistress. There's a bulb here and then it trails."

"Potatoes are a root. Think we can eat it?"

"I don't know. This isn't a plant I'm familiar with. Let's collect the poles for the fog catcher. And the bulbs too, just in case."

"In case we get desperate?"

Iver nodded. "Precisely.

Having collected the peculiar plants, Iver made to pass back the way they'd come, but Petra stopped him.

"I don't think I can get across that ledge again. I was knocking down rocks as I went."

So they worked their way upward into the fog, collecting more pole plants en route. Night fell, miserable and mockingly wet. Petra pried sticky fabric from her flesh, gritting her teeth to keep from crying out. Her skull pounded from the effort. There was no wind, replaced instead by a heavy chill. For Emil, she would push on. For Emil, she reminded herself.

"Well, Mistress—here's camp, unless you've decided to use the path?"

She had not, and so dropped her bag, placing the plants on a nearly flat expanse under a ledge. The wall above could protect them from the worst of the elements, the underside concave. Iver's find appeared nearly as comfortable as the path. It was a better spot than she could have hoped for after her, admittedly unreasonable, demand. This was shelter.

"Okay. How do we make a water catcher?"

Iver shrugged. "I've never built a contraption for converting fog into drinking water, Mistress. However, I have an idea that might work. We arrange a pyramidal structure with the rods. I have plenty of twine to tie them together. Then we need a thin fabric or a net with which to tent them to collect the moisture."

"And then?"

"And then, once it's good and soggy, we ring it out into a pot."

"Do we have a net?"

He shook his head. "No. And her Majesty was all too pleased to claim the fleece, but let's dump our bags, and I'll see what I can come up with."

While Iver sorted through their belongings, Petra arranged the sticks. She dug, plotting each into an angled hole, and filling in gravel to secure them. Tying them together at the crown, her knot would have earned a bemused headshake from a falcon scout, but it should hold overnight just fine. Iver meanwhile, sliced the seams of her remaining shirts, all filthy, and stitched them together. This slapdash quilt, he hung over the frame, pinning and sewing. The finished product looked like a teepee.

"This should work," he said. "Although the water is going to be mint flavored. I knocked over one of the spice jars."

Petra looked around. Sure enough, flecks of green dotted everything from the catcher to the ground to the contents of their sacks. Not being a big fan of mint herself, Petra didn't feel any loss but Iver appeared crestfallen.

"Let's lay out the pots too, in case of rain," she suggested.

Iver complied, circling the fog catcher with dishware. Then they both dug into the mushrooms, of which there seemed many but once consumed, proved unfilling. If they couldn't drink water, they could at least eat, right? Petra regretted not having wiped the mushrooms off beforehand, as the salt residue coating her mouth made her that much thirstier. Without thinking about what she was doing, she started sucking on her sleeve. This had been her habit when she was a toddler, one she'd outgrown just in time to enter the public school system, and one she hadn't thought of in years.

Blessed moisture filled her mouth. It wasn't much but it did wonders to lift her spirits. The teepee would work. Eventually, it would rain. The food situation was bleak but they had those roots, which might prove edible. Treasure hunters had to eat something. They couldn't all have packed enough for the road. As she and Iver hadn't come across any corpses near half-eaten piles of roots, the bulbs were probably safe to consume.

She hoped.

Like the night before Saint Thorlak's Mass, Petra wanted the hours until morning to blip by, so she went to sleep, her sleeve still in her mouth. When she awoke, it was dark. Something had touched her. She was sure of it. Reaching for her flashlight, she flicked it on, revealing a flurry of motion on the ground.

Iver awoke to her scream, and in the artificial light, saw the source of Petra's terror. Bugs. Large furry insects fled from the shine, but roved along the light's shaky border. Iver jumped, kicked off his blanket and rushed to Petra's side.

"Are you stung, Mistress? Are you bit?"

She shook her head, trembling. "No. They were all over me! What are they?!"

He zeroed in on one, wishing it would pause long enough to be examined. "I'm not certain, Mistress. Perhaps scorpions like the one we saw earlier?"

Now that the shock had worn off, and the light shifted the swarm aside, Petra eased herself from her blanket, handing Iver the flashlight. She crawled to the edge of safety.

"No. They're shaped differently—more like beetles but with furry backs instead of wings." She watched, focusing on one of the slower beasties, counting. "They have six legs, so they aren't spiders."

"They might be edible," Iver mused.

Petra swallowed her distaste and forced herself to consider the option rationally. "Maybe. But there are so many. Like bees."

"You're right." Iver agreed, "If we can catch one alone or separate them, maybe we can try it. There being so many here, now, we don't want to draw their ire."

Petra nodded, spooked but grateful to be spared the experience of crunching down on a bug.

"They must like the mint. If they don't eat it all tonight, they'll be back tomorrow for the rest. Judging by their aversion to light, we don't have to worry about them during the day," Iver observed.

"If we keep camp here tomorrow, we have time to make traps to catch them. For food. On purpose." She sighed at the seriousness of her suggestion. "And if we camp elsewhere, we probably won't see them again since we're out of mint."

"That's the sum of it, Mistress."

"I don't know if I can sleep with them so close by," she admitted.

"What if we prop the flashlight like this?"

So saying, he stepped through the milling throng, grabbed the light, then aimed it at Petra, while leaning the handle against rocks and gravel.

"Good?"

"Good. Thanks, Iver."

"You're welcome, Mistress."

Still up, he sidestepped the writhing mass and made for the fog catcher. This he rung over his widest pot. Resetting the cover, he carried it to her.

"It's not much but the catcher is working."

She looked into the pot, her face casting a shadow over the contents. Unable to gauge how much water they had, she accepted Iver's offering gratefully, took a tentative sip, and then a deeper swig. The thirst remained, but Petra passed the pot back to Iver with thanks.

Then, having had his fill, he blanketed himself beside her, and they laid down, back to back. Iver was snoring in minutes. Even with the light, it took Petra ages to get any rest. Then sleep came all at once and she only realized she'd been dreaming when she woke up.

A faint sprinkling drew the duo from their slumber. The flashlight was out. Either they were in for another gloomy day or the sun wasn't yet awake. Petra looked to the scarce droplets darkening her cover with hope. Iver sprinkled more catcher water into a pot. After they'd each had a drink, he funneled the remainder into his canteen and her water bottle.

Breakfast was a paltry affair. They hadn't many mushrooms to begin with and now they were out.

"I think we'll have to give the roots a try if we want to eat later," Iver remarked.

Petra's stomach rumbled as they packed and growled on as she followed Iver skyward. The sting in her feet was more pronounced with every step. Visibility was poor. The fog hadn't dissipated and the rain refused to fall. Between the sprinkling and the mist, Petra's coat was waterlogged. They'd brought the poles, and she was using hers as a staff, for balance. Unfortunately, that meant she couldn't tuck her fast numbing hand into her sleeve.

The slope grew steep, and she crawled, inching towards flatter ground, dragging the stick along. Pulling herself onto a level ledge, she slipped from the slick surface, catching herself on exposed rock below. The rod clattered free, then past, sliding down, to her left. Iver backtracked, his sticks tapping a tune against the stoney path. Petra eased herself up, assuring Iver that she was fine, making to retrieve her stick, but he pulled her back.

"There's a drop there, Mistress."

Petra froze, then crouched down, crawling until a clump of dirt gave way. Blinded by the mist, she couldn't tell the cliff ended. Sopping air licked at her fingers and she turned away, following her friend. Abandoning her makeshift staff, they kept on.

Iver passed her one of his. When the fog cleared, he expected they would find another. The ground was treacherous. One step might find a patch of sand, but the next could slide its way across a smooth wet stone, and over the edge. "Splat," Petra whispered, accidentally knocking a moss clump into the unknown. Iver's every step hugged the rock face, his movements slow.

A loud bout of swearing erupted ahead and Petra came to meet her guide, who put his arm out, blocking her.

"What is it? What happened?"

He sighed, rubbing his brow. "It's another drop Mistress. We can't cross here."

"Okay. A minor setback," she replied, more confidently than she felt. "So what do we do? Follow the ridge the other way until we find a safe crossing?"

"We could, but there might not be anywhere to cross. I can't see the other side."

Nor could she. It seemed, rather than let their tenuous dams break, the clouds were content to gorge themselves until so heavy, they drooped, coating the valley floor. Now it was Petra's turn to sigh. Then she took a step back, sat down, and pulled her bag to her front. From within, she retrieved her flashlight, flicking it on. The light sputtered and died.

Had she thought to pack batteries? She didn't think so. Pulling the contents of her bag apart and sorting the lot, Petra was forced to admit that no, she hadn't brought any spares. They had nothing with which to pierce the fog. Worse, if the bugs returned, she was flat out of luck.

Defeated, Petra forced the contents inside, yanking the zipper closed.

"Okay. Let's backtrack a ways. Once we've got a wall between us and that there fall, we take a right and work our way back up. What do you think?"

"That sounds better than staying here. Shall I lead?" Iver suggested.

"Yes please."

Petra stepped aside and Iver passed her. The smack of stick on stone was convenient when they'd first left camp. Now though, each tap echoed from everywhere. She couldn't rely on the sound to tell her where he was. The mist was so thick, she had to keep within a couple of yards to see him at all. He was moving more slowly than was his custom, but still more quickly than her.

Concentrating on keeping pace with her guide, and not falling off a cliff, took all of Petra's attention. There wasn't any left for mere speech. There certainly wasn't any left for thirst. Or hunger.

Then the rain came and thirst was nolonger issue. First, the wind picked up and Petra hoped it might blow the fog away. Then the sprinkling became a drizzle, became a downpour, all in under an hour.

If visibility was bad before, now standing was hazardous. Petra feared being blown from the mountain. They stopped and huddled, backs to the bluff, half shielded by a protruding mantle. It offered less protection than their recessed campsite but they couldn't walk with the sky coming down.

Petra shouted, "Can you open a cave here?!"

Iver saw her lips move but couldn't connect the sounds, as thunder boomed above. She repeated herself into his ear. Nodding, he stood, wobbly against the turbulence, and held his charm to the escarp. He closed his eyes and she had a mind to hug his knees so he wouldn't be whisked away. Then his eyes snapped open and he sat back down, shaking his head. The message was clear. They'd have to wait out the storm.

Soaked, freezing, and hungry, they huddled under their inadequate overhang. Petra wrapped her bag around her front, her hand in her sleeve, and hugged her knees to her chest, tucking them in her jacket. Iver, his bag at his side, laid pots along the ground, and the catcher quilt over himself. Shivering, with chattering teeth, they waited.

The sky grew dark. The sun must have risen that morning because it was sure descending now, Petra thought. Iver retrieved the roots from his bag. Then, with shaking hands, he cut the first into quarters, removing the tentacle-like offshoots trailing from the central bulb. He kept half and passed the rest to Petra.

"I hope this doesn't kill me," she thought, taking a bite. It was hard. Harder than an apple. Maybe as hard as raw potato, but not so hard as to damage her teeth. The flavor was similar to a yam, if the yam had been rubbed with too much pepper and slow-cooked in a smoker. She took a sip of water. Iver cut up another root. This too, they split. This too, they ate. The rest he saved for morning.

The pots overflowed, thanks to the rain that ebbed and returned in mighty bursts. The wind pelted them with debris, including pole plants, which Iver caught and removed the bulbs from before tossing aside. Neither Iver nor Petra slept a wink and the rain didn't let up until morning. Then her belly was too wet to write on. No matter. They had three days until the next full moon. It had to be enough. She couldn't consider the alternative.

"If we don't catch pneumonia, the rain may have saved our lives," she commented, sinking her teeth into the unnamed root.

They could see what appeared to be a route up. More importantly, with the clouds gone, *they could see*. If again they reached a gap, they could plan a way around it. They had water. They even had food. So far, Petra felt no cramping, no itching. The pain in her feet, back, neck, and nub, was that of someone who'd camped in a downpour days after surgery, rather than symptoms of food poisoning.

The chill was ever-present. Petra's bag and jacket were heavier, soaked through. Iver was forced to leave what water superseded their carrying ability. With luck, they'd collect those pots on the way down. Should their vessels empty again, those were a static water source they could find.

Morale was high. They'd made it this far. They could go yet farther. They could do this. Setting out in the sunshine, the duo thought to themselves, "Today is a new day."

Their optimism dwindled first with the stench and then at the sight of half a man. The top half, anyway. They identified the species by the proportions of the upper body, as any more delicate features had been removed or were sloughing off. He appeared to have died while trying to shield his middle. A leather vest, over a tunic, contained his innards, but exposed organs had swelled, rupturing forth where fabrics wore torn away. He still bore his scabbard, and a dented, bloodied shield. A brume of standard, non-furry flies served as a halo. Writhing pus weaved in and out of the tissue linking his bones—Maggots. Petra's stomach lurched.

"He must have been armed. Only a fool would go up against a griffon empty-handed—" Iver commented, speaking up to be heard over the sound of Petra's retching. "—but I don't see a sword anywhere," he continued, thinking out loud. "The griffon must have taken it back to its hoard."

Wiping her mouth, Petra took another hard look at the deceased. "Maybe. We don't have a sword."

"We do not. Although, I doubt one would do us any good. Have you been trained in how to wield a sword?"

"No."

"Nor have I. What we have are knives, which I am adept with. A slingshot, with which I'd be loath to miss. And an enchanted saddle, a tool specially chosen by her Majesty, Queen Siv, for this quest."

Petra nodded and warily, they resumed their hike. She shuddered as they passed the corpse, turning their backs to a fate well within the realm of possibility for themselves. They expected the griffon at the crest but that carcass indicated a willingness to travel. Maybe the griffon enjoyed the occasional downward stroll.

"Okay. Griffons—a recap. What do we know?" Petra inquired, her voice low in case one was creeping just around the bend.

"We know where they live."

She nodded and spoke her accord. "Here, but higher up. They nest at the peak, where they can protect their wealth."

"That is correct, Mistress. And their nests must be large, because griffon's certainly are."

"Do they live in their nests year round? Because birds don't."

"I'd assume so, Mistress. Otherwise, anyone could rob them."

"But they leave to eat?" she inquired.

"They must, but perhaps, like spiders, they need not eat often. A lone treasure hunter every month or so might be enough to sustain them. That hunter we passed appeared only half consumed, so they may not eat much at all," he ventured.

" Maybe they save food for later like—the alligator, that stores its victim under a submerged log, waiting for the meat to soften, and eating it only in bits?" she recited, pulling from her extensive zoology trivia stores.

Iver tilted his head, considering. Petra forced herself to reflect on the body they passed. There hadn't been much skin left. The muscles, if that was what shrouded those bones, hadn't looked anything like the charts in the doctor's office.

"Could be the griffon is a picky eater. Took the skin and the meat, leaving the organs and the bones. Most people don't like liver. Or kidneys," Petra mused, keeping her discomfort from coloring her words.

"Could be," Iver agreed.

Petra put her hand out for balance, extending her stride over a chasm that cut through the uneven shelf. A small furry shape poked out from a crack in the earth, before retreating anew. When the ground leveled out once more, Petra continued where she'd left off.

"What does a griffon look like?" She let the words out slowly, catching her breath afterward.

Walking and talking simultaneously was becoming more strenuous. Iver considered how best to relay his description so his human companion would recognize the creatures referenced.

"Griffons are large. Their head and front legs are shaped like those of an eagle, while their hind legs and posture are similar to those of a lion. Both sets of feet end in crystalline talons. Feathered all over, their wings are massive, and their tail feathers, long. The males can be quite colorful. You could compare them to Chinese pheasants. I once witnessed a griffon in my youth. I had the luck to be traveling with my clan as the griffons' mating season was coming to a close. Passing through a far more fertile valley than this, we watched while a male took to the sky. He was beautiful," Iver said, nostalgia smoothing his brow.

"A single feather drifted down to us. Canst, a cousin of mine, caught it. He wore it every day leading up to the war," Iver added, more solemnly.

Petra didn't ask if Canst died in battle, nor of which war Iver spoke. As far as she knew, for brownies, there had only been the one. Had Canst only lost his feather, she imagined Iver would have dismissed his reverie on a mellower note.

"And our plan is to loop the saddle onto its back, scramble on up, and command it to let us remove a claw?" she asked.

"Yes, Mistress. That's the goal."

"How do we get close enough to climb its back?"

Iver shrugged. "I suppose one of us will have to distract it."

"How can we? I don't have anything of value to wave in front of it. Are they like cartoon bulls? Do they hate the color red?"

"Red doesn't actually offend bulls, Mistress." She knew this, but deigned not to say so. "However—we are food shaped and not much else here is. If the griffon's hungry, the appearance of either of us should hold its attention."

Petra caught sight of a bleached pole wedged between tufts of tall grass. Straying from Iver's wake, she gave an experimental tug and dropped it again with a shriek. Rather than pulling out a spicy potato, Petra had lifted a bone and in so doing, knocked over others. Some still bore chunks of flesh. Once she'd caught her breath, she called for her friend.

"Yes, Mistress?" he replied, backtracking, and pausing to catch his breath after the light jog.

The altitude was affecting him as well, Petra observed. Seeing the bones at her feet, Iver leaned forward, examining them with a scholarly curiosity.

"Well, those are hooves." And so they were. "Could be this was a satyr—the other half of the body we saw before. Griffons might have a preference for lean horsemeat over fatty human tissue."

Were people fattier than horses? Petra didn't know, but Iver made a pass time of carving critters up. He probably had a better feel for meat quality than she did.

"They're so far from each other. And these look older," she commented.

"Perhaps. I think these have been more thoroughly stripped than the other half. Could be the griffon tore him apart, flinging the head and torso too far to pursue. Mating season only just ended. If the griffon laid an egg, they wouldn't want to leave the nest for long."

Petra didn't even stare at the next body they passed, this one circled by scraps of flesh, their hair still attached. Nor the following two, Alfarians, Iver judged. With their limbs and faces mauled, that was his best guess based on their scale and what fur remained.

They were going to die.

"Iver?" Petra whispered.

"Yes, Mistress?"

"Can we do this?"

He didn't answer immediately, stepping quietly and keeping a wary eye on their surroundings. They would be in sight of the nest soon. If the corpses weren't telling, their increasing shortness of breath was a giveaway that they were approaching the summit.

"I don't know, Mistress, but had you asked me in Kolchus or Polstov, I would have said no and I would have been wrong."

Petra looked at him and then jumped at the sound of a twig snapping underfoot.

"Let's take a break," he suggested. It was getting late anyway, and they'd be at a disadvantage, approaching the nest after dark.

Their nerves were fried and the hike was wearing. They sat back to back at Iver's prompting, the better to see incoming threats. Nibbling at the spicy yams, Petra took small bites to avoid exacerbating her anxiety-riddled stomach. Iver didn't touch his whiskey, wanting his wits about him. The cold seeped into their limbs as they rested, and Petra massaged her stiff joints. That night, they slept in turns, lest the griffon swoop down from the darkness. Come dawn, Petra marked her stomach, before they ate a light breakfast of bulb roots. As recovered as they could hope to be, they set out.

When possible, they stepped purposefully onto lichen and grass, to soften the sound of their movements. Petra breathed slowly through her mouth. This effort served the triple purpose of quieting her breath, filling her lungs more adequately with the too-thin air, and helping her to maintain some semblance of calm. When she had to cross over a break in the ground, she eased over the crevice. Landing a jump would have been too noisy, and with her bag weighing down her lopsided figure, utilized far too much energy.

Petra didn't know what the nest would look like, only that she should expect one. Finally, the frost-covered ground diverged into a curvilinear mosaic of shale colored clay, set with precious stones and jewelry. She stopped. The glittering wall was over twice her height, and Petra could just make out the sheen of silver plumage sprouting high overtop. Iver set his hand on her shoulder.

Nodding, she let Iver lead her down, away from their doom. When they were too far to be seen or heard, she whispered her plan.

"Let's scout the crest now, see where we can hide up there. After dark, you distract him—"

"Mistress, that's actually a her. Males are gold."

Petra nodded, closing her eyes a moment as she adjusted to this information. Female eagles trended heavier than the males, and with lions, females handled most of the hunting.

"Extra big griffon. Got it," she amended. "So, you distract *her* while I climb into the nest. If she sees you, hide where she won't fit. I'll keep a low profile until she comes back. When she returns, I'll jump onto her back with the saddle."

Iver was quiet, mulling over Petra's method. Finally, he spoke.

"Very well then, Mistress. Any preference for how I distract her?"

"Slingshot? If you can pelt her with pebbles without being seen, she should be irritated enough to investigate."

Returning to the peak, they inched from boulders to crags, watching metallic wisps just visible above the mosaic, for a sign they'd been noticed. There was scratching, shuffling from within, but the griffon did not emerge. By sunset, the pair was adequately familiar with the layout of the peak. They considered themselves adjusted to the thin air, but acknowledged they'd be winded when it came time to flee.

The time for questions had passed.

Wordless, Iver inhaled, withdrawing the slingshot from his pocket. Petra nodded, pointing to the saddle, which he passed to her. She slung it over her shoulder. Then they split up, with him headed for cover, and her rounding the nest. There she crouched, remaining still as she heard the first stones strike the beast, followed by its cry. Rising, the griffon cast the gloom darker, her shadow massive as she unfolded her wings before the moon. Her next scream shook the ground, and Petra was grateful she hadn't been standing. As it was, her ears rang and her head hurt.

The barrage ceased, and Petra hoped Iver hadn't ducked into a crag, lest the next quake crush him. The pelting resumed and Petra waited for the shadow to move, for the griffon to leave her next. Instead came another skull-splitting bellows.

"Fool! You know not whom you test. Turn tail at once or your suffering will be unmatched!"

The peppering of debris, against soft feathers and hard mosaic, confirmed that Iver had not turned tail, yet still, the griffon did not leave her perch. More threats followed, and of increasing venom, until neither believed she would be leaving at all. Removing her bulky footwear, Petra peered down, wincing at the moonlit rouge of inflammation, and the yellowed pockets of infection crisscrossing her soles, discharge glistening. She needed antibiotics, but later.

Standing on her backpack would provide a minimal boost. Petra circled back to a waist-height rock outcropping, which she mounted before attempting her climb. Gripping the handles of goblets and swords, clutching sizable crystals, a frame here and a crown there, Petra pulled up with her remaining hand, while pushing with her feet. She nearly lost her grip at every shriek and shuffle beyond the wall, her left arm shaking from exertion, and her nub reverberating with every knock. Her feet burned, and she swore that if she survived this, she wouldn't leave the couch for a week. No, make that a month!

Fingers looped over the curved ridge, Petra yanked herself up and laid flat, assessing the target. Waves of feathers shimmered as the griffon adjusted her stance. Massive, her front claws were hooked over the mound, but her lion's legs were firmly planted on the uneven floor. Her tail was splayed out, like a peahen's, as she reacted to being attacked. Iver had failed to draw her out but she was *distracted*.

Army crawling along the ridge until she was directly behind the griffon, Petra stood, hefted herself higher up the interior wall, double checked her grip on the saddle, and leapt for the beast's back. The griffon chose that moment to thrust forward, swiping menacingly, but ineffectively, towards the concealed slingshot wielding assailant. Given the sudden change of posture, Petra nearly missed the landing, barely grasping a handful of feathers to keep from rolling off the griffin's back. Petra scurried towards the wing joints, to secure the saddle. Wrapping the billet strap around the full girth was an impossibility, as the kelpie's rib cage had been significantly narrower than a griffon's.

Startled, the griffon flexed her wings, curving her long neck to see her attacker. Spotting Petra, the griffon shrieked, shooting upward, somersaulting rider and self both into the sky, the duo casting a serpentine shadow over the crest. The griffon lunged, tossing this way and that, but Petra's arms were hooked tight around each wing joint, feet dug into the beast's sides. She pressed the saddle against the griffon, ready to make demands and have them obeyed, but she couldn't catch her breath to speak. Petra couldn't tell if she was losing vision or if she'd turned from the moon, and she fought for consciousness, to keep her hands and feet in place, when Iver changed tactics. The moment he realized the beast and rider had passed beyond the range of his slingshot, he scrambled over and into the nest, for a means of summoning them lower. Intending to pull free a bow, or perhaps, even better, a gun, Iver found instead two porcelain eggs, barely smaller than himself.

Withdrawing an ax from the hoard, Iver struck the wall, shouting that he would break the eggs. His quick thinking saved Petra from a sure fall to her death, allowing her to awaken fully while the griffon descended. Registering Iver's voice, she struggled to hook the billet straps mid-flight. With one side tied off, Petra attempted to wrangle the other, while calling for the griffon to land, hoping the saddle need not be secured. The griffon obeyed as

Iver raced from the nest, seeking cover. His plan worked too well. As Petra had feared, in lunging for a fissure, Iver was buried by a sudden cave-in, though from the force of the griffon's full weight smashing into the boulder above, as opposed to the quake of her cry.

The force of the landing flung Petra away, slamming her to the ground not far from the nest. Ignoring the griffon's screams, as she seemed not to realize she'd already defeated the brownie, Petra pulled herself up the mosaic wall. She struggled without the boost of her bag, but had never been better motivated. Iver had led the beast from her. Now was her turn to do the same, in case he yet lived. Dropping to the base, Petra examined the eggs. Grabbing the ax Iver abandoned, Petra leaned it against that nearer, and called to the griffon.

"Get back here mama bird! I've got your babies!"

Petra didn't have to repeat herself. She heard what sounded like a million bats at once, and then the griffon towered over her.

"You dare threaten me, puny human? Move aside or die."

"I'm here for a claw," Petra responded more confidently than she felt. "I'll be taking one of yours, or the egg gets it."

She was all too aware that she couldn't hear Iver even though the griffon had quieted.

Before Petra could dodge the assault, the griffon swung a mighty claw, knocking her aside, and slicing through her upper arm. Petra hadn't been bluffing about the egg though, and shattered the shell as she fell. A thorough job—pieces, like glass, splintered outward, wet with amniotic fluid. From within, stirred a sopping chick-cub, who choked at its premature exposure to the elements. The head flopped forward, as it breathed its first and last gulp of air. Petra rushed for the other egg even as the griffon wailed in mourning.

"The claw. Now," Petra demanded, her ax held tightly aloft, the point resting atop the second egg.

The griffon may have relented, given the choice, but in that instant, a second shadow darkened the nest. Without looking up to acknowledge the incomer, Petra used the distraction. She swung at the griffon's massive front foot, slicing free a single dagger-taloned toe, nearly severing half of the next besides. Claiming her prize, Petra slipped from beneath her thrashing, howling victim. Dropping the ax, she rushed to climb her way out even as the new griffon landed, cawing what Petra assumed to be an inquiry.

Letting herself fall beyond the mound, Petra rolled the landing, ignoring fresh pain, and scanned for the saddle. Catching sight of it, she darted, gripping the strap, before racing to where Iver was buried. As best she could, Petra huddled in the blackness between the toppled boulder and rock shards, quietly removing stones and gravel, her progress rewarded by the revelation of faint groaning below. Not far away, she heard the flapping of giant wings, the injured moaning of her victim, and the ferocious cries of their probable mate. As terrified as she was to face her doom, the unknown was worse, so she watched this new griffon circling above, grateful for the darkness and her small stature, and doubly so for the cries that masked the noise of her digging.

Sighting first hair, and then fingers, she released a silent thanks for the wiggle of his hand, every snort and cough, while removing the damp gravel from around his head and shoulders. Now and then, the circling griffon would swoop downward, knocking aside this rock or that, sometimes dipping from view entirely, gliding beneath the peak, before returning once more. Thankfully, such enormous wings were incapable of subterfuge, and Petra paused her efforts, shying deeper into the shadows, whenever she heard his approach, resuming her efforts once he'd passed them by. Presumably, her victim was protecting the second egg, otherwise, she suspected they'd already have been found, and tossed down either gullet.

In what must have taken less than an hour, yet felt like days, Petra cleared enough debris for Iver to riggle free from his near-casket. His face had lost its customary rouge and his eyes shone wet and wide. She caught sight of the red pooling beneath his arm, and then again where she imagined his diaphragm to be, the sheen visible despite the thick layer of grit offering him camouflage. Watching the griffon slip down the opposing edge of the crest, she shoved the claw in her bag, grabbed her friend, and without so much as letting him catch his breath, pulled him into a desperate run.

There followed a ground shaking shriek. Then the arid boom of each wing flap announced a griffon in pursuit. They ran, slipped and slid, hand in hand at an angle growing steeper with every meter—Pursued by the screams of their enemy. Something sharp slit Petra's back, the hook failing to catch. Loose rocks scraped the back of their legs. Iver realized their ledge was coming to an end. He flung his free hand to grip anything that might keep them from falling over, but to no avail. The drop arrived, with Petra spotting it a mere instant before, allowing her no time to reflect on her mortality anew, before they met the next slope. It was on sore and battered rumps that they plummeted from the next, slipping along another, and finally skid to a stop along a gravelly stretch—far below the griffon's hoard.

Petra looked up, her eyes circling frantically for shadows on the hunt. Seeing none, she examined her friend, who groaned, his posture horizontal. Her legs and back felt like she'd been pelted with bricks, and her feet, bludgeoned. Her nub out-hurt them all. She was dizzy, her ears rung, and she couldn't catch her breath, though the air couldn't be as thin this far down.

"Can you walk?" Petra asked, when she could bear to move.

Iver didn't even nod. He just pushed himself up and stepped shakily forward. There was a cry from above. Petra flinched but Iver seemed not to notice it. In moments a second cry sounded, farther off than the first. They stopped, waiting.

When Iver found he could move without quaking, he announced it was time to go. Matching his pace, with every step, Petra missed her shoes. Together, they traced the curve of the mountain, flinching at every crack and cry.

"Can you get us to the portal stone?"

"Yes," Iver replied.

"Good. We have to get you help. Let's head back to the hospital. Come on."

"No," he said, straining. "Not a human hospital. We must return to Josalfar."

With that, he braced his shoulders. He nudged Petra away with his free hand, the other clutching his side. She expected him to sway, to fall, but his stance was sure. When he turned away, his steps were confident.

"Human doctors cannot help me."

Petra suspected speaking was painful for him and refrained from further questioning. They made gradual progress, hugging the rock walls and scanning the heavens for threats. In time, Iver came to a stop after a sharp turn. Before them glowed the open portal.

"Can you wrap my side? My hands—I would like my hands free for this, Mistress."

"Of course!" she piped up.

He nodded, removed his pack, and sat down.

"There is whiskey in my bag. And cloth."

She nodded, pulling out a warped glass bottle and unrolling a spool of beige fabric. Not wanting to trouble Iver for his shears, Petra pulled out her pocket knife and slit a long strip, and then another.

"Okay?" she asked, holding out her selection.

He reached for the whiskey, taking a long swig. Then another, before wiping his mouth on his sleeve, and returning it to her. Grimacing, he nodded an affirmative.

Petra unbuttoned Iver's once pristine jacket, and helped him to take it off. Concerned about time wasted, she didn't bother with such decorum with the next layer. Slipping her knife through his bloody undershirt, she ran her blade down the middle, sawing at the final strip, while he faced away.

"Brace yourself," Petra warned, before pouring whiskey over his wounds.

Iver's muscles grew taut, his expression, contorted, as Petra scrubbed away debris, the alcohol purifying deep lacerations. Then, with dry fabric, she wrapped his chest and abdomen. Blood continued seeping forth.

When finished, she asked if she'd missed anything. Iver let out a long exhale, before opening his eyes and peering down, examining her handiwork.

"My leg got knicked too. I don't know how badly, Mistress."

Petra looked down at his pants and sure enough, there was an inky wetness she'd discounted before as the absorption of fluids dripping from his torso. In moments she had another length of cloth and a shorter piece for cleaning.

"Can you take off your pants?" she asked.

This was no time to be squeamish about looking at a boy's underwear. Iver stood with her help, and removing his belt, pulled his pants from the waist down. The effort pained him and she had him stop once the belt loops were at knee height. Her back chastised the bend. Handless arm bracing him, she cleaned the lower wound too. The gash wasn't as long as the others, but she couldn't doubt its depth given the volume of blood spilled. Once it was bandaged, she helped him to pull his pants up.

"Is that too tight?" she asked, worried her friend would lose circulation in his leg.

"No, Mistress. That's just fine. Now, I will find the way to Josalfar."

Nodding, she stepped back, watching to see if he seemed near to collapse. Unmoved by his suffering, Iver closed his eyes, and sang, his breath bright, sealing the exit. Petra hoped there wasn't a child trapped in there, but they had no choice. Opening his eyes, he clutched at his pendant, and awakened the path to the capital. When the portal shone, he stepped inside.

"Follow me, Mistress."

She complied, meeting his pace while observing his color, the rapidity of his breath, and the continuity of his steps—ready to catch him should he stumble.

Chapter 12

"Could you have summoned the path one-handed?" Petra asked.

"Yes Mistress, but with difficulty," he responded, his words clipped.

The flashlight hadn't so much as flickered when she'd tested it, again. Iver saw just fine in the dark anyway. Neither spoke again until they reached the lip.

"I'll hop down first," Petra said, and did so, letting the saddle fall before turning back to help her friend.

They did not wait for the Alfarians' approach, skirting onlookers as they strode purposefully to the Queen's antichambers. Passersby slowed to observe their trajectory, but made no moves to bar them. Only the guards positioned at the entryway, with their crossed spears, delayed their passage. Ignoring Petra, they barked at Iver, who growling, gestured to his bandaged chest, then to his charge. A low voice yipped from beyond the lit arcade and the guards pulled their spears back.

For Petra's benefit, the voice sounded again, but in Icelandic. "Bring them to me."

An unarmored grey Alfarian stepped from the chamber and bade them enter. Iver complied, striking both guards with his mace-like stare. Petra followed behind, paying neither any heed.

Approaching her Majesty, they stopped short of her platform. Behind Queen Siv stood her customary row of Alfarians, decked out in jewelry and shimmering tops—ladies in waiting or some fairy equivalent, Petra had come to suppose.

"Your Majesty," said Iver, "We have gathered that which you requested."

The Queen raised her chin and Petra placed the saddle on the platform in front of her. Then she removed her backpack and retrieved the claw, flesh and bone still attached. Iver's breath came in starts. They needed to hurry the formalities along.

Queen Siv nodded, gesturing to one of the most ornately clad beside her, who stepped forth, and accepted the Queen's trophies.

"You have done well. I will see to it that your injuries are treated and your bellies filled while the charm is forged."

Petra raised her eyebrows and looked to Iver who looked to the Queen in turn.

"No food nor drink that either of you are provided on this visit shall be enchanted in any way. You have my word."

The pair nodded, Iver, too tired and pained to do much else. Petra however, lacked his lethargy. She hurt, but not to his extent.

"Your Majesty, how long will it take to make Emil's cure?"

"The necessary properties will be instilled in the charm throughout today and much of tomorrow."

Had she shown up the day of, that wouldn't have left time enough to heal him! Luckily she'd arrived a full day before the full moon. Emil would have to hold on a little while longer. Iver thanked the Queen and Petra echoed the sentiment. She might not have, were Iver in less dire straits. Another Alfarian arrived at the arch, and at Queen Siv's summons, was allowed entry. She bade this newcomer lead them to the Healer's quarters, so they departed.

While most Alfarians were lean, their guide was squat, chubby. Petra would've assumed that meant he could sing, like her, that is, until he opened his mouth. His voice was more frog than dog, and he spoke little. Petra paid minimal attention to their route, confident she wouldn't be allotted the opportunity to explore, not that she cared a wit about the secrets of Josalfar. As long as Emil and Iver recovered, the guide could lead her in circles until tomorrow. It made no difference to her.

Entering an ovular abode, lined with shelves sculpted into the stalagmites, the pair was introduced to Healer Stuf. Their unnamed guide left while Petra examined the Healer, who was tall, narrow-waisted, with blond fur so wavy, it appeared windswept, and eyes so close together, they impinged on the piping of his small cleft nose. Petra observed that a pair of glasses wouldn't have been out of place on a face like that. There was a bookish quality to him that was almost human.

Stuf's yip was quiet, his growl low. Iver matched the tone and ran his hands over his wounds, pointing over the fabric. There was a rack of beds against the limestone divider apparently carved from the cavern itself. They were covered with woven frond mats that gave off a fishy odor.

Healer Stuf murmured, patting a bed beside him. Iver unbuttoned his top and took the seat offered. Petra let her mind wander while Stuf removed the bandages, until the scent of blood made any escape impossible. Petra looked to her friend. The scratch across his upper thigh was ringed with bruising, and its center oozed red from cracks in the scab. A month, maybe two prior, and Petra was sure she'd have left the room, gagging, at the sight. She'd have succumbed to night terrors for weeks. But now, everything was different. *She* was different.

So Petra sat on a bed and watched while Stuf wiped away the dried blood, picking clean the gash with metal tools. Iver whimpered, and Petra had a hunch, he was swearing in his native tongue. Yet Iver remained still and took the needling. He was a survivor. Only when his wounds were rebandaged did Healer Stuf turn to and acknowledge the human in their midst. Was she a novelty, she wondered? Or did he treat humans regularly? Would slaves receive medical treatment, or would the be put down, like livestock, if too injured to work? Gunndis' claims implied the more humane resolution, but despite her age, Gunndis was able-bodied.

"Hello," said Stuf.

"Hello," said Petra.

"It seems you've had an adventure," he commented.

"So we have."

"Do you have any injuries that require treatment?" he inquired, head tilted at a curious angle.

"My hand got cut off. Can you grow me a new one?"

"A new hand?!" he exclaimed, aghast. "How would I create a new hand?!"

Petra shrugged. It had been a shooting star in the nightscape of her mind. If such an endeavor were possible, surely Iver would've mentioned it. That he hadn't was telling but she'd had to try.

"With magic?" came her weak response.

Shaking his head, Stuf muttered something unintelligible. Then he raised his eyes to meet her own.

"Magic cannot regrow a limb. Is there anything else that requires healing?"

Petra thought out loud, listing her injuries. "My arm is still sore to the nub, and the other one has a long scratch. I hurt my neck, back, and sides when we fell down the mountain, and my feet are all cut up. Can you help with those?"

"I can't imagine why not. Let's see what we're dealing with."

He removed her cast-like bandages, a precise endeavor involving the utilization of multiple pointed instruments. Doing so released a dank odor, overwhelming the stench of Iver's wounds. Raising a paw in the universal wait sign, Healer Stuf stepped from the room and called to a peer. Returning, he cleaned Petra's arm with a rag and water. He checked her other arm and turned her around, lifting the back of her shirt. She held the fabric in place while Stuf poked and prodded.

"Well," he finally concluded, after cleaning the major gashes and minor scratches, "There isn't much I can do here. You're going to scar, but nothing is out of place. Your back will heal on its own in good time, if you don't push yourself too hard."

Then he cleaned her feet while she tried not to wince.

"Your soles are quite infected," Stuf informed her, his tone casual, conversational.

"Quite?"

Rather than offering clarity, he added, "Take this," and handed her a coin sized pastry from an inconspicuous cranny nestled beside her bed.

Trusting that any charms, placed while under her Majesty's protection, would be removed, Petra popped the pastry into her mouth. She chewed into a crunchy nutty shell full of strawberry jam. Stuf was scrubbing her swollen soles when another Alfarian arrived, carrying a crystalline stoppered vase. Accepting the vessel, Stuf yipped what sounded to Petra like thanks, and the peer departed. Turning to his patient, he opened the vase, scooping out paste.

"It's going to be cold, but this will prevent an infection and help your skin heal faster."

Spreading it, Stuf worked from the nub onward and upward, past the elbow, until her arm was blue. At least, Petra was pretty sure it was blue. What light there was had a hue all its own and the treatment was slow going. This being her first break since before the griffons, and having gone without rest, traveling all the while, Petra was missing words between blinks. The soft tone of Stuf's inhuman whispers did nothing to stave off sleep and Petra soon found herself lost to the blankness.

She was roused awake later by a firm shake and the call of food.

"Breakfast?" she asked, rubbing nub paste around her eyes before remembering her condition, and location.

"Close! Dinner," Healer Stuf replied.

Sitting up, she turned to Iver, still asleep in his bed.

"Don't fret over him. He needs his rest. My apprentice will guide you to the dining galley."

Petra hadn't the foggiest what a galley was and wasn't sure he was using the word right, but hers being one of the seemingly infinite languages at the star people's disposal, she gave him the benefit of a doubt.

"Before you go, put these on. They should fit."

Accepting the offered footwear, she glanced down at her feet. They were as blue as her nub. Following Stuf's suggestion, she pulled the hand stitched leather moccasins over the dried goop.

The apprentice was the Alfarian who'd delivered the vase earlier. Beckoning Petra forward, they offered no introduction and Petra didn't request any. One more day and Petra hoped to turn her back on this cursed underdome forever. What did it matter what anyone called themself? The guide strode quickly, roving at the periphery of Petra's vision, and she took note of the turns en route in case she was ditched on the way back.

The galley was ringed with geyserite, topped with quartz minarets that appeared to burn from within. At a glance, she assumed them hollow, housing lit candlesticks. Her guide led her before a grandiose table of polished obsidian, its legs trailing into the earth, gold filigree framing the plateau. Its surface was overladen with bowls of colored liquids, jellies, berries, nuts, and fruit. Between the sleek table and stone barrier, sat a ring of Alfarians. They varied in color, height, tone, and wear, but not in species. The apprentice bade Petra eat, gesturing for her to take an open seat, before fleeing to sit amongst those posed opposite, as if embarrassed to have shared a human's company.

At either side of Petra sat single-rubied crones, reminiscent of Roth, and neither so much as glanced her way. Being human, she was beneath them all. It didn't matter. She wasn't there to talk. Petra was there to eat, and eat, she would.

She filled her bowl with nuts, berries, and mushrooms, downing handfuls at a time. Assuming the slenderer bowl was intended for beverages, she poured and sipped an unfamiliar liquid. It stung, but she was thirsty and there wasn't another obvious fluid in sight. Alcohol, though not beer, judging by the scent—it was spicy going down, leaving a honeyed aftertaste. She took small sips and didn't have a second glass. Instead, she chose from the juiciest fruits, to slake both thirst and hunger. Petra was famished until she wasn't and then she was far too full. In her mind's eye came a vision of her dad, leaning back in his easy chair and loosening his belt as he complimented her mum's roast duck. Petra had no belt to loosen.

Her bowl cleared, she looked to her neighbors for how to handle her dishes. She'd been so caught up in ignoring her hosts, she hadn't noticed if they were leaving dishware behind or carrying theirs away. Now the galley bore less than half the crowd she'd arrived at. A man-height ebony figure in a metallic vest, stood and backed away, leaving his bowls behind. She'd thought most of the dishes were still in place, but given how many were community plates, had wanted to be sure. Doubtless, some bewitched human would be tidying once the last Alfarian stood. The lazy mongrels wouldn't lift a finger to clean up after themselves.

"Spoiled jerks," she could have spat.

So be it. As she'd suspected, the apprentice hadn't waited. Alone, Petra found her way back to the Healer's quarters, stopping only twice to ask directions, both times citing that she was a guest of the Queen.

Returning to her bed, she sat waiting. Healer Stuf was absent while Iver slept, snoring with a force she half expected to vibrate loose stones from above. She had nothing to read, nobody to talk to, and nothing to do. Not wanting to think, she sought sleep and in minutes, found it.

When Petra awoke again, it was to the unnamed apprentice announcing she and Iver had been summoned by her Majesty, Queen Siv. Iver was sitting up and she couldn't hear his breathing from a bed away. That was an improvement.

"Ready?" she asked, ignoring the apprentice who clearly expected them to leap to and sprint to her Majesty's side.

Petra rose, stretching, and Iver did the same. They paused to pull on their backpacks and don their shoes. Her feet felt less inflamed.

"Ready."

Without a word more, the apprentice headed out, charging ahead. No matter. Iver knew the way. A brisk walk later and they stood before the audience chamber, where two new guards blocked their path. The apprentice barked at them and was away. Iver yipped and the guard to their right raised her paw.

"I shall announce you," she said in Icelandic.

The guard called out to those within, who whistled back in turn. As the spears were lifted, Petra took a deep breath and stepped inside, with Iver trailing close behind.

She just wanted the cure and to go. Cure and go. No more fancy announcements or magic talk or adventures. Just the cure, a straight shot home, and a big fat, *"so long, see you never"* to this Queen and her morally bankrupt city of monsters.

So quick was Petra's step, the ladies in waiting or whatever they were, jumped to shield her Majesty from an incoming assault. The Queen, however, gave no sign of intimidation. Why would she? Petra was eleven, barely armed, and her Majesty had not one, but two hostages. Those who mattered knew Petra would be a very good little girl.

"Welcome, Petra. Welcome, Iver. You're both looking better. I take it Healer Stuf has treated you?"

"Yes, your Majesty. Thank you, your Majesty," Iver piped up, before Petra could say something they would both regret.

Not that she would, intentionally, but ignorance rarely if ever excuses the crime.

"Yes. Thank you, your Majesty," was Petra's careful reply.

"Wonderful. Well then, the Skildus is complete."

In evidence, a figure at the Queen's right stepped forward, parted her claws, and dangled a necklace. The chain was of delicate gold, the pendant white, and the clasp of pale leather. It wasn't difficult to deduce which ingredient contributed where.

"Thanks. Again," Petra said, stepping to the edge of the platform and accepting the charm.

It wasn't warm or cold or glowing. It looked wholly unremarkable considering all they had suffered to earn it.

"Okay. Well, I'll just be off then," Petra said.

Turning from the Alfarians, Petra caught sight of Iver's cringe and his shaking head. What had she done wrong? Unsure how to remedy a flub unrecognized, she faced the Queen again, and attempted to curtsy. How many times did she have to give thanks for *casting a malevolent spell over her brother*—for making Petra choose between *letting him die, risking hers and her comrade's lives* in tasks superseding the ability of a grown warrior, or *handing her baby brother over for a lifetime of slavery*. Was she forgetting anything? Not to mention the Queen had essentially brainwashed and enslaved her big sister. So yeah, thanks for that, she fumed.

"Sorry. I'm in a hurry to get back to Emil. He needs me."

"Very well then, human child Petra. Goodbye. Brownie Iver will see that you arrive home safely and with all due haste."

Freed, Petra raced from the room. Iver stayed back, perhaps to plead forgiveness more adequately, she thought, pausing so he could catch up some minutes later. Matching her stride, he explained about informing her Majesty of the portal in France. Of course—the drop in the playground had completely slipped her mind. Well, it was in the Queen's hands now. No doubt her Majesty would have any number of children working the mines in no time.

"How are you feeling?" she asked, as they darted past dolomite and metalwork barriers.

It didn't matter that she didn't know the way. Petra could see the curved wall stretching to the oculus and leaned into every turn leading out.

"I'm feeling much better, Mistress. Alfarian Healers are gifted. Even at our height, brownies have never been able to match their medical knowledge and practices."

"So that's it then? If they can't fix my arm, then it really will be like this forever?"

"I'm afraid so, Mistress. Perhaps your human doctors would attach a cadaver's hand, but the peoples don't perform such perverse surgeries," he explained, nearing the outer wall.

Petra was quiet as he opened the way home. Iver climbed in and turning back, offered his hand.

"No thanks," she said, shaking her head.

If the nub was forever, then she may as well get used to it. At least it didn't sting anymore. Maybe she should've asked Healer Stuf for a vase of the blue gunk to take home. With less grace than the injured and healing Iver, she inserted arm and nub both. Gripping the glowing ledge, she pulled herself up and in.

They didn't talk much. Petra was too anxious for words, whether verbal or mental. The phrase, "What if we're too late?" kept spinning around her skull. How much could they trust the Queen afterall? And her magic to follow an exact timeline? To keep an inner and outer peace, she counted her steps, tracing the veins embedded in the wall. Reaching the seven hundreds, she lost track and began again. The entry glow dimmed, and they walked blindly on. Petra was tired of darkness. Letting off some anxiety, she treated the flashlight to some good old fashioned percussive maintenance. A few good thwacks later, it shone.

"Mistress?" Iver stopped.

"Yes?"

"I—I'm deeply sorry, but I have to go back."

"What? Why?" Petra asked, surprised.

"I can feel my stitching opening up."

His eyes flicked down to his injuries, concealed beneath his clothes. Healer Stuf hadn't cleared him to go. He'd said Iver should rest up. Petra guessed that message hadn't made it to the Queen. For one thing, she and Iver hadn't communicated it. Not that Healer Stuf had commanded Iver to stay, or made it clear to them for how long Iver was meant to rest. This wasn't a bureaucratic human-run hospital after all. They weren't in France. There were no forms to sign or at-faults to waive. They were dealing with fairies and therefore, chaos.

"Can you make it back on your own?"

"Yes, Mistress."

"Okay then. Well, feel better. And I hope to see you soon."

Was there any reason not to relieve him of his subservience then and there? The adventure was over. She'd have no difficulties finding Leif's from here. Petra had no need for a guide any longer.

"Of course Mistress. I will return to you as soon as I am able."

What if he wanted to stay? She wondered. Either way, this slipshod goodbye wasn't how she wanted to part ways. She had to see him again, if for no other reason than to thank him properly for his assistance. Without him, she would surely have failed.

"Thanks, Iver."

They embraced, gently, and went their separate ways.

She couldn't hear his journey, though, doubtless her progress echoed by. Ignoring the drop in temperature, she thought only of the number of steps left and not of Iver or Emil or death or slavery or anything. Just one step after another until finally, daylight streamed in, the exit in sight.

Petra broke into a run, and upon reaching the lip, slowed, stepping carefully out onto the toothless ground. She'd come too far to die via accidental drowning. What a way to go after besting three actual monsters, though, admittedly, it had been Iver who defeated the kelpie. The way was direct, the only changes since her departure consisting of snow piles lining the shadows of rocks and trees. Before she knew it, Petra was standing at Leif's back door. It was unlocked. She'd hoped it would be. Letting herself in, she called to him.

"Leif? Leif? I'm home. We have to go to Emil! I have it! I have—"

Mid yell, she'd passed through the living room, and stopped, spotting Leif, wide-eyed, stepping from his room.

"Petra?!"

"Yes. I'm sorry I took off. But I'm home now and we have to go. We have to get to Emil now!"

"How did you—I've got to let the police know youre home."

"Fine. After we see to Emil. I have the cure!"

Without waiting for his response, Petra grabbed the keys and ran for the car. She unlocked the doors and set the ignition running. Leif followed after, hopping into the driver's side.

"He's still in a coma. The doctor's don't know—"

"They can't help. Look, whether you believe me or not, just get me to my brother."

Leif opened his mouth, whether to reason or to argue, but shook his head, set the engine to running, and pulled from the drive.

"Tell me about your trip," he finally said, when they'd been on the road for some minutes.

"We don't have time enough for that. After Emil wakes up, okay?"

"How's your arm?"

Glancing down, she pulled up her sleeve and rubbed at the blue smear. Where it flaked off, her skin remained stained.

"It doesn't hurt."

His expression was pained but he kept his eyes on the road.

"This isn't your fault. And it isn't Atla's either. Emil and I made our choices. Had he more information, he would've made a different one, but not me. I don't need my arm, but I need my baby brother."

"He's lucky to have you."

Pulling into the hospital parking lot Leif turned the engine off, pausing before opening his door.

"I want to prepare you for what you're about to see."

"I saw half a dead body the other day. Then the other half a few hours later. That was days after I saw my hand cut off. Let's go."

Struck speechless, Leif unlocked the doors and they both stepped out. Despite her obvious hurry, Leif knew the way and she did not. With exactly zero patience, Petra matched his pace to the lobby, and stood silent, ignoring the eyes on her filthy hair, face, and attire.

"Sir, this is a sterile environment," the clerk commented as he signed himself and Petra in.

"She has a right to see her brother and its important she do so quickly."

The woman's lips thinned but she accepted the form back. Skirting past her desk, Leif led to Emil's room, the scent of rubbing alcohol an unwelcome blast to Petra, who'd grown accustomed to her feral musk. They stopped at an open door and Petra didn't wait for confirmation. She raced inside, and even shrunken under a blanket, a tube in his mouth, more attached to his wrist and hand, she knew him. Before Leif could react, she pulled the necklace from her pocket, and looping it beneath the ventilator pump, Petra placed it around his neck. Leif was at her side as she tied it, hands raised to prevent her from removing the links between Emil and the many machines surrounding them. He gasped as Emil's eyes shot open.

"What the—" Leif exclaimed.

Petra smiled. It had worked! "Oh, thank goodness. How do you feel?" she asked, not sure if he needed to verbally accept the Skildus, but poised to ask him to do so.

Emil's nostrils flared, and he frowned, then grimaced, trying to yell around his tubing, pushing himself up. He had more energy than she'd expected! But obviously, all those tubes, that needle, hurt. The sooner they were removed, the better. Petra leaned into the hallway, calling for a nurse. She announced that Emil was awake. Already, he'd pulled the tubing from his throat.

The second the end emerged from his open, howling mouth, Emil screamed, "Take it off!"

Leif was frozen, unsure if he should restrain the child he'd believed on the verge of death just minutes prior. A nurse arrived in that exact moment. Her expression was one of surprise, which quickly turned to alarm as Emil repeated himself.

"Hey! It's okay. I have to check your vitals first."

She stepped closer, but he seemed insatiable to cease his thrashing. She looked to a single monitor, then shook her head. Emil never stopped screaming, and flustered, the nurse turned for the door.

"Let me go grab your doctor. He should be here." So saying, she left the way she'd come.

Petra inched near, trying to meet his wild gaze but he was looking every which way.

"Do you accept—" she began, but he wasn't listening. Putting a hand on his shoulder, she tried again.

Ignoring her, he pulled something loose from under his blankets, and Petra watched the tube fall to the ground. Whatever it was, removing it hurt, but his fit didn't end there.

"Hey, buddy, they're coming back. Everything's gonna be alright," Leif added, his hands in the air, floating over the fragile child. In his mind's eye, he held Emil in place, then removing his grip when the doctors arrived, saw fresh bruises the shape of his fingers. Shaking the image away, he watched helplessly, calling for the doctor from where he stood.

Emil's expression was twisted in agony, a misery that faded when after pulling free the needle lodged in his vein, his fingers caught on the necklace. Petra moved to stop him but despite the implied weakness of his skeletal arms, he moved too quickly. Yanking it forth, taring the twine in the process, he tossed it to the ground. His expression shifted to one of triumph.

"No!" Petra cried. "Leave it! That's the cure!"

"I need to go back!" Emil announced. He made to rise from the bed, and Leif moved to stop him. That's when the nurse and doctor returned, the doctor gesturing at Leif to step aside, so he could assist. Petra was on her knees, re-tying the twine, praying the charm hadn't been broken. She'd just tightened the knot and was rising to her feet when Emil, who'd been a hair's breadth from the doctor, steps from the bed, collapsed.

The doctor caught his slender figure midfall, and lifted him onto the bed. Then, brows high, eyes wide, he bent over Emil, checking for any sign of life, and finding none, sent the nurse for the AED. Leif and Petra both questioned what was happening, how could this be happening, why was this happening, their words just more background noise to the medical professional trained to pre-serve life. When the nurse arrived with the au-tomated external defibrillator, having been gone barely two minutes that felt much longer, the doctor asked her to remove Emil's family from their presence. Leif complied with the petit woman's kind request, too stunned to weep. He had to grab Petra by the shoulders, and guide her out. She was mumbling about the cure, her eyes only leaving Emil's face when the door closed after her. They waited in the hallway, too tense even to slump against the wall. They could hear the efforts underway in Emil's room, and finally, the ultimate failure. The time of death was spoken in a voice tinged with defeat. Then, the nurse stepped out to notify them, the confirmation they hadn't been mistaken—perhaps overheard similar activity from a neighboring room—etched across her face.

"I'm sorry. He's gone."

She asked if they'd like to come inside, to say goodbye. Leif looked down to Petra, his lips parsed, but he decided against asking, already knowing her response. So at the appropriate march, they stepped in, and looked on in silence while those who, like Petra, had failed, stepped out, allowing them a moment's privacy.

Petra knew there must have been something important to say, or to ask, but the only words circling her skull were those of her Majesty.

"If he accepts the amulet, he will live free."

"If." There it was all along. A ringing doubt, but not Petra's, never Petra's. Because why wouldn't he choose freedom, home, his sister? Why wouldn't he choose to be well, over being cursed, forced to rely on another to fill a hole he couldn't himself. Why allow someone else that power? When there need never have been a hole at all.

Leif set the funeral for that weekend. The police were willing to put off questioning Petra, given the circumstances. Though Officer Arnar insisted they would be back, when things settled.

With Sunday morning came mourning. Officially, that is. Petra's wardrobe had been drastically reduced and unsurprisingly, there was little black to be had. She was no Atla, so she made do with a navy sweater over grey jeans. There wasn't time for shopping. The paper predicted dry weather so she declined to wear her stained, stolen, jacket. Leif offered to make a big breakfast but neither had the appetite. Petra read and reread Emil's obituary over a buttered muffin she was half aware of. The succinct biography concluded with the date, time, and locations for the funeral and burial. Leif asked if they had a family Bible. She shook her head.

"Some families store obituaries in them. I'll give my folks a call about ours."

She nodded, leaving the paper on the table.

They arrived at the parlor early, with night hanging on. That there should be so few hours of daylight was fitting. Walking up a concrete path, crossing a painstakingly manicured lawn, dotted with artfully placed shrubs and flowers past their bloom, Petra pinched herself. Still real, she thought. Snow circled the base of every bare perennial and bush. The funeral home was a simple russet colored house with white shutters and a wraparound porch.

The interior met her vague *funereal* expectations, or so they would have had she any. The lights were warm, the lampshades floral, casting their dour expressions in a somber light. The walls were more window than wallpaper, the glass half-hidden behind floor-length curtains, tied loosely with canary bows, to match the lampshades. Before the pews sat two tables, parallel with the podium and perpendicular to the central aisle carpet. They were lined with white bouquets and photographs of better days. Petra scanned them. Most dated from before the accident. Some included Leif, beaming, laughing at Atla's side. The podium, the pews, and the decor was bland. There was nothing to draw Petra's attention from the sight of a tragically small casket a room's length away—the sight Petra wanted least yet needed most to see. She would give a proper goodbye before this day was done.

Determined, she stepped forward—one foot in front of the other, one hand a fist and the nub offering sensations as if it were the same. Soon, much too soon, she stood before the inevitable. Peering down, she took him in, the words dying in her throat. Petra took in the sight of his pinched face, his cheeks having lost their roundness during her absence. She took in the sight of his closed eyes, unnaturally pinkened mouth, thinner than she knew, bereft of joy. She took in his shrunken stature, for he was little, surely littler than ever he had been, even in his suit with its padded shoulders. Someone had styled his hair, gelling it into place at either side of an artificial part.

Who was this imitation? Not Emil. Not *her* Emil. This grim doll was a child shaped falsehood. It was the antithesis of her brother if ever there was one, for Emil was life and laughter and fun. Not this. Never this.

She was embraced as she wept, wrapped in polyester, by the smell of cologne, and led to a seat.

When her sniffles dried, Leif let go. A pastor rose and spoke. The words flapped and flitted through Petra's bedraggled mind, as she bade her eyes wander from the casket, from the contents therein. The pews were full. At every angle, there were faces, some familiar, but many *un*. When had they arrived? How long had she stood before her baby brother, ignorant to the souls at her back?

A motion called her to the present, to her place at the front of the mourners. Leif was standing, walking to and thanking the pastor, coming to grip the podium himself. He looked lost, eyes wet, and suit wrinkled. His tie was crooked. From nowhere her mum's voice said nobody is ever ready for the death of a child. Why would she have said that? Maybe it wasn't her mother's voice but her own.

Leif pulled a folded sheet of paper from his breast pocket, and unfolding it, put it down, and did not look its way again.

"Hello everyone. Thank you so much for being here today. We shouldn't be here, none of us. This should never have happened, but thank you for sharing in the wrongness, in these losses, Emil's, of his potential, and ours, of him."

He paused, taking a long breath, before continuing. "If any of you don't know me, I'm Leif. I became Emil's guardian not too long ago, but—being a friend of the family, I first met him when he was very little. And he was just about the cutest little boy you can imagine—always smiling, laughing, running amok," Iver laughed, wiping at his eyes.

"When I used to help Atla babysit, Emil was *averse* to napping. Never still, he was always pulling Petra," She started at her name. "—and us into his games. He wanted to be the hero, to save the princess from the dragon, the bank from the robbers, the dog from the net. Everybody had their role, and his was to help. That's all he wanted. When assigned to draw his future profession, one year he drew a police officer. Marta was so proud of his earnest ambition, she hung it on the fridge. The next, he drew a fireman, and Kristjan framed it, for his desk. Emil wanted to grow up, to be strong, and fast—to be the good guy, keeping us safe. But—"

Leif's voice took on an edge, and Petra knew it was self-directed. So too, she knew nothing she could say would change the way he felt.

"When came our time to help him, to keep him safe, and well—we failed. We missed the signs, and then it was too late. When I re-entered his life, when Petra and Emil came to stay with me, he was that same little boy, but trapped in an ailing shell.

And it hurt, to see how he couldn't run, couldn't jump, or play. Even science failed. Emil deserved better. I wish I could tell you what killed him. I wish I could say we learned from this loss, that his suffering led to a cure, a legacy of healing, where no other child need suffer in this manner, but I can't."

His eyes scanned the sea of downturned faces, and when he spoke again, his voice was no longer hard, but somber.

"I wish Emil was given the chance to be the hero he was born to be. In this world of tragedy, of injustice, let us all do our part to be kind, to help rather than cast judgment at the limitations of our peers. We're all struggling, always, but that doesn't mean we can't be there. All we can do is be better, until one day, we can't. I'm sorry Emil—sorry I stayed away for so long, sorry I wasn't watching. And I'm sorry I let you go."

Leif may have said something more, but he was stepping back from the podium. Any sound was obstructed by the distance, and the weeping.

As he settled back into his seat beside Petra, he asked her if she would like to say *a few words* for Emil. The question was half hiccup and half sob, but there was no denying the correct answer.

In truth, she would have preferred not to speak at all, but given the option, she felt obligated to do so. Nodding, she took a shaky breath and walked to the podium, crossing a gap she wished were wider. The pastor offered a wooden box should she need a step to see over, but she was of a height where it wasn't necessary.

Looking out at the rows of faces, some stranger than others, she introduced herself, speaking into the slender microphone perched before her.

"Hi. I'm Petra, Emil's big sister."

The pastor reached over, bending the mic lower. She thanked him, then paused, finding the right words.

"Even though I'm older, I can't remember a time before Emil. He's always been the fun one, the one with ideas, projects, games. The digger. The builder. The maker of messes I'd have to clean—messes I've never minded cleaning because they came from a good place, a place of—" she paused, a stutter looming. "—of joy. Emil's the only person I've ever really wanted to play with, and for the longest time, the only friend I had. I'm going to miss him. I—I just wish I'd gotten home sooner. I'm sorry Emil."

Wiping at her eyes, she found her chair despite the blur. Leif took her hand in his own and together they feigned listening as the pastor continued with the service, telling them how wonderful this boy was, that he had never met, and how great Emil's hereafter would be, in this unseen place he'd never been. Petra endured pats on her shoulder and back, from hands unknown. They didn't matter. The touching ceased. She realized the speaking had as well.

The pastor must have called for dispersing. Perhaps a time and directions were given for the burial. She didn't know, but Leif stood, and made for a space near the exit, where he could individually thank those who had come. Petra and Leif both endured the onslaught of condolences, hugs, and shy shoulder taps. It wasn't over after all. Perhaps the touching would last all day, thought Petra. Glances caught on her abbreviated wrist before apprehensively rising to her face. A neighbor she recognized, let Petra know she'd be in her thoughts, as would Atla and Emil both. Did these people think Atla dead?

"I mean," Petra acknowledged to herself, "in a way she is." Death was a kind of leaving, and Atla wouldn't be coming back.

"Thank you," was all Petra said, with eyes only for the polished casket and the empty hull therein.

Before leaving, Petra stood at Emil's side once more.

"I'm sorry," she repeated, bringing her hand to rest on his icy fingers. "I chose wrong," she admitted where none but the dead could hear. It was a sorry parting gift but she took the doll from her pocket, pressing it beneath the bouquet in his grip. He hadn't wanted the amulet, after all.

Not knowing how long she stood there, eventually, Leif came and led her away. There was a break between the funeral service and the burial, he explained. She nodded, reflecting on her parent's. Atla had hosted at home, busied with the serving of coffee, tea, and dainty sandwiches that were too sophisticated to be filling. Adulthood was putting feelings on hold, Petra had later surmised.

That Leif opted to skip the hostess interim would have been a relief, had Petra considered how this day would go. They found a cafe, a town over, where they were afforded privacy from the funerary guests. Leif ordered them each a tea, black for him and herbal for her, and a handful of pastries to split. Having paid, they selected a round table in a corner with a window overlooking the street.

Tentatively sipping her peeping hot beverage, Petra gazed out the window, observing nothing.

Leif spoke. "I believe you," he said.

Petra turned to him, surprised. "You do?"

"I do. You mentioned in your eulogy that you made a friend. Assuming that's not me, is this friend nearby?"

"You're family, Leif. And he's being looked after right now. A griffon gored him good the other day. Four days ago? They all bleed together."

She thought she'd meant the days, but then, she wasn't sure. We all bleed together, was an unspoken amendment. Or maybe just, *We all bleed*.

"A griffon. I don't even know what that is."

"Neither did I." She looked down, uncomfortable, bringing the worlds together. "They're giant lion birds with medicinal claws."

"Why didn't the cure work?"

Bitterly, Petra pulled the Skildus from her pocket. "He had to choose it."

She handed it to Leif who admired the charm, rotating it in his hands. "How does it work?"

Petra shrugged. "Magic? It protects the wearer from Alfarian enchantments."

"What's this rune here?" he asked, pointing to an engraving at the front.

Petra had been so focused on getting the cure to Emil, she'd barely looked it over, at first. But then he died, and since, she's stared at little but. The rune, if rune it was, looked like a capital Y, wherein that central line continued until it ceased at equal height with its raised arms.

"Haven't the foggiest. Iver would know though."

"Your friend?"

She nodded, returning the Skildus to her pocket. A reminder of how close she'd come to saving Emil, it hurt to hold.

"An officer in Paris described seeing you in the company of a tiny white-haired man with inhuman black eyes. That was his exact wording, by the way. *'Inhuman.'* At least, that's the translation I got. The cameras, when the hospital got around to sharing the footage, didn't show any man though. What do you think they revealed, if you had to guess?"

She sighed, seeing this test for what it was. He didn't believe her. He allowed for the possibility of an incredible truth, which from an adult, was almost as good. It was an agnostic take on her story.

"They saw a cat."

"And so they did. Mad world."

They toasted, burning their tongues.

"Will you stay with me?" he asked. "You did the best you could. You did well. Things just—things don't always work out, no matter how hard we try." He paused then, collecting his thoughts. "But this here, this is your world. You belong in school, going to sleep with a full belly in a warm bed every night. You deserve to be taken care of."

Nibbling at her croissant, Petra responded honestly. "Thank you. For taking us in. For looking after Emil while I was away. For caring. Thank you so much for caring about us."

He made to brush it off, his hands raised in a mid shrug, but she shook her head.

"I mean it. Thank you. But I can't answer that right now. I mean—none of this feels real. Three—Four days ago? I was risking life and limb on a freezing mountain top, all for ingredients to a cure nobody wanted. Today—today I'm eating croissants in a heated cafe with cushioned seats and my baby brother, the person I did all of this for, is gone. Heck, what was it—A month? Two months ago magic wasn't even real. My head either isn't here or it's spinning. I don't know what I'm doing."

Leif nodded. "I understand. If you have to leave again, can you say goodbye this time?"

"Yes, of course. I wish I could've before, but I couldn't risk you stopping me. Emil's life—Emil was on the line."

Leif gave a weak smile. "I know. Did you get word of Atla at all? Is she—is she okay?"

Was it worse for her to be enslaved than dead?

"I met with her. She's happy where she is. She even tried convincing me to bring Emil to them. Atla wanted all of us working under Queen Siv together."

"And if I had agreed, or even just left Emil with her, he'd be alive right now," Petra added, silently.

"Does she know, do you think?"

"I don't know."

"Should someone—are you going to tell her?"

Petra shook her head. "She'd be happier not knowing, but I think the Queen will have her notified."

Leif nodded.

They finished their tea and pastries, watching traffic skirt by. Then Leif looked at his watch.

"Ready?"

"Sure."

The ride was brief. Parking on the street, they found the cemetery. It lined a long stretch of road, but didn't span far from the street. They located Emil's plot in no time. The pastor, with his crimson striped robes, standing over a rectangular hole, was a dead giveaway. Visitors arrived in ones and twos, including Petra's old art teacher, Mrs. Halonen, smelling heavily of wine.

At fourteen hundred on the dot, the pastor jumped back into his sermon. From what snippets Petra gleaned, the man sure had a lot to say about death, heaven, and the Lord but little about Emil as an individual. That was fine with her. She preferred he recite the fables he'd memorized over boasting the qualities of a child he'd only heard of that week. The casket was lowered by a truck, featuring an elaborate pulley system, into the ground. Here and there, adults crossed themselves.

The pastor asked the gathering if they had any momentos they wished to leave with Emil. Petra hadn't expected that, or she might have waited. Leif stepped forward, volunteering an envelope, which drifted to a stop atop the mahogany lid. A boy, perhaps from Emil's class, dropped a toy car that slid off the coffin. Mrs. Halonen moved closer to the opening, a watercolor portrait of Emil in her grip. This she folded into fourths and let loose beyond.

Petra reflected that were Emil there, he'd have said what a shame it was to bury that—what with the mud soiling it. He didn't bury things that shouldn't get dirty. But no matter.

Spying a familiar figure standing resolute, a number of headstones to the side, she eased her way through the smattering of individuals dropping favors, coming to meet her friend. An *I told you so* lay wedged between them, but he swept it aside.

"I'm sorry," Iver said instead, his owl eyes downcast.

"Did she know, do you think?" asked Petra, a hiccup of anger blooming within.

Iver breathed in and out, considering the consequences of his response. When he spoke, he did so with great care.

"It's impossible for us to know precisely all of the methods with which she gathers information. However, yes, I believe her Majesty had reason to believe that your brother would decline the cure."

Well then, that was that. That was her purpose. Of course, she would need to become stronger first. She would need to learn more about the portals, the worlds, and the middle lands. Everything. Petra would need to learn everything, but she was young, and had nothing if not time.

"With my sight, could I be trained to summon the golden paths? Could I learn to navigate by feel, without a map, as you do?"

Iver frowned, sensing the comfort of a warm kitchen, the security of four walls, and a roof slipping away with every word.

It was with dread that he answered, "Yes, Mistress. In our time together, I've perceived nothing that bars you from learning such things."

"Okay," she said, satisfied. "Can you wait by the tree line? I'll be right back."

With a heavy heart, he watched her go, then turned tail himself, dodging ancient salt circles that emanated through the hallowed grounds, before traipsing off into the woods.

Returning to the ceremony, her brother's coffin now hidden beneath handfuls of soil and a slew of momentos, Petra pulled Leif aside. Wordless, she embraced him, her one hand reaching around to wrap her nub.

"I'm going now," she said.

Leif's brows rose and his eyes widened with surprise. "What? Already? Are you sure?"

She nodded.

"Alright then, I guess. Take care of yourself, okay?" He pulled her tight before releasing her again. "And remember—you always have a home with me. Your friend too. You're both welcome."

"Thank you," she said and with one last squeeze of his hand, let him go.

Leif watched her slender form shrink until she'd disappeared into the foliage. Petra didn't look back.

THE END

O nce upon a time, there was a young graphic designer named Jessica Ferrara. She had a passion for creating beautiful designs that could captivate the eye and stir the soul. After graduating from the College of Saint Rose with her Bachelor's degree, Jessica spent three years honing her craft as a tattoo artist in Albany, New York. But Jessica's thirst for adventure could not be quenched by her artistic pursuits alone, and so she set out on an epic journey across the great continent of Europe. She backpacked through ancient cities, explored exotic cultures, and gathered inspiration from every corner of the world. And when Jessica returned to the United States, she found a new home in the heart of Texas. She began a new journey of blogging on her website and reviewing books on Instagram with her return to the States as a way to chronicle her life and open the imagination of potential readers. Here, she could be found writing and painting, pouring her passion onto the canvas and into the written word. Her designs were bold, imaginative, and always spoke to the soul of the viewer, which can be found on her website, Instagram, Facebook, and TikTok .